Grindin'

Grindin'

A Novel

DANIELLE SANTIAGO

ATRIA BOOKS

New York • London • Sydney • Toronto

ATRIA BOOKS

1230 Avenue of the Americas
New York, NY 10020

The Library of Congress has cataloged the hardcover edition as follows:
Grindin' : a novel / Danielle Santiago.
p. cm.
1. Prostitutes—Fiction. 2. African American women—Fiction. 3. Kinship
care—Fiction. 4. Domestic fiction. I. Title.
PS3619.A574G75 2006
813'.6—dc22   2006041778
ISBN-13: 978-0-7432-7760-0
ISBN-10:   0-7432-7760-0
ISBN-13: 978-0-7432-7761-7 (Pbk)
ISBN-10:   0-7432-7761-9 (Pbk)

First Atria Books trade paperback edition February 2007

10 9 8 7 6 5 4 3 2

ATRIA BOOKS is a trademark of Simon & Schuster, Inc.

Manufactured in the United States of America

For information about special discounts for bulk purchases,
please contact Simon & Schuster Special Sales:
1-800-456-6798 or business@simonandschuster.com.

For Kurtrina D. Williams: you were my biggest fan,
and not just because you were my cousin

Grindin'

Vegas Nights

Damn, Nina, how much of that shit did you put in his drink?"

"Same amount as usual. Why?"

" 'Cause his ass looks dead."

Nina glanced at the middle-aged white man lying across the bed. He was in a deep sleep from the mickey she'd slipped him less than thirty minutes ago. "Kennedy, ain't nothing wrong with that man. He looks like that 'cause he drank everything the bar had to offer! Just hurry and finish wiping everything down. We can't afford to get sloppy now."

"I'm through wiping. You hurry up and crack that safe so we can get that shit and be out."

Nina tried but couldn't crack the code to the hotel-room safe.

Kennedy was becoming impatient. "Look, Nina, fuck whatever is in that safe. We got his Rolex and four thousand cash. We need to go ship this shit and catch our flight!"

"Ken, I've always told you patience is a virtue," Nina said calmly, never taking her eyes from the safe.

"Haven't you noticed I'm not big on virtues?"

"Besides, I know this old bastard got way more paper in this safe. You should have seen how much he was spending on chips—about ten Gs a table. His bar tab was a G and he paid everything in cash."

Nina continued to give her full attention to the safe. She looked like a high-fashion runway model, not a hustler and part-time scam artist. All five feet ten inches of her was slim but curvy in the right places. Her 36D cups were perfect for the knee-length red Valentino tube dress that she was wearing. Her legs were especially beautiful in the Manolo Blahnik stilettos. The rich white Vegas gamblers couldn't keep their eyes off her smooth chocolate skin and her shoulder-length jet-black hair.

Once she had worked her way into their rooms, Nina would slip them a mickey while her cousin robbed the gamblers blind.

Kennedy was the mastermind behind the scheme. At twenty-two, she was a genius at crime. If it had been a major in college, she would have graduated summa cum laude.

She'd come up with this particular scheme after the ATF and DEA had raided them. The only thing that had kept Kennedy and Nina from going to state or federal prison was that thirty minutes before the raid, they had been robbed. Nina's boys' father and his brother had hit them for four kilos and all of their firearms. After everything was over, Kennedy considered the robbery to have been a blessing.

Kennedy looked on, aggravated, as Nina continued to try to crack the safe's code.

Nina exhaled. "There, I did it. Told you, ma, just be easy." As she pulled the safe's door open she could not believe what she was seeing. She covered her mouth with a gloved hand to keep from screaming.

Kennedy slid off the bar stool and walked toward her cousin to see what the excitement was about. "Nina, what is it?"

"Yo, it must be fifty Gs in here! And, Ken, look at this black bag. It looks like diamonds, ma."

"Nigga, let me see! Damn, it's like thirty loose stones in here. This nigga must be a criminal himself. Come on, bag all this up. Let's be out."

• • •

Kennedy drove back to their hotel on the outskirts of Las Vegas. She was tired and weary; they had checked in four days earlier. That meant four days of not much sleep and no play.

The night before, she had worked three different casino hotels, getting four different men for their loot. She had cleared forty-five thousand dollars in cash and jewelry. She'd worn a black Gucci minidress. Now she was wearing a white tee and cut-up jean shorts with a crispy white pair of uptowns to replace the Jimmy Choo stilettos. Her beautiful makeup job was gone. Her long reddish-brown hair was pulled back into a neat ponytail. Her lips were covered only by a hint of MAC Lip Glass.

Kennedy had to take No-Doz to stay awake while driving. Nina had already fallen into a deep sleep. Kennedy thought about playing a prank to get her up but decided to let her cousin sleep for the remaining thirty minutes of the ride. Kennedy thought, *Nina did a wonderful job tonight. She was determined to get that safe open.*

After what felt like an eternal thirty minutes, they arrived at the hotel.

"Yo, Nina, get up. We're here. Come on, it's six-fifteen already."

Without opening her eyes, Nina groggily responded, "Just let me sleep twenty more minutes."

"No. Get up! We have to pack all this shit up, ship it, and get to the airport by nine forty-five. In case you forgot, our plane leaves at ten-fifty."

Nina rose up from the reclined seat with an attitude and fresh drool on her face.

"All right, all right, damn! You get on my nerves. Everybody ain't like you! I can't stay up for forty-eight hours with no sleep."

"Nina, I don't want to hear that shit. You can sleep as long as you want when we get home."

"Stop bugging, chick, I'm up."

Inside the room, they got right to the job at hand. Kennedy lined souvenir vases with cash and jewelry. Nina carefully wrapped each one in tissue paper and plastic bubble before placing them in the box.

After they finished, Kennedy stood up and scanned the room to make sure nothing had been left behind. "Is that everything, Nina?"

"Yeah, ma, that's everything."

"All right, then, we only have forty-five minutes to get ready. I'll go ahead and get in the shower! I already have my clothes out."

They finished dressing, packed the rented Suburban, and headed for UPS. Kennedy was glad to see the same black man who had been there each day, working the counter.

He had openly flirted with her, even though he was old enough to be her grandfather. He had even given her a discount on shipping. He began to smile now, revealing a gold crown, at the sight of Kennedy in a pair of tight Chloé jeans, a black halter top, and spike sandals. Her tanned red skin and her beautiful smile entranced him. With his husky voice, he greeted her. "Hey, young lady, I see you came back to see me."

Showing her pearly whites, she responded, "And how are you this morning, sir?"

"I'm a lot better now that I've seen your pretty face. Now tell me, did you come back to take me up on my offer of marriage?" The greasy old man and his gold crown literally made Kennedy sick. But she played along with him, licking her lips and smiling as she answered. "Not this time, baby, but I will let you know next week."

"Girl, you can have all my money."

Kennedy thought to herself, *I'd rather be broke.*

She was tired of playing, so she got to the point. "I have to catch a flight to Louisiana, and I need to overnight these to my sisters in New York. I need to insure both boxes for ten thousand dollars apiece."

"Damn, girl, what you got in the boxes, gold? You wanted the same amount on all those other boxes."

"Only thing in those boxes is antique vases. Only reason I insure them for so much is because I know they won't get messed up or stolen. If anything happens to them, someone will lose their job when United Parcel Service has to kick out ten Gs or more."

"Well, look here, baby girl, just pay for the insurance. I won't charge you for the shipping and handling."

"Okay, that's what's up."

She paid him and turned toward the door. As she walked away his eyes were fixed on her ass. He thought to himself, *I'm going to have some of that sweet young thing.*

When Kennedy approached the truck she saw Nina bending down in the seat. As she looked closer, she saw three white lines on Nina's compact mirror and a rolled-up fifty-dollar bill up her nose. Her nostrils vacuumed the powder trails clean. Kennedy yanked the door open, jumped in.

"What the fuck are you doing?" she barked at Nina.

"Come on, Ken-Ken, with that self-righteous shit—"

Kennedy cut her off. "No, Nina! I don't want to hear that shit. One, how can you even ride around with that shit knowing what we are out here doing? Come on, B, how fucking stupid is jeopardizing everything we came out here for over some fucking blow? Damn, bitch, are you twenty-nine or nineteen?"

Nina couldn't believe how her baby cousin had just blown up at her. "Kennedy, it's not that serious. I always have to toot a little powder before I get on the plane. You know I get nervous about flying."

"That's no excuse. You can get a doctor to prescribe you something for that. How long you been back on that shit? I thought you was clean."

Tears welled up in Nina's eyes as she thought back to a time when crack and heroin had ruled her every move. At the time, Kennedy was only eighteen, but she had helped Nina overcome her addiction after their entire family had given up on her. At twenty-two, she'd been strung-out with two kids. After nearly killing herself and her younger son, she checked into a twenty-eight-day program at a clinic.

No one had expected it to work; she had been there and done that so many times before. While Nina was away for that particular stretch of sobriety, Kennedy had gotten tired of hearing family members talking about Nina like she was some stranger in the street. They were the same people who had kept their hands open for a handout when Nina's money was long.

Furthermore, she was just sick of seeing her older cousin, whom she admired so much, fading away. All of her life she had looked up to Nina: she liked the way Nina got her own paper. While most girls were begging boys for sneaker, doobie, and nail money, Nina was getting her hustle on. Kennedy had always thought that her cousin was the flyest chick in Harlem. Plus, Nina's beautiful dark skin enhanced her beauty.

The heroin addict that Nina had turned into was someone whom Kennedy did not know. At the time, her once-meticulous cousin was wearing the same clothes for days on end. Her smooth chocolate skin had become blotchy and dry. Her long, thick hair became simply long and stringy.

At the end of the twenty-eight days, Kennedy had been there to pick her up. She moved into Nina's house, cooked good meals for her, and took care of her sons. A year later, Nina was back on her feet and clean. She was even more beautiful and healthier than she'd been before the drugs.

She could not deny that Kennedy was one of the few people who loved her unconditionally. Now, as she sat in the Suburban, she knew her cousin was only barking on her out of true love. It had been three years since Nina had closed the book on that chapter of her life.

Nina snapped back to reality. "Ken-Ken, I swear I only toot every now and then. Only when I'm completely stressed or I'm about to fly. And I promise you I'm not fucking with that heroin."

"Look, Nina, I love you no matter what, but I never want to see you go through that shit again. I'm not eighteen anymore. I don't have the energy to go through that shit with you again. And what about your kids? Niko and Taylor are old enough to know now. And Madeline is only two. She needs you to be there for her."

"Kennedy, I promise I'll never go back to that again."

"Aight, ma, whatever you say. But check this: whatever you got left, you need to toss it. I be damned if I get knocked for some petty blow shit."

Home to Harlem

The ride to the airport and the flight home were silent: Kennedy was still upset about the blow. They picked up their luggage and caught the shuttle to the parking deck to pick up her X5.

Once they were on the highway, Nina broke the silence. "Kennedy, I said I was sorry, so can you kill the cold-shoulder act already?"

"Nina, I'm past that already. I'm quiet because I'm exhausted."

"Well, what are you going to do tonight?"

"First, I'm going home and I'm going to sleep, and sleep, and sleep."

"When are you going to Aunt Karen's house to pick up the boxes?"

"Nina, I thought you were going to pick up everything."

"I can't. Once I pick up the truck, I have to drive all the way to Central Islip and pick up the kids from my stepmother's."

Kennedy was too tired to negotiate, so she gave in. "Well, I'll just wait until tomorrow so that the packages we sent this morning will be there, too. Besides, I already have plans for tonight," she said with a sneaky smile on her face.

Nina was curious about that smile. Everyone knew that Kennedy had not had a steady companion since she'd given birth to her son, Jordan, a year ago. "Ken-Ken, who do you have plans with?" Nina asked, still studying the expression on her cousin's face.

"It ain't nothing special. Hassan is coming over to hang with me."

"Hassan who? The rapper from Lincoln Projects?"

"Yes, Nina, the same Hassan."

"You still fucking him? Don't he still go with that same girl he been with forever?"

Kennedy looked at Nina from the corner of her eye. "Yeah, why? You gonna call her or something?"

Nina rolled her eyes. "No, bitch, don't play yourself. I'm just saying, you got mad niggas chasing you from everywhere, with crazy paper, trying to wife you. And you still fucking with this rapping nigga who got a bitch at home? Come on, what part of the game is that, ma?"

Kennedy felt her face turning red. She kept her eyes on the road. "Are you through?"

"What?"

"Are you through expressing your opinion on my life?"

"What are you talking about, Kennedy?"

"Look, ma. I like my relationship with Hassan. The rules are clear and defined. I know he got a girl. We don't lie to each other about the obvious. You heard what Hova said: *'Our time together is our time together.'* And as far as all these niggas out here chasing me, they don't want to do nothing but play with my mind. I've been through all the games before, and I ain't for it now. Plus, I'm not trying to have no frivolous niggas around my son. I've been through too much. What you think I should do? Be like you and Cream? Well, that's not the type of nigga I want in my cipher."

Nina folded her arms across her chest and began moving her neck as she started speaking. "And what the fuck is that suppose to mean, Kennedy?"

"Oh *please,* don't play coy with me, ma. So what, you got a nigga at home! Are you happy with him? Tell me, are you? How can you be happy with a man who punches you in the face whenever you say something he doesn't like? Or better yet, a nigga you caught fucking your best friend!"

An annoyed Nina finally interrupted Kennedy before she could go any further. "Please stop with all that bullshit you kicking! You making it sound worse than what it is. And so what he fucked that bitch? You see who he's with. And don't act like he just be hitting me for no reason because I do provoke him most of the time."

Kennedy nearly crashed the truck from laughing so hard at Nina's last comment. Nina was frozen, holding on to the dashboard. "Bitch, what is wrong with you?"

Kennedy, still laughing, replied, "I don't want you to say anything else to me, just for saying that bullshit!"

"What bullshit?" Nina asked, looking bewildered.

"That stupid shit you just said about you be provoking him. Ma, you really sound like you suffering from battered women's syndrome. That's exactly why I don't want you to call me no more when he choking your simple ass out."

"Oh, so you wouldn't help me if you saw that nigga beating me?"

"Fam, come on, don't even play me like that. Every time I jump in a fight between you two, you go right back to him. And let's not forget that night in Club NV when he was fucking your face up and I hit him over the head with that Hypnotiq bottle. You had the nerve to buck up to me, screaming on me and shit, in front of all those people. I should have duffed your ass. So hell yeah, the answer is no."

"Damn, Ken, I didn't know the shit was that serious."

"Yeah, it's that serious, 'cause I can't understand how a bitch of your caliber be fucking with these bum-ass niggas. And no, I'm not talking 'bout their financial status. I'm talking about their mental capacity."

Nina didn't want to discuss it anymore, so she just let the remark go with no response.

Kennedy was beginning to hate the way the day was going. She and Nina had never argued that much. She really hated it when people tried to analyze her life, especially when they didn't have their own in check.

As Kennedy pulled into the garage Nina began going off. "Damn Cream's ass! Nobody told him to come get my truck and leave this fucked-up shit here." She pulled out her cell phone and made a call, with no luck.

Kennedy asked, "What's wrong with the Lex? Don't you have keys to it?"

"Yeah, I got keys to it, but don't you see all those key scratches all over it?"

"Oh shit, yo, I didn't even peep that."

Nina hopped out of the truck and began tossing her bags into the back of the Lexus. Still heated, she walked over to Kennedy's side of the truck. "I know one of his bitches done keyed his car. I hate him so much. Anyway, what time do you want to hook up tomorrow?"

"Early! The rest of the boxes are supposed to be there by nine. We have to do everything early, Nina, 'cause I'm going down south to get Jordan."

"You driving all the way to NC by yourself?"

"Nah, Kneaka is going to ride with me. Yesterday was the last day of summer school at Fordham."

"I might ride with you, too. I need to go see my mother."

"Well, let me know. I have to go. I'm about to pass out. Holla back."

"One."

Kennedy drove down the hill to her apartment; she did not

even bother to go to the garage to park. She was too tired to walk or catch a cab. She parked on the street down the block from her building.

Kennedy walked into her apartment and dropped everything by the door, including the mail she had picked up from the mailbox, not even bothering to look at it. She fell onto her bed, kicked off her shoes, and within seconds was in a deep sleep.

As Nina pulled up to her building, she saw her Benz truck parked on the opposite side of the street. Cream and about twenty other guys were standing by the truck playing C-Lo.

When Cream spotted Nina, he walked across the street, smiling from ear to ear. "Hey, Nee, baby, when did you get back? Give me a hug, ma." He grabbed her with his six-foot-five, well-built body and hugged her tight.

She squirmed until she broke free of his firm grasp. "Cream, get the hell away from me before I smack fire out your trifling ass. And take this keyed-up shit so I can go get my kids."

"Ma, what the fuck is wrong with you? Why you breaking? Damn, ain't you happy to see your man?"

"I might be happy to see your ass if, when I came home, drama didn't hit me dead in the face."

"What are you talking about, Nina?"

"What am I talking about? Don't play stupid: you know what I'm talking about. That bitch keying your car up like this."

"No, I don't know what you're talking about, 'cause some little punks did that shit."

Nina was becoming furious. She hated when someone tried to play on her intelligence.

"Look, Cream, stop while you are ahead. If your lazy ass ever bothered to check the voice mail, you would know she left me a long message concerning your relationship with her. Oh, you don't believe me? Her name is Tasha Eaton and she said she is pregnant by you. And before she became pregnant, you was all in love with her, spending money, taking her on trips with you and your boys. And the two of you even have a little love nest over in Lenox Terrace. But as soon as she said she was pregnant by you, that is the first time you ever mentioned Mattie or me to her. And you told her she better get an abortion."

Nina gave him the business from the top of her lungs, so everyone in the street was staring. It was already a hot July day. Nina's confrontation had made Cream sweat even more than he was already sweating. His crisp white tee and baggy jean shorts were soaked in perspiration. He looked over his shoulder only to see his boys laughing at him. He turned back to Nina. "Oh, so you don't think we could have discussed this shit in private rather than putting all my business out in the street?"

Nina began laughing like a madwoman.

"You already put your business out in the street when you were flaunting your little whore in front of all your niggas. And furthermore, there ain't shit for us to discuss. I want you to get your shit and get the fuck out of my house." Nina pushed past him, walking toward her truck. All of his boys were staring at her, which really ticked her off. Because they all knew what was going on and yet they came into her house every day, eating her food and smiling in her face. "And what the fuck are y'all looking at?"

They all turned their heads and looked the other way.

Nina got in her truck and merked off, leaving Cream in the middle of the street, looking like an ass next to his keyed-up car.

"Get your shit and get out!" one of his boys jokingly yelled out to him. Laughter roared on the block.

Cream walked back to the corner, trying to laugh it all off. "You know I ain't going nowhere, nigga. All I have to do is buy that big baby a gift and she will be okay."

• • •

The loud ringing awakened Kennedy. Just as she reached for the phone the ringing stopped. She rolled over, and as soon as she closed her eyes her cell phone began to ring. She fumbled around the bed until she found it. "Hello!" she called out, irritation in her voice.

"Dang, girl, where you at?" Nina asked on the other end.

"I was in the state of sleep—a good sleep, too. What time is it?"

"It is a quarter to ten."

"Damn, I been asleep for six hours?"

"You was taking all them No-Doz. When you come down off them things, you come down hard."

"Tell me about it. What up, though?"

"Ain't nothing, packing up Cream's shit."

"Say word."

"Word, my nigga."

"Why?"

"Come to find out he been messing with some young girl from Jefferson the last six months. He moved her into Lenox Terrace. And now she pregnant. So you know she keyed the Lex because he wants her to have an abortion."

Kennedy sat listening in silence. She had known about Cream and Tasha's relationship but had not bothered to tell Nina. Kennedy had learned her lesson about telling Nina things she heard in the street. Nina would go back and tell Cream what she had heard from Kennedy, and then take Cream's word over Kennedy's.

Kennedy's line beeped. "Hold on, Nina, I got another call." She clicked over. "Hello?"

"What up, ma? Where you at?"

"Hi, Has. I'm home. Hold on right quick. Let me get off the other line."

She clicked back over to Nina.

"Yo, Nina, I have to go. That's Hassan."

"Oh, so you just gonna hang up with me like that? For that nigga?"

"Come on, Nee, you know it's not like that."

"Go on, Kennedy, you know I'm just messing with you. Handle your BI and hit me later."

"Aight, Nina, be careful, and don't let that nigga buy his way back in. I love you, ma. Be easy."

"I love you, too, Kennedy. Holla back."

Kennedy clicked back over. "What up, Has?"

"You know I was about to hang up."

"My bad. You still coming over?"

"Yeah, I'm still coming over, but can you come get me off my block? I already put my truck in the garage for the night."

"That's cool. I'll be there in about thirty minutes. I need to take a shower first."

"Aight, ma. One."

Kennedy got up and slipped off her sweaty clothes then turned up the air conditioner to counter the muggy and humid air outside. She took a ten-minute steamy shower, washing away the sticky sweat with peppermint soap.

She felt like a new person after her long nap and refreshing shower. She rubbed her body down with lotion then put on a pair of gray cotton short shorts and a gray fitted tee. She stood in the mirror brushing her hair, thinking, *I need a fresh doobie and maybe a relaxer, too.* Then she was out the door.

When Kennedy pulled up to Hassan's block, everyone turned around and tried to figure out who was in the gray X5 with the gray tints. She rolled down her window and called out to Hassan. "Yo, you going with me?"

"Yo, Ken, what up? I didn't know that was you. Hold up, I'm coming."

Hassan's cousin EB began questioning him. "Yo, who that pretty young thing pushing that X?"

"You remember Kennedy from a Hundred Forty-first and Eighth."

EB squinted to get a closer look. "Li'l thick Kennedy, who used to rap? That's her?"

"Yeah, man, that's her."

"Damn, I didn't know y'all still kept in contact."

"I hadn't seen her in almost two years. I bumped into her last week at the Gucci store, but she was on her way out of town or something."

"You know I could hit that, right?" EB told Hassan with a sly smile on his face.

Hassan just laughed. "Nigga, you couldn't hit that with a bat. Anyway, I'm out. Get at me tomorrow."

Hassan exchanged pounds with everyone on the block before going to the truck.

EB walked over to speak to Kennedy. "What up, girl? How you been?"

"I been okay. What about you, EB?"

"I'm straight, you know, doing my thug thizzle."

"Aight, then, be easy, my nigga."

Hassan got in the truck and gave Kennedy a hug. "What's poppin', Ken? I didn't know who you were pulling up on me like that. I thought you still had the Acura."

"I got rid of that after I had my son."

"Yeah? How's your baby doing?"

"He straight. He down south with my mother. I'm going to get him tomorrow."

"That's what's up. What was you doing out in Vegas, vacationing?"

"Something like that."

"Ma, what you out here doing in the world? And don't lie, 'cause I heard you was doing your thing-thing."

"Come on, you know me, Has. And now I got my son, so I have to grind harder."

"I feel you. Just be careful. You know these streets is ugly."

"Trust me, I know," she replied, her voice full of emotion, then shook it off. "You hungry, Has?"

"A little. Why?"

"Cause I'm going to get something from the Jamaican spot on Forty-fifth and Eighth. I haven't went food shopping, so ain't shit to eat at my house."

"That's straight. Get me whatever you getting, as long as it's not pork."

"Boy, you know I don't hardly eat no pork. I'm getting curry chicken, rice and peas, and plantains."

"Get me that and some half-and-half. Here, is twenty enough?"

"Keep that; it's my treat. You're a guest in my home tonight." She got out of the truck and walked toward the store.

As she walked away his eyes were fixed on her thick thighs. He just sat and reminisced about how good she was in bed, especially that thing she did with her tongue. It had been more than two years since they'd slept together and just thinking about it made his dick hard.

The sound of Kennedy opening the door brought him back to reality.

"Damn, Has, what was you thinking about? You didn't even see me standing here with the bags in my hand."

"I was just thinking about hitting that," he said, slipping his hand between her legs.

At Kennedy's, they ate, drank Heinekens, and talked about

life. Hassan pulled out a sandwich bag filled with weed. "Ken, you ever smoke purple haze?"

"I tried that shit before; it's strong as hell. I just stick to dro and a little Branson from time to time."

"Well, you 'bout to smoke some of this haze with me."

He pulled out an Optimo cigar, cracked it, emptied the contents, and filled it with the haze. Before they had finished smoking the first blunt, he had already rolled another. Kennedy was able to take only two hits of the second blunt.

"That is enough for me. I'm stuck," she said. She got up and attempted to cross over Hassan. He grabbed her by the hips and pulled her in front of him, caressing her thighs with his hands. He slid his hands under her shorts and massaged her throbbing, moist, warm middle.

"Let me take these shorts off, ma."

She could only nod her head up and down as he removed the shorts. The haze had her gone, and it had been so long since she had slept with anyone. The touch of his hands alone simply made her melt. He stood up; his six-foot two-inch frame towered over her five-foot seven-inch body.

He removed his T-shirt and dropped his shorts and boxers. He pulled her tee over her head, revealing her bare breasts. He bent down and began giving her ears and neck wet tongue kisses. Hassan sat back on the couch. He grabbed Kennedy by the thighs and pulled her down on top of him.

She held her breath as she slowly slid onto him, letting out a slight whimper when he was all the way in. She was extra tight after about a year of no sex. Hassan moaned from the tightness and wetness of her walls. The quicker she began to move, the better it felt to both of them.

He stood up, never pulling out, and carried her to the bedroom. He laid her on the bed, placing both legs on his shoulders.

He pulled halfway out and dropped all the way down, causing her to moan.

As he began to stroke her faster, she bit down on her lip to keep from screaming. She was getting wetter and wetter, and he could feel it.

"Ma, you coming?"

Still unable to speak, she just nodded.

"Wait, don't come yet."

He flipped her onto her stomach and entered from the back. He stroked her faster and faster until her body trembled in ecstasy.

"Oh my God, baby," she moaned over and over as she came all over his dick. He pulled out and let off all over her back. Out of energy, he collapsed on her back, gasping for air, heart racing. Once he caught his breath, he got up and went to the bathroom. A few minutes later he returned with a warm rag. Kennedy was laying in the same position, unable to move. Hassan cleaned off her back and in between her legs.

"Ken, you okay?"

"I'm aight."

"Get up and get under the covers."

She lifted her body as much as she could and crawled under the covers. Hassan got under as well and wrapped his arms around her.

"Ma, that shit was bananas!"

Already half-asleep, she responded, "Am I suppose to say thank you?"

"You ain't got to say shit. Just don't get ghost on a nigga again."

"That you don't have to worry about."

Kennedy fell into a deep sleep, still fatigued from the past week. Hassan wasn't tired, but he knew she could not go another round. He rolled another blunt and watched television until he fell into his own nod.

Nina sat on the couch watching episodes she had missed of *Sex and the City* on TiVo. Hours ago she had bathed the kids and put them to bed. She had also finished packing all of Cream's belongings and had set them by the front door. It was 2 A.M. and he wasn't home yet.

Two forty-five, she heard his keys in the door. He saw all his bags packed. Moments later she heard him say, "She can't be serious."

He walked into the living room holding two dozen roses and bags from Chanel. Nina never took her eyes from the screen, even when he tried to start a conversation.

"So you gonna act like you don't see me standing here, huh? Look what I bought you. I got the Chanel sandals and the matching bag that you was looking at."

Nina looked at him, then at the bags, and turned up her nose. "I don't want that shit."

"This shit cost three Gs."

"So what? Give it to that young bitch. And while you at it, get your shit and take it to her house. My bad—I meant *y'all* house."

"Nina, come off it. It wasn't that serious. That bitch didn't mean nothing to me. I love only you, and I am so sorry I hurt you. Now come over here and give me a hug."

Nina was becoming irritated that he wasn't taking her serious.

"Cream, are you listening to me? Do you understand what I am saying to you? I want you to get your things and get the *fuck* out of my house."

"Bitch, I'm not going anywhere! This is my house. I take care of Mattie and them damn boys that ain't even mine! Bitch, you tripping if you think I'm going somewhere!"

"No, nigga, you bugging, 'cause I have never asked you for anything. I got my own paper. And as for Niko and Taylor, I never asked you to support my kids. And everything you do for Madeline, you're supposed to. You're her father. You know what? You are just as pathetic and trifling as Kennedy said you were."

"Kennedy! Oh, so now you listening to that bitch again? Is that who put it in your head to put me out? Since you want to listen to her, see if she's willing to take this ass whipping."

He smacked Nina, causing her to fall backward over the top of the couch. She landed on the floor with a loud thump that woke up the boys. They ran into the living room and saw Cream picking her up by her shirt and punching her repeatedly in her face.

"Mommy!" Taylor screamed out.

Between punches and efforts to fight back, she answered her older son's cry. "Tay, take your brother, go in the room, and lock the door."

Taylor grabbed the phone off the hall table and ran into the room with Niko. His hands shook as he dialed Kennedy's phone number.

Kennedy's phone rang five times before she woke up; she looked at the caller ID before answering.

"Nina, why are you calling me at three in the morning?"

"Ken, this is Tay," a tearful Taylor answered.

"Baby, what's wrong?" Kennedy slid from underneath Hassan's arm and sat straight up.

"It's Mommy. Cream is beating her bad."

Kennedy jumped out of bed, waking up Hassan. "Okay, baby, where are you now?"

"I'm locked in the room with Niko."

"Where is Mattie?"

"She's in her room."

"Listen, Tay, stay in your room. Don't come out until I get there. I will be there in five minutes, okay, baby?"

"Okay, Ken."

"See you in five minutes, bye."

She threw on the first T-shirt and jeans in sight.

"Where you going, ma?" Hassan asked her.

"Cream is beating Nina's ass again. The kids just called, terrified. You can stay here as long as want, the slam lock is on the door."

Kennedy rumbled through her drawer until she found the spare keys to Nina's apartment. She pulled out a 9mm semiautomatic handgun from under her mattress. She checked the magazine to make sure it was loaded.

Hassan saw the gun. "Kennedy, what are you taking that for? Are you sure you don't need me to go?"

"Nah, Has, that's okay. I'll call you tomorrow. I'm out."

Meanwhile, at Nina's, Taylor cracked the door and looked out of the bedroom, despite Niko's protests. He saw Nina and Cream still going at it. Cream was hitting her with hard blows all over her body, but she wasn't taking them lying down. She fought back as much she could, scratching, kicking, and swinging her arms. She reached onto the coffee table, grabbed an iron candlestick holder, and hit him in the eye, causing him to lose his balance. As he fell backward she stood up, dazed, and tried to make it to the bedroom to get her gun. She wasn't quick enough. In one swift movement he was up and right behind her.

He grabbed a handful of her hair, yanking her through the air toward him. He spun her around and began choking her. She wanted to fight back but couldn't. She could only try to remove his hands from her neck.

He released his right hand, pulled back, and hit her with a strong punch, right between the eyes. The punch packed so much power he could not even hold on to her with his left hand. She fell backward, hitting her head on the steel bar that was affixed to the glass dining table.

Glass shattered everywhere, and blood flowed from Nina's mouth and nose. She was unconscious. Cream was frozen with fear. In all of their earlier fights, nothing like this had ever happened. Blood was flowing out so fast. He knew that she had suffered more than a busted lip or nose.

He didn't know what to do. He started to panic and ran to Madeline's room and grabbed her out of the bed. He picked up one of the duffel bags that Nina had packed and ran down the stairs to the car. He laid Madeline down in the backseat, hopped in the car, and pulled off.

As Kennedy drove up to Nina's building, she saw Cream driving away. She thought to herself, *Good, the drama is over.*

She used her key to get into the building then ran up the stairs. The door to Nina's apartment was ajar. She stepped in and called out, "Nina, baby, are you okay? Taylor called me. Where are you?"

From the corner of her eye, she saw Nina lying on the floor. She ran over to her, knelt down beside her, and lifted her head. "Oh God, Nina, wake up. Taylor," she called out, "you can come out now. I'm here, baby. Hurry."

Taylor came out of the bedroom and got a surreal view of his mother.

"Tay, baby, I need you to dial 911. Tell them we need help. Tell them your mommy has been hurt very bad, and she is not moving."

Niko stood over Kennedy and Nina, his face covered in tears and mucus. "Ken, he took Mattie."

"He did? I didn't see her in the car. Well, we'll get her back. Niko, baby, I need you to go get me a glass of water and a wet rag."

Nina started coughing and gagging and more blood came out of her mouth. She looked up at Kennedy. "Ken-Ken, take care of my kids, please. Don't let nobody take them."

"Nina, stop talking like that. You're gonna be okay. The ambulance is on the way."

"I can't, Ken. The pain is too bad in my head. I want you to take my kids. Please promise me."

"I promise. But you're going to be okay. You can't leave me yet. I won't let you get off the hook that easy."

"Tell my kids I love them so much. And I hope I didn't upset you."

Kennedy had tears streaming down her face.

"Ma, I'm not upset with you."

" 'Cause you were always right about me. You were the only one who kept it gully with me. I love you."

"I love you, too. Now stop talking. Save your breath."

"Ken, please don't be mad, but I . . . I can't make it." Nina's eyes closed as she took her last breath.

A cool breeze ran through the room, causing the hair to stand up on the back of Kennedy's neck. She shook Nina's lifeless body. "Nina, wake up. No, Nina, you are not leaving me now. Come on, ma, we have too much to do."

Kennedy wiped the blood from Nina's mouth and tried CPR to no avail. Niko and Taylor looked on, crying, as Kennedy continued to talk to Nina. She rocked back and forth with Nina in her arms. "Nina, why, why, sweetie, why didn't you call me? Why didn't you call me? I would have come. I was only playing when I said don't call me."

Moments later, the paramedics and police rushed through the door. The police took Kennedy aside for questioning. She answered their questions to the best of her knowledge. She continued to watch as the paramedics worked on Nina with no success.

Kennedy looked over and saw Niko and Taylor on the couch. Niko had his head buried in Taylor's chest; Taylor was trying to console his younger brother. He was crying just as hard as Niko.

Kennedy attempted to wrap up the conversation with the police. "Can we finish this later? The boys—they need me."

The short, round lady officer who happened to be a mother empathized with Kennedy. "That is perfectly fine. We'll be here for a while, but I need you to give me a recent picture of Madeline. And we need to speak to the boys once they settle down a little. Is there anyone I can call for you?"

"No, my aunt is on her way here now."

Kennedy went and sat down between the boys, pulled them close, and wrapped both arms around them. They sat still while the EMTs bagged Nina's body and took her away. Kennedy stared straight ahead as she spoke to the boys. "This is why you never put your hands on a woman. Always honor your mother's memory, and never hit a woman. Promise me and your mother right now you will never hit a woman."

Tearfully they answered, "I promise."

Later that morning, everyone gathered at Karen's house. Of Kennedy's seven aunts on her mother's side of the family, Karen was the strongest. Whenever something went wrong, she was the one the family called. Kennedy was her favorite niece and everyone knew it. She had favored her ever since Kennedy was a child because Kennedy reminded her of herself.

Karen could see from the other side of the living room that Kennedy looked run-down and tired. She saw others attempt to talk with Kennedy and not receive a response. She knew that Nina's passing was going to tear Kennedy to pieces sooner or later. Karen decided that it was time for her to get away from the crowd. "Kennedy, baby, come on, you need to go lay down."

"I'm aight, Auntie. I just wish she would have called me."

"Sweetie, you can't carry on like this. You can't blame yourself."

Kennedy laid her head on Karen's shoulder and broke into tearful sobs. "Auntie, you don't understand. We had an argument about Cream when we came back from Vegas. I told her not to call me the next time he was beating her. I didn't mean it; I just said it in the heat of the moment."

"Baby, I know you didn't mean it, and Nina knew you didn't mean it. You were always there for her, even when the family gave up on her."

"I know, Auntie, but we were more than cousins. She was my sister."

"I know, baby, I know. Have you talked to your mother again?"

"She called me from Auntie Klarice's house. She said Auntie Klarice was in denial."

"I can only imagine what she is going through, losing her oldest child at the hands of that low-life nigga."

"My mommy said they will be here sometime tonight. She was going home to book plane tickets for them and Grandma."

Karen fought back the tears as she looked down at Kennedy, lying in her lap like a child. For the first time, she noticed that Kennedy's dark jeans and hot-pink T-shirt were covered in blood.

"Kennedy, let me take you to your house so you can take these clothes off. You need to get away from all these people for a little while."

As they got up to leave, Cream's mother, Vivian, walked through the door, holding Madeline. Kennedy took Madeline out of her arms and hugged her, glad to have her back safely. She sat back on the couch and placed Madeline on her lap.

Vivian was very humble. She apologized many times for Cream's actions and explained that Cream had dropped Madeline off around 5 A.M. Vivian honestly felt bad and humiliated, so she didn't hang around any longer than necessary. "Mattie, honey, come give Grandma a big hug. I'm getting ready to leave now."

Madeline attempted to get up, but Kennedy wouldn't let her go. For the first time, Kennedy looked directly at Vivian. "Miss Vivian, please don't take this the wrong way or don't think I'm trying to disrespect you when I say this. But the next time you talk to your son, you need to tell him his best bet is to turn his self in to the police. Because if me or any of my cousins see him, you'll know exactly what my aunt Klarice is going through right now. But then again, he won't be safe on Rikers, or any jail in the state of New York, will he?" Kennedy smiled coldly and let Madeline go. "Go give your granny a hug so she can go."

Vivian hugged Madeline quickly and walked so fast to the door she almost ran.

Kara, Kennedy's mother's snooty rich know-it-all sister whom no one got along with, especially Kennedy, looked at Kennedy and shook her head. "Kennedy, you ought to be ashamed, talking to that nice lady like that, after she came over here so humble. I swear you have no couth."

Kennedy got right in Kara's face. "Kara, take that snooty, I-got-my-master's-degree shit back to Queens and shove it up your tight ass! I'm not for it today, not when my cousin, my sister, my best friend, just died in my arms."

Kara was scared to even breathe.

Karen placed her hand on Kennedy's shoulders and gently pulled her away. "Come on, Kennedy, sweetie, don't do it. She is not even worth it."

Kara was fuming. "Karen, why are you taking her side? She was rude and disrespectful to Vivian, and now me."

Karen stepped up to Kara's face. "I want you to leave her alone. She may have been crass in her approach, but she was right. We're glad Mattie is back, but Vivian knows where her son is, and I didn't appreciate her coming in here with all her self-serving apologies either. Come on, Kennedy, let's go."

"That's okay, Auntie, I'll drive myself. I'll take Mattie with me and get her cleaned up, too." Kennedy picked up Madeline and walked out of the door, slamming it behind her.

Kennedy placed Madeline in the backseat of the car and strapped her in. She got into the car, put on her seat belt, but could not move. After a minute or so, she took a deep breath and started the engine. She drove down Lenox in a daze, feeling like the world was moving though *she* wasn't.

She sat at the red light on 139th and Lenox, looking at all the kids in the park playing with not a care in the world. Their innocent faces were so beautiful, so full of hope. She continued to watch them play, wondering what they would be when they grew up. Her thoughts were interrupted by Madeline's tiny voice.

"Ken-Ken."

"Yes, baby?"

"Can I have an icy?"

Kennedy looked at Madeline, who was watching the kids outside, lined up at the icy cart. "Yeah, li'l mama, I'll get you one by my house after you eat some food. Okay?"

"Okay."

Kennedy turned around in time to catch the light turning green, but Madeline wasn't finished talking.

"Ken-Ken, are you taking me home?"

"We're going to my house right now. Why?"

"I want my mommy."

Kennedy had not given any thought to how she was going to explain Nina's death to Madeline. *How do you tell a two-year-old she will never see her mother again?* With tears streaming down her face, she gave the only response she could. "Baby, I want your mommy, too."

I Wish, I Wish, I Wish

Big Ma was nothing to play with. She was a God-fearing, strong black woman. Big Ma knew the Bible like the back of her hand. She could quote the Scripture verbatim. In the next breath she could curse like a sailor on leave. Big Ma's husband, Daddy James, had moved their family to New York in the forties. They traded in living under Jim Crow laws and the KKK for the equally racist NYPD.

At age seventy-five, Big Ma had seen everything—lynching in the South, rioting in the North, and the eighties crack epidemic. After Daddy James's death in 1992, she'd decided she had seen enough. Big Ma moved back to Charlotte, North Carolina. A year later Kennedy's mother, Kora, and Nina's mother, Klarice, followed, taking their children with them.

Kennedy and Nina had hated the idea of leaving New York. When they moved to Charlotte they rebelled in every way possible, until Kora and Klarice gave in and sent the girls back to New York to live with Karen.

Now, as they sat on the plane, Kora was regretting the decision she and Klarice had made. *We should have put our foot down and made those girls stay in Charlotte. They would not have gotten in so much trouble over the years. And poor Nina wouldn't be dead.*

Big Ma sat between her daughters with an ache in her heart.

Before today, she could not have fathomed what it would mean to lose another grandchild. Nina was the fourth grandchild she'd lost to violence in twelve years, the first granddaughter. Big Ma's grand girls, as she called them, were special to her. She had only five granddaughters, compared to eleven grandsons, and three of the surviving eight were in prison.

The first time Big Ma had lost a grandson, it had nearly torn her apart. By the time she lost her third grandson, she'd learned to accept death as God's will, and this she never questioned.

Losing her oldest granddaughter was an altogether different hurt. The pain she felt for Klarice was intense. She'd cried only once, when she first learned of Nina's death. *I have to be strong for Klarice. Lord, I have to be really strong for Kennedy. This may take her sanity.*

Big Ma had already witnessed Kennedy nearly go insane after the death of her boyfriend Pretty Boy.

Kennedy was fifteen when she'd met Pretty Boy. He was eighteen, and already a gangster's gangster. They had fallen hard for each other. Pretty Boy had been her first boyfriend. Kennedy was the only thing he loved. He was the product of a prostitute and a pimp. He had been in and out of foster homes the first ten years of his life. The streets had literally raised him.

Kennedy and Pretty Boy had met at the rink in Jersey. Kennedy knew who he was, but she wasn't checking for him. Every young girl uptown was sweating him, and even some older women. He had beautiful brown skin, gorgeous full lips, and pearly-white teeth. He wore his curly, jet-black hair in a very neat small Afro. The fact that Pretty Boy was getting money only made him all the more attractive to women.

Pretty Boy had watched Kennedy as she danced while skating round and round. She looked like candy to him. Kennedy was only fifteen, but her body was twenty-five. Pretty Boy had seen her around uptown in her parochial-school uniform. Usually he would see her when she came through the block to visit her cousin Alex. Pretty Boy had always admired her from afar.

That night Kennedy had on her favorite pair of red stretch Parasuco jeans. They made her voluptuous behind look even bigger. Her microbraids were pulled up in a ponytail, showing off her cute baby face. Her huge doorknocker earrings were the perfect accent. As Kennedy skated by him, Pretty Boy reached out and grabbed her. "What up, shorty?"

"Nothing. You looking for Alex? He should be here in a little while."

"I'm not looking for Alex, I'm looking for you."

"For what?"

"I want to take you out tomorrow."

This cannot be happening. The hottest nigga uptown wants to take me out. Okay, answer him, stupid! "Where do you want take me?"

"I was thinking we could go to the movies and out to eat."

"That's straight. What time?"

"Tomorrow, around six-thirty. Meet me by the train on a Hundred Forty-fifth and St. Nick. Wear something like that. Don't wear that Catholic-school uniform."

Oh my God. He has been watching me! "Okay, it's a date. I'll see you tomorrow."

The next day Kennedy and Pretty Boy had gone out. They clicked immediately; it was as if it were meant to be. From that day forward they were inseparable. Pretty Boy would come to her house and walk her to school in the morning. Kennedy would meet him on his block every day after she got out of school. It was truly young ghetto love.

After a year of dating, things began to run smoother and faster for Pretty Boy. He started to control a few more blocks. With his added responsibilities, he didn't get to spend as much time with Kennedy as he'd done before. Some mornings she would come out the house and Pretty Boy wouldn't be there to walk her to school. One morning Kennedy came out of the building and he was sitting in a brand-new Chevy Tahoe.

"Pretty, whose car are you driving? I hope it ain't some crackhead that owe you money."

"Hush, girl, and get in."

"No. Not until you tell me who it belongs to."

"It's mine. I bought it. Now get in."

Kennedy was a little apprehensive, and then she finally got in. "I'm glad you showed up this morning."

"Come on, ma. Please don't start with the time thing again. You already know what time it is. Niggas is grindin' right now."

"So what am I suppose to do now—come second to your paper chase?"

The hurt spread across Pretty Boy's face. "That ain't even fair, Ken-Ken. You know how I feel about you."

"No, I don't know! I never see you anymore."

"I know a way we can fix this. Do you feel like skipping school today?"

Kennedy thought about it. "For what?"

"I have a surprise for you; I was going to show you after school. Since I see you need some attention, we can go get it now."

Pretty Boy drove Kennedy to the Delanor Apartments. He pulled into the back parking area. "Get those keys out the glove compartment."

Kennedy followed Pretty Boy into the building. *Where in the hell is he taking me? I should've gone to school.*

Pretty Boy led her to an apartment on the fifth floor. "Unlock the bottom lock with that red key."

"Hell no! Pretty, whose apartment is this?"

"Kennedy, what the fuck is wrong with you today? Why are you so paranoid? Never mind, give me the damn keys." Pretty Boy opened the door and stepped inside. Kennedy hesitated before walking into the empty apartment. Pretty Boy grabbed her arm and pulled her inside. "Welcome home, mama!"

"What?"

"This is our home."

"Our?"

"Yes, *our!* I just thought with the way things are going lately, we should live together. That way we can see each other at night and wake up to one another every morning."

"Damn, Pretty, I didn't know you felt like that."

"That's 'cause you think you know everything." Pretty Boy playfully tugged at her plaid skirt. "Do you wanna christen the place right now or wait until the furniture gets here in two days?"

"Boy, you are so nasty. We will have to wait. I have to go to school today. I forgot I have an English test fifth period."

"Here, drive yourself," Pretty Boy said, handing her a Honda key.

"Damn, you doin' it! You bought two cars and a new apartment?"

"Stop clowning and come downstairs so you can see it."

The car was a hunter-green, '96 Honda Accord coupe. The interior was beige. Kennedy was grateful for it. "Thank you, Malik."

Pretty Boy blushed; he loved it when Kennedy called him by

his government name. "You welcome. It's only a year old. It has like twenty thousand miles on it. Don't worry, give me a couple of months. I'll get you something nicer for your graduation."

"Why? I like this. I mean, I know women in their thirties and forties who've never owned a car."

"That's why I love you, 'cause you appreciate a nigga."

Six months later, Kennedy graduated. True to his word, Pretty Boy bought her a BMW M3. Business was booming for Pretty Boy. The crew he ran with had locked a few spots in Maryland, Virginia, and South Carolina. Pretty Boy went from making two thousand dollars a day to making between ten and fifteen.

With the success of his come-up came the jealousy, the haters, and the grime, even within the crew. They were a tight crew, with the exception of one loose screw, Tony. Tony, Pretty Boy, and a few other young heads were led by Sazaar. Sazaar treated Pretty Boy and Tony like they were his sons. Pretty Boy was committed to Sazaar and the dynasty they were trying to build. That's why he went to bed late and got up early, sometimes never sleeping. Pretty Boy's commitment made Sazaar respect him and show him favor. That made Tony jealous. Tony wanted all the rewards with no sacrifice. The crew noticed Tony's jealousy and began to call him Cain and Pretty Boy, Abel.

One blazing hot August morning, Pretty Boy came back from South Carolina and instead of going home had gone straight to the block. Kennedy could not believe it when she saw him on the block holding court with his crew. She double-parked and hopped out the car. "Yo, Pretty, can I holla at you?"

Pretty Boy turned to walk toward her. *Damn, look at her face. I know she is pissed off.* When he got in front of her, he wrapped his arms around her. Instead of returning the hug, she shoved him away.

"What up, baby girl?"

"What's up with you, playboy? How long you been back?"

"I got here like, um, two hours ago."

"And this is where you came to first?"

"I had some important business to take care of."

"I can't wait until the day I become as important as your business. Why do we even live together?"

His constant absence was driving Kennedy nuts. When Pretty Boy was in New York he had to take care of the blocks he ran. Most nights consisted of him coming home around 3 A.M. and getting up at 7 A.M. Kennedy was sick of it.

Pretty Boy could tell by the look in her eyes that she was fed up. "Kennedy, you know there is nothing in the world more important than you to me. I have to take care of my business so we can maintain."

"Malik, I don't think *we* are maintaining right now."

"What are you trying to say?"

"I think I should move out. You know, get my own place." *Damn, did I just say that? Maybe he will see shit is real and give me the attention I deserve!*

"Come on, Kennedy, not today with this bullshit, aight. What the fuck do you want to move out for? Don't I provide well for you? Give me a valid reason why you want to leave. Are you fucking wit' another nigga?"

Yeah, nigga, grovel, see how I feel. "Don't play yourself; you know I would never cheat on you. Yeah, you give me more than what I need materialistically. I need you more than I need any of that shit. I want to move out because I saw you more when we didn't live together!"

Pretty Boy saw straight through her charade. He didn't like putting their business on front street by debating on the block.

He put his arm around her and walked her over to the driver's side of her car. "Kennedy, right now is not a good time for this. You are talking from emotions. Go do what you have to do. Let me wrap up all my shit on the block. Meet me at the crib at five-thirty so we can go out and talk about all of this."

"You cannot be serious." Kennedy was laughing uncontrollably. "Wow, this is unbelievable. Mr. Pretty Boy himself wants to take the train."

"I thought it would be a good idea so we can spend some time together. Since you think it's such a joke, fuck it!"

"No, baby, that's straight. Let's go."

Pretty Boy addressed the issues that Kennedy had presented to him earlier that day as they walked down Lenox toward the 2 and 3 train. They continued to talk during the ride downtown. By the end of the ride, they seemed to have resolved everything. Pretty Boy even sealed it with a promise to take Kennedy to Jamaica in a month.

The two enjoyed a movie, dinner, and a long walk through Central Park. They returned home around 1 A.M. and made love before falling into a deep sleep.

One hour later Kennedy was awakened by unfamiliar voices. She tried to open her eyes, but they were covered with duct tape; so was her mouth. Her wrists were taped together, as were her ankles. She panicked when she heard, "Shoot him now, nigga."

Kennedy wanted to cry or scream, but she could do nothing. The two loud blasts in her left ear deafened her. She felt warm, thick liquid on her skin. *Oh God, did they shoot me?* She placed her bound hands on Malik's chest, where she felt even more blood. *Oh, no, Malik, please no!*

Kennedy just laid her head on his shoulder and prayed that someone had heard the shots and would call the police. Uptown, gunshots were so normal that sometimes no one even bothered to dial 911.

Another gruesome scene unfolded that night at Sazaar's home in Queens. As Sazaar approached the house he heard his wife moaning in pain. He switched his direction. Instead of using the front door, he crept through the side door with his gun drawn. Sazaar watched as one guy paced around his wife, who sat in the middle of the family room tied to a kitchen chair. Her face was badly beaten and smeared with blood. Her nightgown was ripped open, exposing her bare chest. Sazaar felt a little comfort knowing his two young sons were away for the night. The second intruder sat next to Sazaar's daughter. She had the body of a eighteen-year-old, but she was only thirteen. Her face was battered. Tears came to his eyes, just knowing they had touched his little girl.

Sazaar let off two shots. He hit the boys in places he knew would take them down but not kill them. Other than his brothers, no one knew he had once been a trained assassin for the Panamanian government. Sazaar moved in quickly, disarming both boys and tying them together. He then freed his wife and daughter, securing them in the master bedroom. He went back downstairs and snatched the masks from the heads of the two intruders. Sazaar was utterly shocked to see two of his youngest soldiers.

Benji and Deon worked under Tony. Sazaar took a seat in front of them. He lit a cigarette and took a long drag. "Who sent you?"

Knowing death was imminent regardless of his answers, Deon said, "Fuck you, nigga, we sent ourselves."

"Why did you come for me?"

"We want your food."

"I still don't follow. I've been generous with all my workers."

"How the\fuck are you generous? You living out here in this big-ass house and we in the hood *starvin'*."

"*Mijo,* you make a couple of Gs a week. You call that starvin'? I'm tired of talking to you. It's useless." Sazaar shot Deon once in the head. Benji emptied his bowels in his pants as he made eye contact with Sazaar. Sazaar put it to him simply: "I'm not going through the twenty fucking questions with you. Who sent you?" He already knew the answer; he just needed confirmation.

With a nervous voice Benji answered, "You already know it was the modern-day Cain. Only Tony thought he could take out his brother and God in the same night."

Sazaar raised his gun once more, pulled the lever back, and silenced Benji forever. Then picked up his cell phone and called his two older brothers, Meza and Salazar. They rushed over to help him secure his family and dispose of the bodies.

Salazar drove Sazaar's family to a safe location while Sazaar and Meza dismembered the bodies in the basement and tossed them into the furnace. Benji's statement kept running through Sazaar's head. Suddenly he realized. "Oh my God, he put a hit out on Pretty Boy, too!"

Meza looked up at him. "What?"

Sazaar explained everything to Meza as he repeatedly tried to call Pretty Boy. As soon as Salazar returned they headed toward Harlem.

As Meza drove, Sazaar sat slumped in the back of his brother's black Impala. They crept through the blocks, looking for any sign of Pretty Boy. The fifth time they rode down Pretty Boy's street, Sazaar spotted Nina walking away from Pretty Boy's building. Salazar cut her off as she crossed the street. Meza jumped out and grabbed her.

Nina was shaken until she saw Sazaar. "What the fuck, Zaar?"

"I'm looking for Pretty Boy."

"Damn, you didn't have to go all postal and have niggas snatch me up and shit! Hell, I been looking for Kennedy all morning."

"When was the last time you heard from Kennedy?"

"Last night."

"Wasn't you just leaving the apartment?"

"I came through and rang the bell after Kennedy didn't meet me at the hair salon this morning. What in the hell is going on, Zaar?"

"Nina, someone tried to pull a hit on me last night, in my own home. I think Pretty Boy and Kennedy may be in trouble."

Nina's head and heart dropped. "I have keys to the apartment. We can go upstairs and check on them."

Nina entered the apartment, followed by Sazaar, Meza, and Salazar. The living room was in perfect order. Nina heard the bedroom television blaring. She pushed the bedroom door open; the sight made her fall to her knees. She crawled over to the bed. Sazaar ran in.

Pretty Boy and Kennedy's naked bodies were covered in blood. Nina lay down on top of Kennedy and wept. Her crying woke Kennedy up. She jerked and moaned. Nina jumped back. "Zaar, she is still alive!" She slowly pulled the tape from Kennedy's eyes and mouth.

It took Kennedy a few minutes to open her eyes. Once she did, everything was blurry. She shook nervously as she tried to figure out who was releasing her. She desperately clung to Pretty Boy's body and grew so hysterical that Nina had to slap her. "Kennedy, it's me! What happened?"

Sazaar pulled the sheet from the floor and covered her naked body. "Kennedy, sweetheart, it's me—Sazaar. Who did this to you?"

After eighteen hours of lying in the bed with a dead body, Kennedy was in shock, confused, and restless. She sobbed loudly and shrugged her shoulders.

Nina thought it might be better if she asked the questions. "Ken, are you sure you don't know anything? Can you just tell us what happened?"

"I . . . I don't know . . . we went to bed and then I heard voices, but I couldn't see anything . . . Malik, baby, get up," she wailed, falling on top of his body.

Sazaar looked over at Nina. "I have to go now. Call 911 in about half an hour. Call me later on today and keep me posted. Tell no one that you saw me or that I'm alive. Kennedy, anything you ever need, call me." He kissed Kennedy on the top of her head, then left.

Two days later Kennedy stopped talking altogether. She didn't like talking anymore, because every time she opened her mouth she cried. After Pretty Boy's funeral, Big Ma took her to Charlotte. She stayed secluded in a back room for six months. During those six months, she barely ate, and she didn't speak a word to anyone. Kennedy just sat in the room and wrote in her journal.

As their plane landed in New York, Big Ma, Kora, and Klarice were all thinking the same thing. They never wanted to see Kennedy go through anything like that again. Big Ma had one goal: to keep Kennedy from going back into that deep, dark hole again.

When the trio of women walked off the plane, Karen and Janice, Big Ma's second-oldest daughter, were waiting for them. The lost look on Klarice's face made Janice extend her arm to her first. "How you holding up, Klarry?"

The sisters embraced and Klarice answered, "I'm . . . I'm okay, I guess. I really need to know how do I go on living after today. I mean, how did you go on after you lost Alex?"

The question made Janice's heart so heavy her eyes filled up with tears. She cleared her throat. "I had all of you, and a whole lot of prayer. And we're going to do the same for you, sweetie."

Kennedy sat on the love seat watching everyone in disgust. *Look at all the nosy motherfuckers. I swear to God, if they don't stop asking me questions, somebody is going to get cursed the fuck out!*

A lady with a plate in her hand who was eating a chicken leg, and smacking real loud, walked over to Kennedy, sat down, and started talking. "Now, Kennedy girl, tell me what happened?"

Kennedy looked at her like she was crazy. "Don't you think you should mind your fucking business, you nosy-ass bitch." She got up and walked toward the front door. She opened it and immediately became happy. "Big Ma!" She threw her arms around her grandmother.

"How you, sugar?"

"I'm better, now that you're here."

"Is that the only person you see?" Kora asked.

"Sorry. Hi, Mommy. Hi, Jordan." Kennedy hugged her mother and took Jordan out of her arms. "Hey, big boy, did you miss Mommy?"

"Yeah." He answered with the softest little voice.

"Mommy missed you so much." Kennedy passed Jordan back to Kora when she saw Klarice coming up the hall. She embraced her aunt. They held each other for a few moments.

Klarice whispered in Kennedy's ear. "Baby girl, I know you're not okay, 'cause I'm not either. I want you to be strong. I've been thinking about you ever since I found out this morning."

"Auntie, y'all don't have to tiptoe around me. I'm not going to crack up again. Yes, I feel like I lost a part of me, but I'm older now."

"Kennedy, get up and get dressed. You are being so ridiculous right now."

"Mommy, you and Kneaka can take my truck and go on. I will catch a cab over to Auntie's after the wake."

"Kennedy, just explain to me why you don't want to go to Nina's wake."

"Look, Mommy, I don't think I'm being disrespectful. One, I can't do it two days in a row. Two, you know how Harlem wakes are. Everybody walking around, talking, and laughing. Niggas showing up to see what chickens they can pick up. I can't do it. I might flip out and spaz on someone."

Just then Kneaka walked into the room and handed Kennedy the cordless phone. "Big Ma wants you."

Kennedy rolled her eyes as she put the phone to her ear. "Hi, Big Ma."

"What's this I hear about you not going to Nina's wake?"

"Big Ma, I'm not feeling it today."

"Baby, I was just calling to see if you was all right. Everybody over here making it seem like something's wrong with you. No, baby, you don't have to come today. If you don't think you can handle it, that's right, stay at home."

"Thanks, Big Ma."

Big Ma hung up the phone and everyone in the house waited anxiously to hear her report Kennedy's decision. "Kennedy has her own reason for not going to the wake. It ain't nobody's damn business. So when she get here later don't ask why she wasn't there."

That night Kennedy did not sleep. She lay in the bed and observed Jordan as he slept. He looked so angelic. As she watched him she pledged to keep out of the streets.

Around six-thirty, she finally dozed off. When the clock struck eight, Jordan was up and hungry. She dragged herself out of bed and picked him up. "Good morning, booby," Kennedy cooed, placing kisses all over his face and neck. "How did Mommy's boy sleep? I bet you slept better than Mommy." She tried to place Jordan in his high chair. He arched his back and kicked, out of protest. "Come on, J, not right now."

Once Jordan had settled down, Kennedy handed him his favorite breakfast—dry Cheerios and fresh strawberries. Kora entered the kitchen yawning and stretching. She saw Kennedy's face and gasped. "You look terrible."

"Good morning to you, too, Mommy. I know I look bad. I didn't get any rest."

"I can take care of Jordan. Go get you some rest."

"It's no use in going back to sleep now. I'm going to go get a doobie, then to Ninety-sixth Street to get a facial. 'Cause makeup can't do nothing for these bags."

After showering, Kennedy looked in the mirror. *Damn, Mommy was right. I look a hot-ass mess with these red eyes and dark circles.*

Six hours later, the Abyssinian Baptist Church was filled to capacity and Kennedy looked dynamic. She wore a sleeveless, black linen dress by Theory that stopped midknee. On her feet were the prettiest Casadei black stiletto pumps and she carried a black Chanel bag. Her black, wide-brim hat was tilted to the side so that it covered the right side of her face, and she sported silver Dior shades. Her jewels were a diamond tennis necklace and matching bracelet; both had been gifts from Nina.

She stood over Nina's coffin. Everyone looked on with sympathy as Kennedy smoothed Nina's hair with her hand. She arranged it the way Nina had always worn it. Kennedy still wasn't satisfied. "Look at you, Nina. You don't look like you're resting or in peace. Even in death you're still a fly bitch. You looking good in that cream Donna Karan linen. How ironic is it that cream was always your favorite color."

Kennedy felt someone come up behind her. "Well, Nina, I guess I have to take my seat now. Other people want to see you. I brought you some things to take home with you." She pulled a few items from her black Chanel bag and began placing them in the coffin—a gold hugs-and-kisses set; three teddy bears, one for each of Nina's kids; childhood and recent family photos; a letter she wrote to Nina the night she died; and one white long-stem rose.

Finally, Kennedy bent over and kissed Nina's cheek. She let her fingers glide along the cherrywood coffin as she turned to walk away. Kennedy stood frozen in her steps when she saw the woman in front of her.

The woman was dressed similar to Kennedy, in a black linen dress. It was easy to tell that she was prissier than Kennedy, by her black three-quarter-length gloves, pillbox hat with hair pulled back in a neat bun, and pearl necklace. Her bare arm displayed the same tattoo as Kennedy's and Nina's—the name Sanchez, a pair of praying hands, and the words *Death Before Dishonor.*

Kennedy thought, *My mind must be playing tricks on me. No, that's her. After all these years, the prodigal child has returned home.* Before Kennedy stood her sister Kenyatta. They had not spoken in more than five years. Standing with Kenyatta were

Kenyatta's three daughters: Jazz, thirteen; Jada, eleven; and Jalyn, three.

Yatta had severed all ties with Kennedy and Nina after a vicious argument with Nina. She'd been more enraged with Kennedy for taking Nina's side in the disagreement than with Nina herself.

The two women stared at each other for about forty-five seconds. It seemed more like five to ten minutes. *I've already lost Nina. I'm not about to let some dispute from five years ago keep me from cherishing every moment I have left with Yatta.* Kennedy slowly stepped toward Yatta and embraced her. "I am so glad you came."

"I should have come sooner."

Kora was sitting on the front pew. No longer shedding tears of grief; now her tears came from the joy of seeing her two girls finally speaking again. *I wish Yatta and Nina could have straightened things out before Nina passed.*

Kennedy barely cried during the church service. Even though seeing Nina in her coffin made everything real for her. The graveside service was another story. Hearing the words *Ashes to ashes and dust to dust* caused Kennedy to pass out momentarily. When she came to, she didn't want to leave Nina's grave. It was a heart-wrenching scene. Not Kora, Klarice, Janice, or Karen could get her to walk away from the casket. Kennedy did not leave until she was ready. That was forty-five minutes after the graveside service was over.

Yatta's return took most of the unwanted attention away from Kennedy. The family and mourners went to Karen's house for the postfuneral dinner. Everyone was excited to see Yatta. She had been living a secluded life in a wealthy Boston suburb. Kennedy walked past as everyone surrounded Yatta and bombarded her with questions.

"Kennedy, come in here for a minute, baby."

Big Ma was in the kitchen, along with Kora, Klarice, Janice, Kara, and Karen. "What's up, Big Ma?"

"We're in here talking 'bout what we're going to do with the kids. Your mother says she can help Klarice with Niko and Mattie. We want to know if Taylor could stay up here with you."

"No, Big Ma, we can't separate them like that. I can keep all three of them up here. Anyway, I made a promise to Nina that I would take care of them."

Klarice walked over to Kennedy. "Baby, I cannot let you burden yourself down like that. They're my grandkids. Once I retire next year, I will be able to handle them by myself."

"Auntie, it's not a burden. It's what Nina wanted."

After the custody discussion, Kennedy excused herself from the room. She grabbed a Heineken and stepped onto the balcony. Yatta was already sitting out there drinking a glass of wine. This was their first time alone since their reconciliation.

Yatta looked at Kennedy. After a long pause she said, "What's good, little sister?"

"You know, same movie, different script."

"That little boy of yours is off the meat rack and he is so handsome."

"Girl, please, my nieces are gorgeous. What are you going to do when little niggas start knocking at the door?"

"Show them my P89!"

They both laughed as they looked for the right words to say. Kennedy stopped laughing and got serious. "So, Yatta, how come you never called me? If only to let me know that you were okay. Didn't you at least want to know how I was doing? Did you really hate me that much for voicing my own opinion?"

"For the same reasons you ain't picked up your phone and called me in five years. We're both stubborn. Now, you know I kept up with you through Mommy and Kneaka. I really thought you would at least have called me when you had your *first child.* Plus, the real story is longer than that."

"Well, we have all night!"

"Kennedy, don't act like Mommy hasn't already told you some of the story, if not all."

"Yatta, don't take this the wrong way. I told Mommy a long time ago, I didn't want to hear shit about you unless it pertained to my nieces. So go ahead and spill the beans."

Yatta poured a glass full of wine and took a few sips before she began to speak. "I wasn't still holding that grudge against you and Nina. The last five years with Petey have been hell. He has been so mentally abusive toward me. He put his bitches before me. He humiliated me in every way possible. I could not have any friends. All he wanted me to do was take care of the girls."

"Are you serious?"

"Yes, girl. So for the last year I have been secretly stashing money in a bank account. I bought new furniture and hid it in storage. I moved most of the girls' and my clothes out and he didn't even notice."

"Damn, I didn't know Petey had changed like that. So you were leaving him?"

"Hell yeah, I just wanted to make one clean move back to New York. I knew once I was back here with *my* family, I would be safe. 'Cause all he used to tell me is if I ever left he would kill me." Yatta swallowed the remaining wine in her glass. "And one morning, like a blessing in disguise, Bernice called me. She was the one friend I was allowed to have 'cause she was his partner's wife. I was dropping the girls off at day camp when she called. Bernice said she turned on my street and saw the feds raiding my house."

"Say *word.*"

"Word. She met me around the corner, I got in her car and we watched the entire thing from down the street. I don't wish that shit on nobody, but when I saw them bringing Petey out, I was smiling on the inside. Them feds ain't no joke. They got his ass for everything in the book! They got him for conspiracy, murder, kidnapping, extortion, and interstate trafficking."

Kennedy was blown away. "So the feds took everything from y'all?"

"Not really. I mean they got like a million and a half out of the house. After I saw them taking Petey away, I emptied out all of our joint bank accounts. I emptied out all the accounts with just my name on it. I took money to his lawyer. I took some to his mother and put the rest in safe-deposit boxes. Later that night Bernice and I snuck in the house and removed as many clothes as we could fit into her Suburban."

"So what are you going to do now?"

"What I had already planned to do. I bought a remodeled brownstone."

"That's good. You know *I am glad you're back.*"

"I'm glad to be back. I just wish I could have made things right with Nina."

Tears clouded Kennedy's eyes. Yatta reached over and hugged her. "I love you, little sis."

"Don't ever leave me again, big sis."

"Never, sister. I will die before I dishonor this name."

"You and the girls are more than welcome to stay at my house tonight."

"Thanks, but I already moved into my place. I'll be over to your house, since Mommy thinks she can't leave your side."

"Yeah, everybody thinks I'm going to crack up or some shit like when Pretty Boy died. I really can't take much more of all these people here. I'm going home to lie down. I know Mommy not ready to go, so can you bring her?"

"Now, you know you didn't even have to ask me *that*. Go on and get out of here, girl."

Kennedy moved quickly and quietly through the crowded apartment so no one would get in the way of her early exit. She waved good-bye to a few guests who were standing outside on the stoop smoking. She slid into her truck and started the ignition. The sound of R. Kelly's *TP-2.com* CD came blasting from the speakers. *Kneaka must have driven last, 'cause I know Mommy ain't listening to R. Kelly.* She listened to the CD as she drove up Eighth Avenue.

As the song played, she unconsciously sang along. Once she realized the words she was singing, tears began flowing down her face, but she continued to sing. *"I wish that I could hold you now. I wish that I could touch you now. Wish that I could talk with you. Wish that I could walk with you, be with you somehow."*

Is It Too Soon to Love You?

Two months after Nina's passing, Kennedy had finally wrapped up all of her cousin's personal business. She set up educational and mutual funds for Nina's kids with Nina's half of the money from Las Vegas. Nina had left over $2 million to her kids in insurance money. Kennedy found close to $100,000 in a safe-deposit box. She gave Klarice all of it, every last dime.

Kennedy moved into a four-bedroom brownstone in order to accommodate the kids. Her new home was next door to Yatta's. Having Yatta back in her life felt like old times, but it also reminded her too often that Nina was gone forever.

Cleaning out Nina's apartment was something Kennedy was not looking forward to. She knew she needed to get it done before the kids returned from North Carolina for school. Kennedy and Yatta agreed to let the kids miss the first week of school.

While they were packing Nina's things, Yatta came across an old photo album. "Look, Ken-Ken, here are the pictures from the last time we went to the bike rally in '96."

"Wow, look at us looking like some chickens."

"No, Kennedy, look at you and that crazy-ass Guyanese nigga! What's his name?"

"Dwight. That was my first boyfriend after Pretty Boy died. I was loving him, too."

"Loving? Y'all was two simple muthafuckas. Remember when he caught you on that nigga bike from Baltimore? That shit was too funny when Dwight chased you down the strip and snatched you off the bike. Your crazy ass was really buggin' when you tried to knock him and that girl off his bike with a bat."

"That was my baby. He was the first nigga to break my heart. It was for the best, though. 'Cause at the rate we was going, we would have ended up like Nina and Cream. Most likely he would be the one in the body bag."

Yatta noticed the sad look growing on Kennedy's face, so she changed the subject. "Where are these pictures from?"

"These are from Memorial Day weekend 2000. That week was crazy. Nina wanted to go to Cancún and I wanted to go to Miami. So we did both. Yo, we was buggin', doing some extra shit as usual. That was Nina and me." Kennedy turned and walked away so Yatta wouldn't see her cry.

Kennedy and Yatta arrived in Charlotte around 5:30 A.M. that Tuesday. Everyone in the house was asleep. Exhausted from the ten-hour drive, the two sisters fell asleep in the den. A few hours later, Kora came into the room screaming, "Turn on the television . . . turn on the television!"

Kora's screaming scared Kennedy out of her sleep. "Mommy, what is it? What's wrong?"

"A plane just hit the one of the Twin Towers."

"*What?*" Kennedy and Yatta asked in unison.

Once Kora got the digital box on, she turned to MSNBC. The sisters saw the answer to their question for themselves. "What in the hell was that plane doing flying so low?" Yatta asked, talking to no one in particular.

Kennedy saw something creeping onto the left side of the television screen. "Oh my God. Look y'all—it's another plane."

They couldn't believe their eyes as they witnessed the second plane slam into the north tower. Yatta stood up. "Hell no, this shit ain't no accident."

Kora thought about her youngest daughter as they watched the terror unfold. "Somebody please call Kneaka. Call and make sure my baby is all right. Call my sisters and check on them, too."

Kennedy pulled out her cell phone. "I'll call, Mommy. Don't worry, Mommy, everybody is going to be all right." *Lord, please let everybody in my family be okay. I don't think we can take another tragedy.*

Their fear and anguish grew when they could not reach their loved ones in the New York. The attacks didn't stop in New York; two more planes were hijacked. One of those planes crashed into the Pentagon. The fourth plane mysteriously crashed in a field in Pennsylvania.

Kennedy could not bear to continue to watch the repeated images of those planes slamming into the towers. She took a break and went outside to get some fresh air with Jordan. The town was entirely too quiet. Charlotte is the nation's second-largest banking center, so the city was under tight patrol.

Jordan was sleeping in Kennedy's arms as she slowly rocked him back and forth. She looked down at his innocent face. Jordan had the prettiest pecan-tan complexion. He had the biggest, brightest eyes and they lit up like lightbulbs when he smiled.

The first thing Kennedy had ever said to Jordan the day he was born was: "You are so beautiful. I will give my life before I let anyone harm a hair on your head." Tears streamed down her face now as she wondered, *What type of world did I bring my child into? How do I protect him from terrorists?* Kennedy felt vulnerable and naked; that is the loneliest, most hopeless feeling anyone can experience.

Yatta had been standing in the doorway watching Kennedy. She stepped out onto the porch and sat next to her on the steps. "Are you okay?"

Kennedy quickly dried her tears with the back of her hand. "No, I'm not. First Nina, now this. I just don't know what to do."

"I don't know either, Ken-Ken. All we can do is turn to God."

"I never turned away."

"At one time I did . . . Anyway, it looks like we couldn't go home if we wanted to."

"Why?"

"They closed all bridges and tunnels into the city until further notice."

"This shit is really bugged out. Did Mommy get in touch with Kneaka yet?"

"Yeah, she talked to her. Kneaka said everyone is okay."

"Thank God for that."

After a month Kennedy settled into her new role as a mother of four. It was demanding, but that was the good part. The kids took her mind off Nina and terrorism. Kennedy tried to put all her time and thoughts into the children, especially Taylor. She tried to instill in him life lessons, since he was the oldest.

Kennedy sat him down often and told him things that she one day planned on telling Jordan. "Rule one: treat girls and women the way you want men to treat the women in our family. Rule two: there is nothing feminine about dressing neat and cleaning a house. No woman wants a lazy, messy-ass man."

Kennedy even began training Taylor and Niko in financial matters. "Taylor, I'll give you twenty dollars a week. Niko, I'll give you fifteen dollars a week. That will be your allowance. You can spend half of it on whatever you want. The other half goes into a savings account. At the end of the year, you can take the money out of savings and buy something big."

Taylor's face lit up. "Can I get an electric scooter?"

"I want one, too," Niko chimed in.

"Wait, boys, let me finish . . . Or you can take that money and invest it. That means you put it into another account, which will make you even more money."

"I want to make more money," Taylor said.

Kennedy smiled at him. "You are definitely Nina's son."

Hassan was standing in front of Dr. Jays on 125th Street exchanging jokes with his entourage when he turned and saw three girls coming out of the store. One of the females looked familiar.

When the girl got closer, Hassan realized that it was Kennedy. "Yo, Ken-Ken, what up, ma?" He grabbed her and pulled her in for a tight hug.

Kennedy smiled because she was happy to see him. "What's good, Has?"

"I don't know. You tell me. You act like you can't hit a nigga back. Don't tell me you back on that bullshit."

"Not at all. I've had some difficult days lately."

"I'm sorry about Nina. I know how close the two of you were."

"Thanks for the beautiful flowers and the cards you sent. That was really nice of you."

"That was nothing, ma. But what's up with you wearing these big-ass clothes and dark shades. This not even you, Kennedy."

"Come on; not you, too. I have four kids now; I don't have time to be cute every day."

"I didn't say you wasn't cute."

"Why, thanks," Kennedy responded sarcastically. "I have to be going now. I'll give you a call later."

Hassan grabbed her hand before she could walk away. "Do me one better. I want you to come hang out with me, at the 9/11 fund-raiser. T.O.N.Y. Records is throwing it this Sunday."

Kennedy thought about it for a couple of seconds. "Nah, that's okay."

Kneaka, who had been with Kennedy in the store, jumped into the conversation. "Ken-Ken, stop acting like that. You know you want to go. Besides, I want to go, too."

Damn, her li'l nosy ass is always in my conversations. Kennedy shot Kneaka an evil look. Hassan smirked at Kennedy. "See, your girl wants to go."

"Excuse me for being rude. These are not my girls. These are my sisters, Kneaka and Yatta. I thought you had met them before."

Yatta shook his hand. "It's nice to finally meet you and I'll make sure she gets to that party. It will do her ass some serious good to get out the house."

"Damn, I'm starting to believe this is a conspiracy," Kennedy responded. "Well, I guess you win, Has. If big sister say I'm coming, I'll be there."

As soon as they walked away, Kneaka tore into Kennedy. "I know you're going through a lot right now. But do you *have* to look like that? And what happened to going out on dates?"

"Kneaka, mind your young-ass neck."

"No." Yatta broke into the conversation. "Don't tell her to mind her business. She is concerned about you just like I am. I know life seems pretty fucked up right now. But you have to pick yourself up and keep it moving."

"And I am fine with that, but everybody keeps acting like a part of that is getting or having a man."

"Kennedy, companionship is only natural and you shun it every chance you get."

"Look, Yatta, and Kneaka, I shun men because I can't deal

with the heartache of having another one die on me, fill my head with lies, and break my heart. I will never love hard again."

The 9/11 fund-raiser was filled with A-list celebrities. It was a world that Kennedy had once dreamed of being a part of. She once dreamed of being a rap star. Kennedy was sixteen when Foxy Brown and Lil' Kim came on the scene. She'd loved their style; they were fly, and they spit like dudes. Before them her favorite rapper had been Roxanne Shanté.

Over the years, Kennedy had honed her rap skills. She'd even appeared on several mix tapes. An excellent writer, she would have made a great female rapper. She was the total package: she was pretty, she could flow, and she had a presence that commanded attention.

Those dreams now seemed like a lifetime ago. Watching her sisters mingle brought her back to reality. The two glasses of champagne Kennedy had drunk were making her feel a little light-headed. She laughed at herself. *I'm up in here drinking like I ain't on crazy meds.*

Kennedy looked gorgeous. Yatta had picked out her clothes when she caught her trying to wear all black, digging in Kennedy's closet until she found some color. She outfitted Kennedy in a burgundy leather button-up blouse, a crisp blue-jean micro miniskirt, and a pair of matching burgundy knee-high stiletto boots. Kennedy's hair was braided straight back in cornrows that hung down to the middle of her back. Her makeup was immaculate. Still afraid to show her eyes, she wore a pair of tinted brown-and-gold Chanel frames.

All sorts of famous men had been hitting on Kennedy all night—actors, rappers, CEOs, singers, and athletes. To her sisters' dismay, she didn't give any of them the time of day. There was one guy, though, who caught her eye.

For another minute or so, Kennedy tried to figure out what it was about him that made her want him. There was nothing special about the guy's gear. He had on the regular rapper/block-boy gear. That is, an oversize white T-shirt, baggy blue Evisu jeans, and an iced-out platinum chain. Maybe it was the way he was watching her from under the brim of the two-tone, red-and-white Philadelphia 76ers hat he wore.

Kennedy knew that he was watching and whispering about her to his man. This made her move in a more delicate and sexy way. What she didn't know was that he was trying to gather his strength to walk over and talk to her. All night he'd watched her turning away famous men. He figured, *What chance do I have?*

He finally stepped away from his crew, whom he'd been holding up the wall with, and stepped to Kennedy. "Can I get you another drink?"

Although nervous inside, Kennedy kept it short, with an attitude, and answered, "No."

"Can I talk to you for a minute?"

"Can you?"

"Yo, shorty, what's up with all the hostility. I just wanted to holla at you. You look real nice and shit, I guess you don't have the personality to match," he said, turning to walk away.

Kennedy reached out and grabbed his arm. "Look, I'm sorry. Right now all this isn't for me. I'm Kennedy, and you are?"

"I'm Chaz, but some people call me Schiz."

"Well, I like Chaz; that's my son's middle name."

"That's a good thing. Where you from?"

"Uptown. Where are you from, *Chaz*?"

"I'm from BK."

"Oh, what part?"

"Bed-Stuy, Lafayette Gardens."

There was an awkward moment of silence, and then Chaz

asked her, "What brings you here tonight? Do you work for one of the labels?"

"Nah, my sisters and I are guest of Hassan's."

"Oh, is that your man or something?"

"Not hardly. We're friends from the same hood."

The guy Chaz had been talking to earlier walked over to him. "Yo, come on, man. Strick is calling for you."

"Aight, Rob, tell him I'm coming. Let me finish up here." He turned his attention back to Kennedy. "Ma, can we exchange numbers?"

Kennedy hesitated, but there was something about him. "Sure." They both pulled out their two-way pagers. Chaz smiled at her. "I love a woman up on her technology. Beam me your information."

Rob interrupted them again. "Come on, man, we have to go now!"

"Chill, I'm coming right now. Kennedy, I'll call you tomorrow. Maybe we can go out for lunch or something." Chaz was whisked away immediately, followed by ten guys.

Kneaka and Yatta walked over to Kennedy. "Who was that?" Yatta asked.

"I don't know him. He said his name is Chaz."

"He looks real familiar. Chaz must be pretty special to get Miss Thang's number," Kneaka teased.

Kennedy rolled her eyes at Kneaka. "Look, Has is about to perform."

"I'm sure you've seen him perform a million times," Yatta said, with enough humor to make even Kennedy laugh.

"Look, we can talk about all this later, because after this, I'm leaving."

After Hassan left the stage, Kennedy walked over to him and waited patiently. Every time he turned to talk to her, someone else vying for his attention would grab him. Finally she grabbed him and hugged him. "Thanks so much for inviting us. I have to get home now."

"I wanted you to come home with me."

"Not on a school night. I have to get the kids ready in the morning."

"Can I come to your crib?"

"I don't care. How long are you going to be?"

"I'm leaving here in twenty minutes. I just want to see this next kid perform."

As Kennedy and her sisters headed for the exit, Derrick "Strick" Strickland, the CEO of T.O.N.Y records, was onstage giving a speech about his new protégé. "After a vicious bidding war with other great labels, we finally got this talented young man over at Top Of New York Records. He brings a very refreshing flavor to the label. And following in the path of other great Harlem and Brooklyn relationships, such as Puff and Big, Dame and Jay, I can comfortably say this will be another great one. So without further ado, give it up for Schiz."

Kennedy almost tripped going out the door. Kneaka smiled from ear to ear. "I told y'all he looked familiar. I saw him in *The Source.*"

Kennedy took one look back at the stage. *Boy, I sure do know how to pick 'em. Always the ones running game.*

Every morning after dropping the kids at school, Kennedy and Yatta would retreat to one of their homes and share their morning routine. That routine included drinking coffee, reading the papers, and talking. On this Monday morning they were ironing out Thanksgiving plans; the holiday was only a week away.

Kennedy had been pondering what her next move in the game would be. Before hooking up with Petey, Yatta had been a hustler's dream. She could move any product given to her. Drug dealers who wanted to hustle upstate or outside of New York would send Yatta to get in good with the locals. Once she found out how the town ran, they would come in and lock it down.

Naturally, Kennedy sought out her advice. Yatta was reading the *New York Post,* sipping coffee from a small blue-and-white paper cup, from the corner bodega. Kennedy was reading an article in the *Daily News* that had captivated her. The article was about students from New York attending college out of state. They were getting money by buying wholesale guns down south and in the Midwest, then defacing the serial numbers. They would sell them in New York at half the retail price and still make a good profit. The only flaw in their plan was that defacing the gun no longer concealed the serial numbers. New technology allowed the police to raise and look at the numbers.

"Yatta, did you read this article about these college kids running the guns?"

"Yeah, I read about they dumb asses."

"They only dumb 'cause they bought the guns in their own names."

Yatta could look in Kennedy's eyes and tell she was scheming on something. "Kennedy, what are you thinking?"

"I'm thinking I need a new hustle. My expense money is getting low. I refuse to start dipping in my stash—my stocks and bonds or my mutual funds."

"How bad is it? Do you need me to front you some dough?"

"Nah, it's not that bad. I'm sitting decent. I was thinking about getting back into the dope game. All that shit is on fire right now after Bin Laden's ass came through. I bumped into Noodles the other day and he had the nerve to ask me to start running bricks for him again."

"What did you say?"

"I told him, if I did, I need five thousand per brick and it's a five-brick minimum. And I need five thousand for any off weeks."

"Why don't you take some of your money and go back to college? If you get out the game now, you'll come out on top."

"Don't start with that school shit, Mommy number two."

"Why not?"

" 'Cause school just ain't for me, man."

"Go for something you like. How come you don't get back into your writing? You could even start writing music again. There's a lot of money in that shit. You could even start rapping again; get Hassan to put you on."

The conversation was cut short by the ringing of Kennedy's cell phone. "Hello?"

"Can I speak to Kennedy?"

"Who is this?"

"This is Chaz. Is she available?"

With a hint of sarcasm in her voice, she answered, "This is she."

"What's good, ma?"

"What brings this call a week later?"

"Let me tell you, ma. As if my life is not complicated enough right now, my two-way froze up on me. I had to send it off to the company to be fixed. I just got it back today."

"Is that so?"

"Yes, *that* is so. I'm sneaking into the city in a minute. I wanted to go get something to eat."

"Is that an invitation for me to join you?"

"That was kind of the point."

Kennedy debated on it in her head for a few seconds. "Yeah, we can have lunch. Where do you want me to meet you at?"

"I can pick you up."

"How do you know I want you to know where I live?"

"Aight, ma, I'm feeling that. Meet me in an hour at Carmine's."

"See you in an hour."

Kennedy, usually not one to let her feelings show, closed the phone with a smile on her face. Yatta could not help but notice her sister's instant mood change. "What are you smiling so hard for?"

"What? Ain't nobody smiling hard. That was that boy Chaz from the party. I'm going to meet him for lunch."

"You? Going out? This sounds promising. And please don't wear black."

"This sounds promising for what? I'm not trying to turn this into anything else. I'm never loving another nigga hard, *true story*."

She is prettier than I remember, Chaz thought as the hostess directed Kennedy to his table. Kennedy had chosen a hunter-green sweater, butterscotch leather pants, and boots. She wore her hair hanging, the front pulled back by a clip in the top middle of her head.

Chaz stood up and embraced her. "How you feeling? You look real nice today."

"Thank you. I'm doing okay. And how are you?"

"I'm good. I can't complain."

After ordering the food, Chaz started with the twenty questions. "So, mystery lady, I tried to do a background search on you and came up empty."

"That's what you get for being *nosy*."

"So what do you *do*?"

"I'm a businesswoman."

"What type of business?"

"Business."

Chaz laughed, showing off his immaculate teeth.

"What are you laughing at?" Kennedy asked, becoming annoyed.

"That's the same answer I used to give when I hustled."

Kennedy blushed. "So when were you going to tell me who you were?"

"Why? Would you have given me more play, instead of attitude?"

"No, I would have given you more attitude."

"Why?"

" 'Cause, I already did your type."

"My type?"

"Yes, *your type.*"

"And what is that?"

"Street niggas, athletes, rappers . . . et cetera, et cetera. They're all the same."

"That's kind of harsh, ma. I'm not even going to touch that one."

Kennedy, knowing how to pose questions without stating the obvious, asked him, "So, do you have any kids?" She thought to herself, *What I really mean is, do you have an overdramatic baby mother or mothers?*

It wasn't that easy to get over on Chaz. He already knew what she was trying to ask. "Yes, I have two daughters. They're eight and six years old. And no, I'm not with their mother.

"What's the story with you and your baby's daddy?"

"Ain't no story. He's in prison doing a five-to-ten."

"Are you bidding it out with 'im?"

"Hell no, *see him when they free him.*"

"Damn, baby girl, that's ugly."

"We were not together when I got pregnant. He treated me

like shit while I was pregnant, and after I birthed his son, he denied him without ever seeing him. If he'd done right by his son, he wouldn't be locked up now."

"How do you figure?" Chaz asked with a confused expression on his face.

"It's very simple. If he had done right by his child, bad things would not have happened to him."

The waitress set their drinks in front of them. Chaz took a sip of his tea before speaking. "Damn, that's deep. So it's just you and your son?"

"No, I have three other kids."

Chaz's face looked like he was searching for the nearest exit.

Kennedy took a long swig of her strawberry lemonade before speaking again. "I didn't mean to alarm you." She laughed. "I can tell by the look on your face what you're thinking. Don't stress yourself. I adopted my little cousins after their mother passed away."

When the words escaped her lips, Chaz breathed a sigh of relief. "I'm sorry to hear that. Was she sick?"

Kennedy opened her mouth, but nothing came out. Suddenly tears were rolling down her face. She found herself still unable to speak about Nina's death without crying.

"Kennedy, are you okay?" Chaz asked.

After taking five deep breaths, she was able to speak. "Yeah, I'm fine. I guess I'm still not over losing Nina. We were really close and it has been so hard the last few months."

Chaz and Kennedy sat and conversed for two hours after eating. Kennedy told him everything about her and Nina's relationship up until the day Nina died. He shared his feelings about how his life had changed since he got his record deal. "Ma, everything is so crazy right now. I mean, I'm not complaining. I just thought once I was getting that legal paper, shit would be gravy."

He looked at her and shook his head. Just talking about it frustrated him. "When I was in the streets, I broke day almost every day. Now there are days I don't even see my house. My baby mother act like I wasn't getting money before. Now every time she call, it's about money. And niggas that I could have sworn were thorough be on my dick like a bitch."

The conversation would have carried on for hours if Chaz's producer had not called and reminded him that he was two hours late for his session. He walked Kennedy to her truck and was impressed by her choice of wheels. They hugged and promised to see each other the next day.

Later that night, around 1 A.M., Chaz dialed Kennedy's number.

She answered on the third ring. "Hello?"

"Ma, I can't wait until tomorrow. I need to see you now."

"Come on over."

Upon entering Kennedy's home a short time later, Chaz was further impressed. He liked the vintage white chaise, chairs, and oversize beige upholstered sofa that sat in the living room. He fell in love with the black-and-white poster-size picture of Kennedy and Jordan. In the picture, Kennedy was nude from the waist up. Jordan was completely nude and Kennedy held him so that his tiny body covered her breasts. The picture was tastefully done. "You have a nice home, Kennedy. I might have to hire you to decorate my new crib in Jerz."

Kennedy liked conversing with Chaz as much as he liked conversing with her. It felt like they had known each other for years. She even found it easy to talk about Pretty Boy's death, something she rarely discussed with anyone except Big Ma.

Chaz even shared his feelings about growing up without his mother. "She was always in and out of rehab. Then one day she killed a white executive. She said he was trying to rape her.

What's a black junkie's word against a rich white man? My mother was sentenced to fifteen years. She came home last year." He took in a deep breath, like it was too heavy to even talk about. "She came home last year," he repeated. "I looked out for her. I put her in a nice apartment out in Canarsie and bought her a Honda Accord. I never want to see her turn into that junkie from my childhood memories. I keep money in her pockets and food in her fridge. I don't want her to have any reason to run back to the streets. I'm trying to build a relationship with her. That's something we never had."

Kennedy listened intently, thinking, *I could never live without my mother.* They were still talking as the sun was coming up. Kennedy never brought any men around Jordan, but she knew Chaz was tired. "You can lie on my bed. I'll sleep on the couch in my room. You have to stay in the room. I have to wake the kids up in two hours and I don't want them to see you."

"Are you coming to my house?" Yatta asked Kennedy when they were returning from taking the kids to school.

"Not this morning, sister. I have company."

"Who?"

"Chaz, nosy."

"Say word." Yatta was shocked. She had expected Kennedy to say Hassan.

"He came over to talk to last night. We didn't go to sleep until this morning."

"I bet y'all didn't."

"Now, you know it wasn't like that. Anyway, I'll be over when he leaves."

Kennedy returned home to find Chaz already awake. He was in the bathroom washing his face. She walked up behind him. "You leaving me already?"

"Yeah. Do you have any extra toothbrushes?"

"Look in the medicine cabinet."

"I'm sorry, ma, but I have an important session this morning. You can come to the studio with me if you want."

"Nah, I don't want to come through and take your shine," Kennedy said jokingly.

"Take my shine. How?"

"When I get on the mike."

"Quit playing, girl, you can't spit."

"Yes I can!"

"Let me hear something."

Kennedy smiled and began rhyming. "These chicks are quarter water I'm Cristal's daughter/I'm coppin' bricks they coppin' quarters/That's ounces, OT when I bounces/In the six with my One Forty-first cuties/And I meant OC we out the country/New York chicks in Atl actin' country?/They fuckin' dummies!/Unlimited accounts in Prada/Cash we got a lotta/Mischievous fam fifty mil or more you're just a low-price whore/And don't come to me with dick on your breath/I rocks it to death/Jacob on my wrist glistening, turns your eyes to slits/I burn like Al Green and grits/Hard nipples firm tits/Your man wanted to lick my clit/Feel some type of way?/Then see me bitch/One Forty-first and Eighth find me and big Sanchez/Every nigga we date get cash or move that weight!"

Chaz stood there, stunned. "I knew it was more to you than you were telling. That's why you were at the party. What label are you signed to?"

"I'm not signed to anyone, true story. I gave all that up after Pretty Boy died."

"You shouldn't have. You sound like you have skills from that little bit I heard."

"All of that was a lifetime ago. I have three new priorities now."

"I'm trying to make you my new priority," Chaz said with a sneaky smile.

Kennedy walked him to the door. He turned to her. "Seriously, ma, I'm very particular when it comes to chicks. But you I'm interested in. I want to see you a lot more."

Blushing, she answered, "I definitely think we can arrange that. Now go on and get to the studio. I don't want to be the reason you're late."

"Believe me, it would be a good reason," he said, kissing her on the cheek and wrapping her in a tight hug.

"Bye, Chaz. Call me later." She watched as he walked up the street and got into his car. Kennedy was impressed with his black CL600. It was beautiful, with sheer black tints on the window, black leather interior, and eighteen-inch Mercedes rims.

Chaz couldn't get Kennedy off his mind as he sat in traffic on the FDR. He sang along with the new Faith Evans CD. *"Is it too soon to love you? When I just met you the other day. Why do I believe it's perfect?"*

Kennedy was blasting the same song from her stereo. She was in the shower thinking of Chaz and singing along. *"Could it be I'm scared to take a chance? Thinking we are moving fast and I don't know where we stand. I don't know where we stand."*

Dreams Do Come True

A month had passed since Kennedy's first date with Chaz. Their relationship blossomed. Just when they'd gotten into a comfortable routine of seeing each other on a daily basis, Chaz had to go to work in California for three weeks. Kennedy hated that he would be gone for the holidays.

The night before Chaz was to leave for California, he and Kennedy went through their normal ritual: Chaz came over after the kids went to bed. He ate his plate that Kennedy set aside for him every night. They watched a few television shows, the news, and a DVD. Afterward they talked until they fell asleep. Usually Kennedy got up in the morning and took the kids to school while Chaz slept.

This morning, when the alarm clock woke Kennedy, she sat up and did not see Chaz. *I know this nigga did not leave without waking me up and we're not going to see each other for three whole weeks.* She was so busy fussing in her head she almost missed the small red box sitting on the pillow.

Kennedy reached over and picked up the box. A small piece of paper was attached to it. It read simply: *Merry Christmas, Chaz.* Kennedy cracked the box like a little girl and peeked in. Inside were a pair of two-carat solitaire diamond earrings. *Oh my, these are beautiful. He is too sweet; he might just fuck around and make me love him.*

Kennedy picked up the house phone and dialed Chaz's number. When his voice mail picked up, she looked at her diamond Chopard watch. *He must be on the plane already.* As she waited for the beep, she looked down at the earrings and began to smile again. "Hi, Chaz; it's Kennedy. I got the earrings you left me. Thank you so much, they are so beautiful. Call me when you touch down."

The relationship was new and Kennedy didn't know quite what she should buy him for Christmas. She decided that some nice clothing would make a great gift. She told herself, *I'll buy him some things that are not too significant but not too insignificant.* So she went to Philadelphia and purchased him three Mitchell & Ness throwback jerseys and fitted baseball caps to match.

To Kennedy, the jerseys and hats were not significant enough. She wanted to buy him more. She went to Gucci and purchased Chaz a belt, a wallet, and a pair of sneakers. *I still need to get him one more thing,* she thought. Kennedy found him a beautiful blue Lacoste sweater. She bought him a pair of blue-and-green alligator sneakers to match. *Now, that is significant.*

Chaz was getting some of the best rest he had gotten since he'd arrived in L.A. when the loud banging on the front door of the three-story rental condo interrupted his peaceful sleep. He continued to lie in bed, hoping one of the other ten guys would answer the door. The knocking started all over again. "Damn, I know them muthafuckas hear the door."

Chaz opened the door just in time to see a FedEx deliveryman returning to his truck. He yelled out to him, "Yo, my man, you got something for this address?"

"Yes, I'm looking for Chaz Harris."

"That's me."

"I need your signature here." He handed Chaz the electronic clipboard. "I would have left it by the door, but it was signature release only."

"Thanks, my man, good lookin' out."

"Merry Christmas, Mr. Harris."

"Same to you."

Chaz retrieved the box from the man and walked back into the house. *Who in the hell sent me something way out here?* he wondered as he went to the kitchen to get a knife to open the box.

Chaz smiled when he saw the note sitting on top. *Merry Christmas! I hope we can bring the New Year in together. With much love, Kennedy!*

Chaz took each item out of the box, one at a time, getting more and more excited about each one. He grabbed his cell phone, scrolled down to Kennedy's name, and pressed talk. She picked up on the third ring. "What up?"

"You, ma! Thanks for my gifts. That was so nice of you. No other girl, not even my baby mother, ever did anything nice like this."

"You're welcome. I'm glad you like everything."

"I would fly to NC from here, but I have to get back to New York to record the last four songs by the fourth of January."

"I'll be back in New York on New Year's Eve. I'm letting the kids spend the rest of their vacation down here. So we can have some time alone."

"That sounds like a winner, ma." Chaz looked up to see his road manager and childhood friend, Rob, coming down the stairs.

"You know you have to be at the studio in thirty minutes."

"Nigga, I know that." Chaz rolled his eyes, turning his attention back to his conversation with Kennedy. "Aight, ma-ma, I have to go take a quick shower so I can get to the studio. But again, good looking out on the gifts."

"You got that, baby boy. Call me when you have time."

Rob was busy rummaging through Chaz's gifts. "Ol' girl spent some serious dough on your ass. You must have blew her back the fuck out!"

"Come on, man, it ain't even like that."

Rob studied Chaz's face for a few moments. "Hold the fuck up. You bought those expensive-ass earrings for a bitch you not even fucking?"

Chaz became tight in a matter of seconds. He stood up, coming face-to-face with Rob. "Don't ever disrespect her again. And don't worry about what I buy with my money."

"My bad. I didn't know it was like that. I thought she was some groupie."

"No, my man, she ain't nobody groupie. She got her own shit, and if she didn't, I would still fuck with her off of GP."

January fourth had come and gone. It was the fifth and Chaz's CD was lacking its last track, a duet with a female rapper named Lady Heroin. Chaz, Strick, Rob, and Shy, the producer, sat around the mixing board. Chaz was mad because Lady Heroin's label would not give her clearance to do the record. "Can't we get somebody else? Who the fuck they think that bitch is anyway, Foxy or Kim? If anything, I would be helping *her* career."

"Calm down, man," Shy told Chaz. "I'm going to see if we can get Eve or Remy. But I think both of them are on the road and we need to get this done today. I don't care if we have to get a nobody and write her lyrics for her."

"Who else do you have in mind, Shy?" Strick asked.

"I need a real fly chick with that attitude to match. I mean, I want her to be able to stand up to Chaz on the track. And this shit is going to be the first single, so she has to be a little hot to make jump off."

Everyone quietly thought of other female rappers who could be called on. "Oh shit! I know who we could get," Chaz blurted out.

"Who?" everybody else asked at the same time.

"My girl. I can get her to do the track. She can spit."

"Oh boy, here he goes again about his imaginary girlfriend that nobody else has seen." Rob chuckled.

"Fuck you, fat boy. Anyway," he said, ignoring Rob and focusing his attention on Strick and Shy, "ma spit like a nigga and she a little fly uptown chick."

Strick thought about it. "Who is she signed to?"

"Nobody. She not even trying to get on. She used to rap when she was younger. She did a few mix tapes throughout the city."

"Call her. 'Cause this shit needed to be done yesterday."

Rob smiled at Chaz. "Yeah, call her, man, so we can see if she really exists."

After convincing Kennedy that he had an emergency at the studio, Chaz went downstairs to meet her. When she pulled up he immediately went into begging mode. "Ma, please do me this one favor. I need you to get on track with me. This CD is starting to stress me. I just want it to be over with. I would rather be spending time with you and be able to hang out with my daughters before I go on this promo tour."

Kennedy stared at him with a serious expression on her face. Then she broke a smile. "I'll do it for you, booby."

Chaz reached over and hugged her. "That's what's up, ma. Good looking out."

• • •

When Chaz entered the studio with Kennedy, it was plain to see why he'd kept her hidden. The way her Seven jeans hugged her ass made the men drool in her face. Strick could tell she had a style all her own. Kennedy was rocking a white fitted tee, a blue mink baseball jacket and cap, and a pair of blue Dolce & Gabbana lace-up stiletto boots.

"She is perfect," Shy said. "Now, if she can rap like you say she can, we can pull this shit off." He played the beat for Kennedy and explained the concept of the song to her. "It's basically a ghetto breakup song. Chaz has been caught cheating on the girl who has been down with him for years and helped him accumulate his wealth."

"I think I can put something together for that."

Kennedy listened to the beat a few more times before writing her verse. She wrote several different verses before she came up with one that she felt fit the beat. "Aight, Shy, I'm ready."

"Get in the booth and get this shit poppin'." Shy called everyone into the recording room as Kennedy was stepping into the recording booth.

Being inside the booth felt natural to Kennedy. *This feels so right.* She placed the headphones on her head, then looked out through the glass and locked eyes with Chaz. He smiled at her and winked. She blushed and winked back.

Kennedy said a quick Hail Mary while Shy cued up the instrumentals. She closed her eyes so she couldn't see the eyes watching her. Her heart was racing as she began to rap, but it all came out cool and confident. "When I met you, you had nada, zip, zilch, zero/Not a dollar on a fuckin' hero/You was huggin' the block servin' rocks/Lettin' every other crackhead suck your cock/That shit had to stop/Started rollin' wit' me/Took you from pushin' OZs of trees to powder-white Ks/Niggas never saw the likes of me/The way I left 'em duct tape in they Vs/On the strength of me you rock that platinum shit/Fuck Nikes, nigga, I put you in Prada kicks/Off of all my trips cocaine numbing my clit/Now you OT fuckin' with some next bitch/Now you suck my dick you leaving all my shit/Plus my name still on the title to that hot-ass Six."

Strick was feeling Kennedy's flow. He wanted to hear more. When she stepped out of the booth he told her, "I want to hear you spit some more. Shy, throw on some different beats."

Kennedy rapped different songs off the top of her head for the next thirty-five minutes, songs that she'd written over the last ten years. Strick fell in love with her flow, too. As she continued to rap he saw a star in the making. When the tenth beat finished and she stopped rapping, Strick told her, "I think you're a perfect package, ma. I want to sign you to a deal. I can turn you into an overnight celebrity."

"I don't know if I have time for a music career now. I'm raising four kids."

"Look at it this way: you'll never have to worry about being unemployed."

"No offense, but I'm not worried about that now."

"I guarantee you that I can make you see more money than any other female rapper out right now."

Before she could come back with a quick response, she heard Nina's voice in her head. *Ken-Ken, this is your dream, ma. This is your chance to leave the streets behind.* Kennedy snapped out of her trance, "Aight, Strick, I'm game," she said as she walked back into the booth to redo her verses.

Strick told Chaz and Shy, "That girl has all the qualities of a star. I'm going to make her one. That's my word."

Two weeks later, Kennedy was quietly celebrating her birthday with Chaz. He had taken her to a posh little resort in upstate New York. Chaz was falling harder for Kennedy every day. She was so laid-back—she didn't take herself too seriously. Chaz loved those things about her, but he especially loved her sense of humor. Earlier in the day, she had dragged him up to the ski slopes, even though she couldn't ski herself. Every time she fell down, she would fall out laughing.

The night of her birthday, they dined at the resort's four-star restaurant. For the first time Chaz was nervous about giving a female a gift. From his point of view, Kennedy was independent and could purchase anything she desired herself. After they finished eating, he handed her a card. "Baby girl, I didn't know what to get you. I know you like to shop so . . . I thought this would be a bangin'-ass gift."

Kennedy opened the card; it contained three gift certificates of one thousand dollars each for Barneys. The card read: *Baby girl, I have never met anyone like you. You are so beautiful inside and out. Happy birthday, li'l mama, I pray that we will share many more.*

The lyrics to an old Etta James song came to her. *"At last, my love has come along. My lonely days are over."* A single tear ran down the right side of her face. "Thank you so much, Chaz. I love the gift, but I love the card more."

"Why are you crying?"

"You make me so happy—something I haven't been in a long time. I think you gonna fuck around and make me fall in love with you."

"Ma, you know you got my heart."

The wait staff came toward the table singing "Happy Birthday." The first waiter was carrying a cake with twenty-three burning candles. When they finished singing, Kennedy was blushing red with embarrassment. She took a deep breath and blew out her candles. Chaz asked her, "What did you wish for?"

High off the four martinis she had drunk, she answered, with sex in her eyes, *"You."*

Just then Chaz's two-way went off; he opened it and read it.

"I'll be right back. I need to go up to the room and use the phone." He looked up and noticed the "negro, please" look Kennedy was giving him. "Ken-Ken, you know, don't neither one of our cell phones work good out here."

Kennedy eased up a little. Chaz slid her his platinum American Express. "Go ahead and pay the bill. I don't want these assholes thinking I'm running out on it."

After twenty-five minutes and two more martinis, she was growing impatient and returned to the room. Standing by the door, she heard Chaz yelling. Kennedy unlocked the door and cracked it open so she could hear what he was saying.

"Fuck you, too. Yo, you are the most simplest *bitch* I know. Next time anybody in my family come to get my daughters, you better let them go. You are so petty! All the fucking money I give you, B. You better learn the rules to this shit. 'Cause in a minute I'm gonna file for custody of my daughters and your ass won't see another piece of my paper."

He slammed the phone down, sat down on the couch, and dropped his head into the palms of his hands. Kennedy walked over and stood next to him. "Chaz, what was that about?"

He was a little startled. He hadn't heard her come in. "Nothing, man, my dumb-ass baby mother. She wouldn't let my sister and mother pick up the girls today all because I left her five Gs instead of eight. She pissed because that delayed her in getting her furniture."

Kennedy didn't press him for any more information. She had never seen him this mad before. *I hope it's really over between you and her,* she thought. She sat down next to him and wrapped her arms around him. "Let me take your mind off of that. Here, I brought you a bottle of Grey Goose from the bar." She fixed him a vodka straight and poured a cranberry juice and vodka for herself.

"Here, have a drink. Get your mind off that bullshit, baby."

Kennedy pressed play on the CD player. Mary J. Blige's *No More Drama* CD began playing. She sat down on the couch next to Chaz and raised her glass to him. "Here's to no more drama."

He sat his drink down and laid his head in her lap. Kennedy could feel how tense he was; she massaged his temples as they talked and listened to the music. *I like this song,* Chaz thought. "What track is this?"

"I think it's number three."

"I'm feeling Mary on this one. Let's just steal away."

"No, I'm feeling Mary on *this* one," Kennedy said, picking up the remote and skipping over to track thirteen, "Never Been." By no means was Kennedy a singer, but she leaned over and playfully sang into his ear: *"Pardon me, excuse me, I can't help it. But I see the energy between you and me and I'm selfish. Don't want no other girls calling you never ever. 'Cause I want us to stay together forever."* She kissed the top of his ear and licked his lobe with the tip of her tongue. Chaz's dick shot straight up.

Finally—the moment they had been waiting for. Kennedy had been craving him sexually, but she hadn't wanted to seem too forward. From their conversations, he could tell that she had been hurt in the past. He didn't want to rush her into anything or make her feel obligated to have sex with him.

Chaz grabbed her hand and stood up, pulling her up with him. He led her over to the bed, then pulled her in close and began kissing her as he unzipped her suede tube dress and let it fall to her feet. Kennedy reached down and unbuckled his pants. He stepped out of them and moved back to pull off his shirt. Kennedy bent over and unzipped her boots.

"No, leave them on," Chaz told her, removing her strapless bra while kissing her neck and shoulders. He laid her flat on the bed and pulled her thong off. "I just want to touch you." He ran his hands over her entire body, massaging every curve and taking in the tender feel of her skin. Chaz rubbed her inner thigh, running his hand upward until he found what he wanted. He parted her vagina lips with his middle finger and gently pushed it inside of her. The wetness and tightness of her inner walls aroused him further.

His hands alone felt so good that Kennedy thought, *He can skip the foreplay and just slide it inside of me. God, please don't let him have a little dick.* She slipped her hands inside of his boxers. *Oh shit, he's packing. Maybe a little too much for me.*

Chaz continued to bring her pleasure with his hand as he planted wet tongue kisses on her neck. He worked his way down to her nipples, sucking and gently biting them. He knew exactly what he was doing, circling his finger around inside her and gently stroking her clit with his thumb. The way she was grinding on his finger, he knew he was bringing her to ecstasy.

I am about to cream all over his hands. "Oh, Chaz," she shrieked while coming all over his hand. In one swift motion he removed his boxers and slid his large dick inside of her. Kennedy winced a little as he went deeper. "You okay, baby girl?" he whispered.

"Yes, please don't stop." The feeling of him going inside her while she was coming was like nothing that she had ever felt before. Chaz wrapped his hands around her three-inch heels and pushed her legs back until she was spread-eagled. He stroked her insides, dipping up and down so smoothly it looked like he was dancing. Chaz rolled her onto her stomach without pulling out. Kennedy let out a giggle, thinking, *Wow, that's one move I never experienced before.*

He pulled her body to the edge of the bed until she was standing. The stilettos made her ass sit up perfectly as she bent over on the bed with chest lying flat against the sheets. The visual alone almost caused Chaz to cum early. He squeezed each cheek as his strokes picked up more and more pace. The more comfortable Kennedy became with the size of his dick, the more she got into the rhythm of his strokes and began to throw it back at him.

Letting her know that he was still in control, using his body, Chaz laid her flat onto the bed and continued to pump all his strength into her. He licked the back of her neck, causing her to cum all over again. The liquid exploding onto him from her was so warm there was no way he could continue to hold on. "Ma, your pussy feels so good."

"So does your dick. Are you ready to *cum*?" she asked, tightening her muscles.

"I am now." He rolled her onto her side, pulling her leg up to her chest. His strokes became faster and longer. Kennedy grabbed his free hand and put her mouth around his middle finger and began sucking it. Chaz's entire body shut down as he bust a long hard nut inside of her. Kennedy gently slid her body from beneath him and turned to face him. She kissed him on the cheek.

"Ma, that was so beautiful," Chaz told her.

"Was it worth the wait?"

"Of course it was. Shit. Was I worth the wait?"

"You were worth every single minute. Now, are you ready for round two?"

Kennedy had never imagined that recording that song would change the course of her life. Funk Flex introduced the song to New York City and he showed it so much love. Strick called Kennedy, excited. "Yo, Ken-Ken, Flex is dropping crazy bombs on the song. Mad A 'n' Rs are two-waying me wanting to know who you are and if you have a deal yet. Didn't I tell you I was going to make you a star?"

Strick wanted to get the visuals out to the public immediately while the song was new and hot. He knew that a video would catapult the song to the top of the charts. He scheduled the filming of the video for three weeks after the single was released to radio.

Kennedy arrived at the video set at 5 A.M. It was her first taste of what the music industry was really like. After her hair had been flat-ironed and her makeup was done, the stylist Strick had hired for the shoot arrived. On sight, Kennedy was not feeling her. The biggest problem she had with the girl was the way she was hanging all over Chaz when they came through the door and laughing extra hard at his jokes.

Strick walked the stylist over to Kennedy. "Ken-Ken, this is your stylist, Tameeka."

"Hi, Tameeka."

"It's nice to finally meet you. I brought you some great things to wear today. I'm going to lay them out on the table so we can go through them." She yelled over her shoulder, "Chaz, can you bring those bags over here, sweetie?"

Kennedy rolled her eyes, thinking, *Sweetie? This bitch must be trying to test my fuckin' patience.* Chaz walked over, sipping on a large morir soñando. He stopped in front of Kennedy. "What's up, baby girl?" He bent over to kiss her on the cheek.

Kennedy moved her face so that he wouldn't make contact. "So you just now making your way over here to speak? I didn't sleep with you last night."

"Come on, Ken-Ken, I know you saw everybody stopping me to talk."

"Yeah, but you sure made your way over here when your little friend called you. Go on over there and help her with her bags, *sweetie.*"

Chaz walked away mumbling, "Here she go with the bullshit."

Once Kennedy's hair was finished, she walked over to the wardrobe area. She looked at Strick and frowned. "I'm not wearing none of this wack-ass shit."

"What?" Tameeka squawked.

Kennedy leaned back and placed her right hand on her hip, using her left to punctuate her words. "You heard me the first time; I'm not wearing none of this cheap shit. Strick, how much money did you give her to work with? It couldn't have been a lot 'cause this shit look like it came off of Fordham Road."

Tameeka rolled her eyes and said, "Well, I never."

"And you never will . . . dress me, that is. Strick, you couldn't get Misa, June, or whoever dresses Charlie Baltimore? I got shoes that cost more than all this shit put together. You could've told me to bring something out of my closet. She can dress them other chicks," Kennedy said, pointing to the extras, "but she not dressing me."

Tameeka, growing tired of the insults, told Strick, "I'm good at what I do. I don't have to take this shit from some wannabe diva."

"Chill. Y'all just be easy," Strick pleaded, standing between the two women.

I'm not trying to hear this shit Strick kicking. Kennedy opened her cell phone and began dialing. "I'm not even entertaining her last remark. I'm calling my sister. Trust, she can style circles around this bird." She waited for Yatta to answer. When she did, Kennedy could tell she'd been sleeping.

"Kennedy, it is early on a Saturday. What do you want?"

"I need you to get up and go to the Village to get me some clothes. 'Cause this shit this broad brought up in here is hideous."

Kennedy closed the phone. As she walked past Tameeka she told her, "Stick around. You could get an education in styling. And, Strick, I suggest you get a refund." She walked out into the cold winter air smiling.

She didn't know Chaz was walking behind her. "Kennedy, what the fuck is up with that jealous shit you just did?"

"That wasn't no jealous shit. I didn't like the clothes and now I don't like the bitch."

"I know what it might've looked like when we walked in, but she didn't know you was wifey."

"And why is that, Chaz? What am I, your dirty little secret?"

Chaz didn't say anything.

Kennedy stared at him, waiting for some type of answer. For the first time she let her insecurities show. "I knew this shit was going to happen if I started fucking with you."

"What shit, Kennedy? What the fuck are you talking about?"

"Chaz, I'm going to my trailer to lie down. Please show Yatta where I'm at when she gets here."

Kennedy turned and walked away. Chaz called out to her, but she kept walking, scared that if she turned around she would break down and cry.

Yatta showed up at Kennedy's trailer door with eight oversize bags from Limpas', Petit Peton, Versailles, and Shoe Fetish. Kennedy was so relieved. "Thank you so much for coming."

"It's nothing, li'l sis. Here, take some of the bags."

Strick walked in behind Yatta. "Is this little cutie your sister?"

"Yeah, this is Yatta, and Yatta, this Strick."

"It's nice to meet you, ma," Strick said, looking at Yatta like he wanted to eat her up.

Yatta returned an equally lustful look, which didn't go unnoticed by Kennedy. Strick loved the clothes that Yatta had purchased. He thought to himself, *I've found myself a new stylist and maybe a new shorty.*

All eyes were on Kennedy when she walked onto the video set. She was wearing a navy-blue leather hooded halter top. The matching skirt looked like a piece of loincloth. But her boots sent the outfit over the top; they were baby-blue-and-navy thigh-high stilettos.

Tameeka rolled her eyes at Kennedy and Yatta caught it. "What's her problem, Kennedy?" Yatta asked, pointing at Tameeka.

"That's the fake-ass stylist bitch I was telling you about."

"She *is* hideous and who the fuck she thought she was styling with that horrible dry wet-and-wavy weave?"

The two sisters fell out laughing. The director yelled out from his chair, "Everyone take your places."

Chaz walked onto the set followed by his usual entourage. He had a fresh haircut and his goatee was trimmed to perfection. His well-kept physique looked terrific in the Evisu sweater and jeans he wore. Even though she was still pissed, Kennedy couldn't help thinking, *My booby is fly as hell.* She wouldn't dare let him know that and rolled her eyes as he approached her.

"You feeling better?"

"I'm straight," she answered, with her nose in the air, as she walked away to take her place on the set.

Chaz looked over at Yatta. "What's good, ma?"

"My sister, and if you hurt her I'm going to fuck you up!"

The tension between Kennedy and Chaz made for a good video, given the point of the song. Kennedy was a natural in front of the camera. By midnight, she was tired and filming wasn't close to being over. She continued to put forth her best effort, even though her head was throbbing and her feet ached like hell.

Around 5 A.M. the director yelled, "It's a wrap."

I never knew I would be so happy to hear those three words, Kennedy thought as she washed the makeup off her face inside her trailer. She was so ready to get home to her bed. She threw on her clothes. The comfort of her Nike Air Max felt like good sex.

She gathered all of her things and rushed out the door to find Strick and Chaz standing outside.

Strick grabbed her and gave her a huge hug. "You did your thing today, ma, especially for your first video." He handed her a card. "This is a gift certificate for you to the Bella Spa. Take the next three days off and pamper yourself, 'cause next week we're kicking this shit into high gear. I'm talking 'bout performances, promo tours, and a whole lot of studio time."

"Thank you, Strick. This is so nice of you. Is the car service here yet?"

Chaz interrupted. "I told Strick to cancel your car. You can ride home with me, if that's okay with you."

"I don't care. I'm just ready to lie down."

Kennedy took off her coat and jeans, dropping both in the middle of Chaz's bedroom floor. She wasted no time getting into his king-size bed. She was drifting off as soon as her head hit the pillow. Chaz got into the bed and began rubbing on her thighs and kissing her neck. Kennedy groaned at him. "Not now, Chaz. I'm too tired."

"Turn around and look at me."

"*What?*"

"Look, I'm not those other niggas. I'm not cheating, I'm not lying, and I'm not going to leave you."

"You know, Chaz, it all sounds good. But I heard it all before."

So Emotional

Auntie, Auntie, your video is number one on *106 and Park*."
Jazz ran into Kennedy's room, waking her up from some much-needed rest.

"It is! Okay, wake me up and let me know what number it is on *Direct Effect*." Kennedy rolled over and went back to her pill-induced sleep. Since the single had made it onto the *Billboard* Top Ten, her life was no longer her own and the road had become her new home.

Traveling, at first, was cool. Then came the stress. Chaz had his entire crew and she didn't have anyone. Kennedy missed her kids dearly, especially Jordan. Even more, she missed the quality time she and Yatta had begun spending together.

The worst part of being on the road was watching the groupies all over Chaz at the after-parties. After a while Kennedy started showing up at them and staying for one hour, which she was required to do by contract. Chaz told her, "You're being petty about the after-parties. If the groupies bother you that much, why don't you stay next to me during the parties?"

"Them hos don't give a fuck. If I'm standing next to you, they'll still try to suck your dick and tell me to hold it for them."

• • •

The after-party at Club Dream in Washington was the best so far, and Kennedy had consumed numerous alcoholic beverages. She found solace on the dance floor away from the VIP, Chaz, and his groupies. She'd even found a great dance partner, Drico.

Drico was from the Bronx. Kennedy had seen him a few times around New York at different events and parties. The familiarity and the liquor made her dance a little sexier and closer than usual. They were even whispering and laughing in each other's ears.

What the fuck? Chaz thought as he looked down from the VIP and saw Kennedy on the dance floor. *She done lost her fucking mind.* "Yo, I'm ready to go," he told his entourage. On the way out he yanked Kennedy from the dance floor.

Kennedy protested all the way to the parking lot. "Who said I was ready to go?"

"I said you was ready to go. You was being a little too cute dancing all close with that nigga. What was you doing dancing with another nigga anyway? As a matter of fact, don't dance with no more niggas."

"Chaz, who the fuck you think you talking to? I'm not your child and I don't say shit when these hos be grinding up against your dick night after night."

"Kennedy, don't start with that groupie shit again. Get your ass on the bus."

"Oh, you getting real offensive. Did I strike a guilty chord? You think I don't know you fucking them groupie-ass hos?"

"Damn, is it time for your period or something? Lately all you do is nag the hell out of me. You'll make a nigga cheat."

Kennedy knew Chaz was drunk, but she still took his comment to heart. "Oh well, if that's how you feel, baby boy, beat ya fuckin' feet, my man, 'cause I'll never beg a nigga to stay where he don't want to be."

"I didn't mean it that way, Kennedy."

"Whatever." Kennedy got onto the tour bus and didn't say a word to anyone on the ride to the hotel.

Once she was back in her room, she got all her bags together and called a cab. Kennedy hurried downstairs to the lobby, avoiding anyone from the tour. She had the cabdriver take her to the bus station, where bought a ticket for the 6 A.M. bus to New York.

When Kennedy arrived in front of her brownstone that morning, she instantly spotted the cream Bentley sitting out front. *Who the hell is this?* she wondered. She paid the cabdriver, retrieved her bags, and rushed inside. When she opened the door Strick and Yatta were sitting next to each other on the couch.

Yatta jumped up. "Ken, where have you been? Why didn't you let anyone on the tour know you were leaving? And why haven't you been answering your phone? Everyone's calling, worried about you."

"Damn, Yatta, slow down. I left my phone charger in the hotel room. My battery been dead since last night." Kennedy ignored Yatta's other questions and turned her attention to Strick. "What up? What you doing here?"

"I'm trying to figure out why my artists are pulling disappearing acts on the road."

Kennedy plopped down on her chaise and began to explain the previous night's events to Strick and Yatta. She went on to share how lonely and stressed she felt while out on the road.

Strick took everything Kennedy said into consideration before he began to speak. "Look, Ken, if it's one thing I know about you, I know you understand business. You have to apply the same rules to this industry that you apply to the streets. One of the most important rules is never let your emotions get in the way."

Kennedy knew that he was right, and that was the exact reason she had vowed to never fall in love. Her train of thought was *being all soft over a nigga is never good for business. If you're worried about where he at and what he's doing, you can't concentrate on what's most important—your money.* Now here she was so emotional over Chaz, totally disregarding her own number one rule.

Strick continued giving her his speech. "Ma, I'm not mad at you. I understand what you're going through. The next time you go out on the road, take a few of your girls with you so it's more comfortable for you. Is that straight with you?"

"That's what's up!"

"Aight, go get dressed. I want you to take a ride with me."

Kennedy sat down on the extra-soft leather inside the Bentley. She looked around the car and was thoroughly impressed. Strick noticed. "You like this?"

"Actually, now that I'm inside, I do. I mean, I always thought they were overrated; still do a little."

"I could see you in an Aston Martin."

"What's that?"

"The meanest luxury sports car. You would stop the show in that, ma. I can call up my car dealer and see if he can get you one."

"Nah, I'm cool. I can tell by the way you talking about it that it cost an arm and a leg."

"Did I say anything about you paying for it?"

Strick pulled his car into a garage on East Twenty-eighth Street. He still had not told Kennedy where they were going. Once the attendant took the car, he led her inside the office building next door.

"Strick, I trust you, but where are we going?"

"Fall back, Mama, it's a surprise."

"What kind of surprise? How do you know I even like surprises?"

"All women like surprises. And don't worry, it ain't nothing bad. Someone wants to do a song with you."

"Who?"

"Didn't I say it was a surprise?" He pushed the up button for the elevator; he gave her a taunting smile all the way to the tenth floor. When the doors opened they stepped off the elevator into the Hip Rock Studio. The receptionist buzzed them through the glass door and then through the steel door, which led to the recording rooms.

Kennedy smiled at the sight of Hassan bent over, enthralled in a game of C-Lo. She walked over and tapped him on his shoulder.

"Give me five minutes and I'll be ready to record my verse. I'm on a roll right now," Hassan responded, thinking it was the pesky studio engineer.

"You ain't winning no real money."

Hassan turned around, and when he saw Kennedy, he grabbed her and hugged her tight. "What's good, ma?"

"Ain't shit, playboy. You know me, just trying to maintain."

"You making big moves and not even hollering at your boy."

"Stop it, Hassan. You doing ten-million-dollar deals. I'm small potatoes to you."

"Well, you ready to jump on this track with us?"

"Who is us?"

"Me, S.C., Joaquin, and Kicks. Have you ever met them?"

"No."

"Let me introduce you to them."

Hassan led Kennedy into a mixing room where the three rappers were sharing a blunt. Hassan took care of all introductions.

The three guys gave Kennedy a warm reception. They all told her they had her on various mix tapes and how they thought she had a bright career ahead of her. She was so happy to hear these things coming from three of her favorite veteran rappers.

Eight hours later, Kennedy had finally finished recording her verse and ad-libs. She stepped out of the booth and sat on the couch between Strick and the CEO of Vegas Records, Caz. "I'm done, finally!"

Caz looked at her and smiled. "I like you, ma; you a fly little bitch. Come holla at me if this nigga Strick not paying you your worth," he said with his overcocky demeanor.

Hassan and Strick laughed at the look on Kennedy's face. She had to admit she was a little amused by his cockiness, but too tired to indulge it. "I would love to stay and kick it with y'all, but I'm tired."

"Give me thirty minutes and I'll be ready," Strick told her.

"No, Strick, you stay. Can you give me thirty cash so I can get a cab uptown? I left my wallet in my other bag."

Before Strick could answer, Hassan grabbed Kennedy by the arm. "That's aight, Strick, I got her."

Strick watched them closely as they exited the room. Chaz was more than an artist to him; they had become close friends. He could tell from the way Hassan was acting that there was more to him and Kennedy than she had let on. Strick had no plans on running to tell Chaz anything, but he wasn't going to stand by and let his boy get played either. Kennedy wasn't flirting with Hassan. But Strick couldn't tell if that was because he was there or because whatever they might have had was really over.

In the elevator Hassan leaned up against Kennedy and wrapped his arms around her waist. "What's good wit' you? You not fucking wit' a nigga no more?"

"Come on, Has, you know I'm with Chaz."

Hassan backed away from her. "No, I didn't know."

"Now you do, and you know when I'm messing with someone that's the only one."

"I thought it was gonna be you and me."

"You can't be serious. How is it going to be you and me and you have a girl? I'm not into playing second to another bitch for the rest of my life."

"I'm not even wit' my baby's mom no more."

"Oh, so now she just your baby's mom."

The elevator door opened and Chaz was standing there. He observed the serious expressions on Kennedy and Hassan's faces. "What's up?"

"What are *you* doing here?" Kennedy asked.

"I came to meet Strick. Where were you on your way to?"

"Hassan was just walking me out to catch a cab."

Chaz reached out and gave Hassan a pound. "Good looking out, my man. I got it from here."

"It's nothing. Kennedy is my homegirl. We go way back," Hassan said with a sly smirk.

Chaz tried to talk to Kennedy about small things on the ride uptown, but she wasn't having it. He rubbed the top of her hand. "What's wrong? You still mad about that D.C. shit?"

"Ain't nothing wrong with me. I'm just tired and don't feel like talking."

"You always tired when it's convenient for your ass. But you revved up when it's time to get in my shit with your false accusations! I'm the one who should be pissed after your bullshit in D.C."

"Well, that's your business."

"I'm getting real sick of your smart-ass mouth, too."

"Why you still here, then, Chaz?"

"Maybe I'm still here 'cause I love you."

Hearing those three words made Kennedy's heart melt. She loved Chaz, too, but she wasn't about to let him know it. She had already let her guard down too much. "That's real *nice,* if you mean it."

Chaz pulled the car over in front of Kennedy's brownstone. She hopped out and turned to him. "You not coming up?"

"I don't have a reason, do I?"

"I *know* you're not going to drive to BK or all the way to Jersey tonight."

"Who said I have to do either?"

"Well, do whatever the fuck you want to do."

Chaz pulled away from the curb, not even waiting to see if she got in the building okay.

He drove downtown and checked into the W Hotel. Any other night he would have fallen asleep as soon his body hit a comfortable mattress. But tonight was different. Thoughts of Kennedy filled his head. *Why am I loving this chick like this? I think I'm going to fall back for a while. That's exactly what I need to do, just fall the fuck back.*

The sound of his cell phone woke him early the next morning. Without opening his eyes, he patted around the bed until he found the phone. He flipped it open and put it to his ear. "Speak on it."

"What up, dun-dun?"

"Jay?"

"Yeah, nigga, it's me."

"Jay! My nigga, what's poppin'? You hit the bricks yet?"

"Yeah, nigga, I'm free! Chaz, I ain't going soft on you or nothing. But good looking out on all the shit you did for me the last two years while I was on lock."

"That's nothing, Jay, you got that. Real recognize real. I already know when the heat is on you'll be one of the very few holding me down." Chaz's line beeped; he looked at the caller ID. "Yo, Jay, I'ma come through and scoop you in like an hour. I need to take this call. This nigga been ducking me about my paper for a minute."

"Handle your BI. I'll be at my baby mom's crib. One hundred."

"One hundred." Chaz switched lines and his attitude. "What is it?"

"Yo, this Macon."

"I know who this is, nigga! I hope you calling about my paper."

"I'll have all that for you in two weeks."

"Have my fuckin' paper in five days or your ass is gonna have problems." Chaz terminated the call.

Chaz cruised through downtown Brooklyn and his old stomping grounds. He pulled up to the place that had raised him—Lafayette Gardens—to pick up Jay. The police were everywhere. They had a blood-soaked area taped off. In the middle of the tape was a pink-and-white bike identical to the one he had bought one of his own daughters for Christmas. He stepped out of the car and watched the crime lab work the scene.

"Yo, what up, baby?" Jay asked, walking up on him. They exchanged a quick hug and a pound.

Chaz turned his attention back to the crime scene. "Yo, what happened here?"

"You remember old-ass crazy Bill from when we was little?"

"The one who used to beat his wife and kids all the time?"

"Yeah, him! You know all his kids bounced as soon as they were old enough. His wife finally decided she'd had enough; her oldest daughter came to move her out this morning. Bill came out the building and started blasting at them while they were getting in the car. He completely missed them and hit Lanae's little girl instead."

"*Word.*"

"*Word,* my nigga."

A paramedic walked out of the building carrying a small body covered by a small white sheet in his arms. Two long thick pony-tails with a purple ribbon were hanging from beneath the sheet. It was a horrific sight for any parent to watch. As he watched, Chaz's heart broke. "Come in, Jay, I can't take this shit."

"I thought we were going to Manhattan," Jay commented, notic-ing the direction they were traveling in.

"We are, but after seeing that shit, I have to swing by and check my daughters."

"I feel you, dawg. When I saw that baby laid out on the curb like that, I had to run back upstairs and hug my little shorties up."

Chaz parked his car in front of his baby mother's building in the Clinton Hill section of Brooklyn. His two daughters were outside playing hopscotch. Eight-year-old Tiki and six-year-old Chasity ran over to him and jumped in his arms. "Daddy!" they screamed in unison.

"What's up with daddy's girls?"

"Can we go to your house today?" Chasity asked.

"Not today, baby. Daddy has work to do."

"But we miss you, Daddy. Only time we get to see you is on TV," Tiki whined.

"I promise you next weekend we'll do something special. Whatever you girls wanna do."

Chasity started jumping up and down. "Ooh-ooh, Daddy, can we go to Disney World and see Mickey Mouse?"

Chaz couldn't say no to the pound-puppy face she was giving him. "Sure, li'l mama, if that's what y'all want."

"Thank you, Daddy!" they cheered in unison.

"Where's your mommy?"

"Upstairs cleaning."

"Come on, let's go upstairs and get her."

Chaz entered the aging building holding on to each of his daughters' hands. The walls along the hallways could have used a couple of fresh coats of paint. The older ladies in the building did their best to keep it looking neat by sweeping and mopping three times a week. Chaz's daughters' mother, Ria, was standing in the doorway when they got to the second floor.

She was wearing the usual cleaning gear, a T-shirt and cutoff sweatpants. Short and slim, Ria was nice and curvy in all the right places. Her beautiful pecan-tan complexion was set off by beautiful brown slanted eyes that made her look exotic. Her short hair was always immaculately done.

"What's up, Ria?" Chaz asked, walking by her into the apartment.

"Nothing. What brings you by?"

"I wanted to see my daughters. You know, it's not safe to let them be out there playing by themselves."

"I was watching them from the window. How do you think I saw you? And why you bringing that frontin'-ass Jay around here?"

Chaz rolled his eyes at her. "Tiki, take your sister in the room to watch cartoons." Feeling she was about to ask for money, he beat her to the punch and offered. "What you need for the girls?"

Pleasantly surprised, Ria answered, "I need money for their spring and summer clothes. Its getting warm and they only have a few pieces from last year."

Chaz pulled out a knot containing two thousand dollars or more. "Here, that should be a G for each of them."

"Thank you."

"No need to thank me; those are my daughters." He paused and said, "Ria, I still want you to move out to Jersey."

"I told you before; I really don't want to leave Brooklyn. All my peoples are here."

Chaz looked at her like she was crazy. "Your peoples? Fuck your peoples! I'm talking about my daughters' safety. We didn't have a choice but to grow up in this zoo. I just saw a little girl Chasity's age being carried away covered by a white sheet. If you really want to stay in Brooklyn, I'll buy you a house in Canarsie near my mother or somewhere way out."

"I thought you wanted us to move to Manhattan so you could see the girls when you left the studio. You must don't want your bitch from Harlem to know about us."

"Your simple ass will never change. My girl don't have nothing to do with this situation. The reason I'm telling you to move to Jersey is because I have a house there now. I no longer have an apartment in Manhattan." He pulled out another knot of cash. "This should be enough to get you started. Call and let me know if you need some more."

"Can you bring me some cash so I can trade the car in and not owe anything?"

"Trade it in for what? I just bought you that truck last year."

"I want the new Lexus 430."

"Yeah, whatever. I'll bring it next week when I pick up the girls to take them to Disney World. Kiss them good-bye for me. I don't want them out here crying."

Chaz walked back to the car feeling good about seeing his girls. But he was frustrated by Ria. The little girl's death was still weighing heavy on his heart. Growing up in Brooklyn, he had seen plenty of tragedies, even caused a few. But having kids put things in a new perspective.

• • •

Yatta walked into Kennedy's living room eating a bowl of farina. Jay-Z's latest CD, *Blueprint,* was blaring from the speakers while Kennedy ran top speed on the treadmill. Perspiration caused her clothes to stick to her body and her hair to stick to her face.

Yatta knew her sister's extra-hard workout ethic was due to Chaz's absence in her life. She also knew if Kennedy was hurting she would never show it. Yatta picked up the remote and turned the stereo down. She stood in front of the treadmill. "Have you called Chaz yet?"

"Has he called me? Fuck him, I'm not sweating him."

"Didn't nobody say nothing about you sweating him. You hard on a nigga. He tells you he loves you and you go cold. But I know you love him. If you didn't you wouldn't react the way you do."

Kennedy slowed the treadmill down, bringing it to a complete stop. She grabbed the towel hanging on the rail and wiped the sweat from her face. "I'm done talking about Chaz. If he wants to talk to me, he knows where to find me."

Kennedy and Yatta were sitting under the hair dryers flipping through fashion magazines at their favorite Dominican hair salon, Marisol's. When Kennedy received a call on her cell phone, Yatta could tell from the pissed expression on her face that it was serious.

"What happened?" Yatta asked once Kennedy hung up.

"That was Taylor's teacher. She's having a problem with him. She wants me to come over and meet with her right now."

"I wonder what's going on. Taylor never gives anyone trouble."

"I don't know. He's been real cranky with me lately. I figured it was because I'm gone all the time."

Kennedy tapped lightly on Mrs. Shooda's door. The petite lady rose from her desk. She was around forty-five and gorgeous. Her sun-bleached blond dreadlocks went perfectly with her beautiful smooth chocolate skin. Mrs. Shooda's proud West Indian heritage shined through in her attitude. She opened the door, and before she stepped into the hallway, she turned to the class. "Class, continue reading until page 201, and no talking. Good morning, Ms. Sanchez. How are you doing?"

"I'm fine, and you?"

"Ms. Sanchez, Taylor threatened to cut a student. This is my second year teaching Taylor and he has been one of my best students in the twenty years I've been teaching. That is one of the reasons I didn't turn this matter over to the monsignor. The other reason is, I know this has been a very traumatic year for him."

"He *what*?"

"He threatened to cut a student and he planned to make good on his threats today with this." Mrs. Shooda pulled a lime-green box cutter from her pocket.

The box cutter belonged to Kennedy. "Mrs. Shooda, I am so sorry. I had no idea."

"I truly believe the boy is still grieving the loss of his mother. He needs attention. Maybe other children have teased him about his mother. Maybe that's why he brought the blade to school. Whatever the case, Ms. Sanchez, I have zero tolerance for thuggish behavior. I want you to keep him home for three days. I put all of his assignments in his bag. I also included Teresa Weston's phone number. She is a highly recommended child therapist and a great friend of mine."

Kennedy was overwhelmed with guilt. *How did I miss all the signs? I've been too wrapped up in my new career to pay attention to the kids' needs.* "Thank you, Mrs. Shooda," she said in a barely audible voice.

"No need to thank me. I just wanted to give you a chance to rectify the problem before it gets out of control." Mrs. Shooda opened the classroom door. "Taylor, gather your things and come out, please."

Taylor slowly walked out the door. He could tell by Kennedy's glare that she was fuming. Mrs. Shooda stopped him, placing her hands upon his shoulders. "Remember our little talk. You are a special young man. Do not mess up now." Taylor nodded in agreement, too afraid to speak. Mrs. Shooda embraced him tightly before turning him over to Kennedy.

She didn't say a word to him as they walked to the car. Kennedy yanked the back door open and nearly pushed Taylor in before she climbed into the front passenger side.

"What happened?" Yatta asked, sensing her sister's anger.

Kennedy dropped the box cutter in Yatta's lap. "Billy badass here threatened to cut another little boy." She turned around and stared at Taylor. "Yo, what's wrong with you? Are you trying to get kicked out of school forever? What would've happened if Mrs. Shooda didn't confiscate that blade from you? Would you really have cut that little boy?"

"Maybe," he replied, unable to look up at Kennedy.

"Then what? You go to Spofford and start a life of endless trips to jail?"

Yatta interrupted. "Calm down, Kennedy. Let me talk to him. You're too upset. Tay, what did this boy do to you that was so bad you wanted to cut him?" She handed him a tissue. "Here, clean your face and talk to me like a big boy."

Taylor composed himself. "Li'l man was telling everybody that my mother was a crack whore. And he said my own grandmother don't want us, that why we live with Kennedy."

Yatta made eye contact with Kennedy. Kennedy dropped her head. *Damn,* she thought, *why did I go so hard on him before hearing his side?* "Taylor, he only said those things to hurt you. You know as well as I do that none of those things are true. No one loves you more than your grandmother. So don't ever let lies hurt you. Your mother was a wonderful woman and you have every right to defend her honor, but not with violence. Now, next time you have a problem, bring it to my attention or Yatta's attention. Okay?"

"Okay."

"Give me a hug. I love you."

"I love you, too, Kennedy."

Kennedy's stress level was about to go from bad to worse as she sat in an image-and-marketing meeting with Yatta, Strick, the label's staff, and her nemesis, Brooke Colbert. Brooke, the president of marketing for T.O.N.Y. Records, was the epitome of the black yuppie. She even had a degree from Yale University to go along with her attitude that she was better than most black women.

The hatred between Brooke and Kennedy was mutual. Kennedy believed Brooke was intentionally trying to ruin her career. "I think you should tone it down a bit with all the *gangsta* rhymes," Brooke suggested.

"Ma, stop while you're ahead. Everything I rhyme about I'm qualified to rhyme about, because I lived it. Your skin may be black, but you don't know shit about being *black.* And you don't know shit about hip-hop."

"I know marketing!"

"And that's your fucking business, *bitch*!"

"Okay, okay." Strick interrupted. "Brooke, let Shy and myself handle the music. You just get the product pushed once we get it out."

"Okay, but what about her image?" Brooke asked.

Kennedy interjected before Strick could answer. "What about it?"

"Well, it's my job to give you a style that's marketable."

Everyone in the room knew Kennedy was ready to flip out. "Let me explain something to you, *ma*. You can't even join a conversation with me on style. This chick sitting next to me is my stylist, and not because she's my sister, but because she is the flyest bitch I know. There is nothing you can tell either of us about style. We been fly since the cradle, courtesy of Kora Sanchez. You can't even dress yourself with those go-to-hell acid-wash jeans on. This meeting is adjourned for me."

"Kennedy, in my office *now*!" Strick demanded.

Brooke and her assistant gave Kennedy dirty looks as she and Yatta left the conference room. She shot them back an even dirtier look.

Kennedy followed Strick into his office. He put on his baseball cap and grabbed a few small items from his desk. As she watched him Kennedy said, "Strick, I thought you wanted to talk to me?"

"I just wanted to get out of that meeting, too. You know I had to front on you, though. I can't let you spaz on my staff like that and have them thinking I don't get on you about that shit. Seriously, can you ease up on Brooke a little?"

"Nope. She hates me and I hate her more. I'm going to dig into her ass every time her and her little pissy-ass assistant try to get slick!"

"Kennedy, your ass might really need anger management. Come on, I got something that will make you feel better."

• • •

"This shit is bangin', Strick," Kennedy said, examining a beautiful gray sport coupé. The burnt-orange-and-gray interior fasci-
nated her; she had never seen such an exquisite car. "This shit is
nuts. What kind of car is this?"

"This is the Aston Martin DB7 Vantage."

"Damn, I see what you was talking about now. This is the most
luxurious car I've seen. You gotta let me push this sometime."

"You can push it all the time. It's yours."

What did he just say? "Huh?"

"It's yours, Kennedy. It's a gift from the label."

Kennedy hugged Strick and rocked him side to side. "Thank
you, thank you." She stepped back and stared at the car for a moment. Then a solemn expression fell upon her face.

Strick noticed the mood change. "Ken-Ken, what's wrong?"

"I was just thinking about Pretty Boy. He surprised me with
my first car, a Honda Accord. He was a beautiful person just like
you."

"Thanks. Come on, let's be out before you get all mushy
on me."

Kennedy zoomed through the streets of downtown Manhattan.
She dipped in and out of traffic, nearly giving Strick a heart attack. "Kennedy, you drive like a nigga. You're going to kill the
clutch."

"I love this car and I usually don't like selfish cars."

Chaz, Jay, Shy, and Rob were standing in front of the building
where the studio was located when Kennedy and Strick pulled
up. It was the first time Kennedy and Chaz had seen each other in
a week, since they had argued. "Strick, you done copped another
hot whip?" Shy said, checking out the car.

"Nah, homey, that's Ken-Ken's."

"Say word! Ma, this is a real good look for you."

Kennedy couldn't even respond to Shy's comment. She was too occupied in a staring match with Chaz. Jay asked Chaz, "What's up wit' homegirl? Strick hittin' that?"

"Fall back, that's *wifey.*"

"Oh, that's Kennedy. She's even prettier in person."

When Strick got out of the car, Chaz jumped in and just stared at Kennedy. *Here he go with his bullshit,* Kennedy thought. "What?"

"You ate?"

"No."

"Let's go get something."

Kennedy pulled away from the curb and drove in silence. Chaz continued to stare at her. "What's up with you, Red?"

Kennedy couldn't help but to blush; she loved when he called her Red. "Nothin' much. How've you been?"

"I've been aight. You could've called a nigga."

"Did you call me?"

"So now you on some ol' tit-for-tat shit."

"I have to protect my feelings."

"Protect them from what?"

"From getting hurt."

I know I said I was going to fall back. But fuck that, you only live once, he thought. "Kennedy, how many times do I have to tell you I'm not them other niggas? I'm not out here chasing skirts. I did that already; I don't want those headaches anymore. I just want to come home to you and for you to trust me the way I trust you."

Emotional conversations always overwhelmed Kennedy. She pulled the car over. "Chaz, I know you're different. That's why I love you." *There, I said it,* she thought. "I know I act like a bitch, but I'm so afraid of being hurt again."

"Ma, please believe me when I say you are like no one I've ever met before. You got me and I'm not going anywhere." He sealed his words with a long deep kiss. "What do you think about Disney World?"

"Huh?" she asked, laughing.

"I'm taking my daughters to Disney World tomorrow. I want you to come."

"I can't."

"Why?"

" 'Cause Yatta and I have been promising our kids that we would take them to Disney. How would that look if I go with you and your kids?"

"You can bring Yatta and the kids. My sister and her son are coming, too."

"I still can't go and not bring Jordan and Mattie. They're still in Charlotte with my mother."

"Here." He handed her a black American Express card. "Call your mother. She can meet us down there and just pay for whoever is going."

Kennedy looked at the card, shocked. "You have one of these now? You have to spend a lot of moola just to get invited to have one of these."

By the next morning, Kennedy's house had been turned into *Romper Room.* Seven kids high off of syrup were running through the house. Kennedy was just about to lose her mind. "Chaz, I can't wait on the car service any longer. We're just going to have to take two cars and leave them at the airport."

"You read my mind."

Kennedy felt a little hand tugging on her shirt from behind. "What is it now, Niko? Oh, I'm sorry—Chasity. What do you need, baby?"

"Can I call my mommy? She didn't give me my inhaler."

"Sure, baby, the phone is right over there."

In Brooklyn, Ria rolled over and read the caller ID on her ringing phone: *Kennedy Sanchez*. She answered, "Hello?"

"Mommy, you forgot to give me my inhaler."

"No, I didn't. I gave it to your daddy."

"Oh! Okay, bye, Mommy."

"Chasity, don't hang up. Where are you at?"

It was too late. Chasity had already hung up. Ria looked at the caller ID again. *Kennedy, Kennedy. Oh hell, no! I know he don't have my daughters around his bitch.* Ria picked up the phone to dial his number. Then she thought about it. She had big plans this weekend. There was no way she was going to get into it with Chaz and give him a reason to bring the girls home. She copied the number down from the caller ID and saved it for future use.

Jealous One's Envy

Who *the hell is calling me at six-thirty in the morning?* Kennedy reached over and grabbed the phone off of the nightstand. "Hello?"

"Put Chaz on the phone!" an angry female voice demanded.

Kennedy sat up. "Who is this?"

"Bitch, this his baby mother! Now put his ass on the phone."

Chaz rolled over. "Kennedy, what's wrong? Who is that?"

Kennedy held up the palm of her hand toward him and continued to speak into the phone. "First off, this is not Chaz's house. If you wish to speak to him, address me the correct way, you disrespectful slut. And since you called here being cute, you damn sure ain't talking to him. And keep playing with me, I'll stomp a hole in your ass."

Ria let out a loud laugh, "Bitch, *please,* you better ask Chaz how I get down. I'll bring it uptown."

"Well bring it, ma, 'cause I guarantee you won't leave the same way you came. Hey!"

Chaz snatched the phone from Kennedy. "Yo, why the fuck is you calling here? I'ma see you about this dumb shit. That's my word." He slammed the phone down. He didn't even want to look over at Kennedy.

As she went to the bathroom she told him, "You better check that bitch 'cause I don't do baby mothers."

• • •

It was just one of those days that started out bad and was destined to end worse. Kennedy was at a photography studio in SoHo, getting her makeup done for a photo shoot. Yatta was laying Kennedy's clothes out. Meanwhile Yatta's phone kept ringing. Kennedy tried to ignored it, but couldn't. "Dang, Yatta, answer that shit! Put it on vibrate or something. It's irking my nerves."

"I'm not answering it. That ain't nobody but Petey calling, making empty threats."

"For what?"

"He mad 'cause I sent the girls with his mother. He wants me to come visit him."

The phone started ring again. "Hand me the phone," Kennedy told Yatta. "What's the problem, Petey?"

"Who is this? Oh shit, I know this not little tough-ass Kennedy. Now don't go filling Yatta's head up with all those ideas like you did Nina. I heard you might be the reason she dead. Telling her to leave her man."

Kennedy waved her makeup artist away. "You 'bout a ignorant motherfucker. I don't know why you so worried about what Yatta doing out here. I hear all the bodies they trying to stick to you, you got one foot in the electric chair."

"Ha ha, that's real cute. Bet y'all evil-ass bitches won't be laughing for long." Petey slammed the phone down.

Chaz filled Jay and Rob in on the morning's events as they drove through midtown on the way to the studio. Rob was jealous of the relationship Chaz had with Kennedy, and jealous of Chaz in general. "What you flip on Ria for? That's your daughters' mother. She can call you anytime she get ready," he said to Chaz.

"She sure can call me anytime. On any of my phones, but not Kennedy's."

"I'm tired of everybody actin' like Kennedy don't do dirt."

"Shut up, nigga," Jay said, cutting his eyes at Rob.

"Nah, Jay, I want to know what the fuck he talking about," Chaz said.

"He ain't talking about nothing," Jay pleaded, trying to squash the conversation.

Against Jay's wishes, Rob continued talking. "Man, the way I hear it is, it's more to her and Hassan than she telling. That nigga cousin, EB, told me Hassan been hitting that since that nigga Pretty Boy died. They was still fucking when y'all met at that party."

Chaz got heated on the inside. He made a drastic U-turn in the middle of the street. "Yo, where you going?" Jay asked.

Chaz didn't answer as he drove in the direction of SoHo.

Jay turned and looked at Rob in the backseat. "That why I don't fuck with you now. You been li'l pussy-ass nigga since we was young. Always got your name in the middle of some gossip, just like a bitch."

Chaz stormed into the studio and snatched Kennedy off the set. He shoved her through her dressing-room door. His glare scared and nearly silenced her. "Baby . . . baby, what's wrong?"

"You're a fucking liar, that's what's wrong!"

"What? I never lied to you."

"Yes you did! You lied about you and Hassan. You said he was just your homeboy. Do you fuck all your homeboys?"

Kennedy dropped her head.

"Look at me, damn it!" Chaz yelled at her. "Why did you lie?"

"I didn't lie. You never asked me if I was jaying him."

"Yeah, this shit is becoming real clear to me now. That night when y'all was on the elevator, you was on the way to fuck him. Wasn't you?"

"Yo, you are unbelievable B. Wasn't shit going on between him and me that night. And I haven't fucked Hassan or anybody since we been together."

"If you not fucking him, why didn't you keep it gully with me from the door?"

"Do I have to tell you every nigga I've fucked before you? Shit. Do you name every groupie you've fucked? Instead they write me letters."

Chaz backed Kennedy into the corner. "I swear to God, if you fucking that nigga, I'm going to choke the shit out of you. I ought to knock the shit out of you for playing games with me anyway."

"Who do you think you're talking to? I don't have to explain shit to you. And you're dead wrong if you think you're ever going to put your hands on me. Just get the fuck out! I don't care if I ever see your petty ass again!"

"I'm not going anywhere!"

Kennedy picked up a pair of cutting shears. "Get out or I will stab you."

"Fuck you, Kennedy. You dirty bitch."

"If I'm such a dirty bitch, Chaz, why you here?"

Yatta entered. "What is wrong with y'all?"

Chaz turned to leave. "Ask your sister. She might not tell you, though. She real good at keeping secrets." Chaz backed away, never taking his eyes off of Kennedy as he left the room.

"Kennedy, what is he talking about?"

"He found out about me and Hassan."

"What do you mean he found out? I thought he knew."

"He knew we were friends. I didn't volunteer any extra information." Kennedy reached in her purse, pulled out a prescription bottle, and took one pill. Yatta picked up the pill bottle and read the label aloud. "Effexor XR, one hundred and fifty milligrams! Kennedy, you're going hard with the pills lately."

"Whatever it takes to get me through the day."

"Well, an addict is an addict, no matter the drug of choice."

That night Kennedy lay naked under her warm duvet listening to the humming sound of the central air unit. The house was empty and the quietest it had been in a long time. Yet she was unable to fall asleep or to get Chaz off of her mind.

Kennedy got up and went into the kitchen. She poured a glass of wine before rummaging through the kitchen drawers. "Got it." She smiled once she located her emergency stash of sleeping pills. She popped one in her mouth and chased it down with the wine. Within ten minutes she was down like a baby.

"Ain't that your baby's daddy?" Nee asked Ria.

"Where?"

"Over there."

"Yeah, that's that motherfucker. I wonder if his little rapping bitch in here."

Nee suddenly became excited. "Ooh, girl, I knew I had somethin' to tell you."

"About what?"

"Girl, you know Kisha's sister was doing hair at that picture studio. She said Chaz busted in there and drug that bitch off the set. She said you could hear him screaming on her throughout the building. Something about her fucking Hassan."

"The rapper?"

"Exactly!"

"I told him about messing with them bourgeois uptown hos. Them scandalous, gold-diggin' bitches."

• • •

The club Slate was filled to capacity with industry insiders for Triad Records' annual party. Strick, Chaz, and Jay were talking to S.C., Kicks, and a few other guys when Hassan and a few of his boys walked up. Hassan exchanged pounds with S.C. and Kicks. When he got to Chaz with his hand raised in the air, Chaz looked at him like he was crazy. *I should knock him out on some real live Brooklyn shit. Just leave it alone for now, don't fuck up this man's party,* Chaz told himself as he turned to walk away.

"Damn, Has, what was that shit all about?"

Never the one to let someone play him, Hassan addressed the problem immediately. "That nigga must be mad 'cause I'm fucking his bitch."

As Chaz moved through the crowd he felt a small hand grab him from behind. He knew it was the touch of a female and hoped that it was Kennedy. He was surprised and disappointed to see Ria. "What are you doing here?" he asked, frowning.

"The same thing you're doing here."

"I doubt that, and where are my daughters at?"

"Why? You're not watching them."

"Ria, don't play with me! I haven't forgot about that bullshit you did this morning."

"My aunt Sheryl got them. Enough of all that, I heard your little girlfriend is fucking all the rappers."

"Mind your fucking business, Ria."

"Why don't you just come home to your family? I heard that bitch already got like five kids anyway, and this the bitch you abandoning us for?"

"Are you serious? Do you know how stupid you sound? We're not together 'cause you're a fucking whore and you burnt me. We'll never be together!" Chaz walked away.

Upset, Ria was ready to go. Since she'd driven, that meant her friends were going to have to be ready, too. After dropping her friends off at their homes, Ria arrived at her own and retreated to her bedroom. She grabbed her cordless phone and pressed *67 before dialing Chaz's cell-phone number. When he answered she didn't say anything; she just listened to his surroundings. Judging by the loud music, she knew he was still in the club. *Perfect,* she thought, hanging up the phone to dial another number.

The shrill ringing of the phone scared Kennedy out of a deep sleep. She was mad at herself for not turning the ringer off. "Hello?"

"It must be real lonely in that bed tonight, since my children's father is home where he belongs."

"Ria?"

"Yeah, ho, it's me."

"I don't give a fuck if he is there with you. You can have his bum ass, 'cause you need him. I made myself, so I'll never need a nigga. Since he's there with you, he can never come here again. Now lose my number, bitch, and die slow." Kennedy slammed the phone down. Her feelings were hurt. *I bet he been messing with that bitch all along. I should've gone with Hassan that night.*

A few seconds later the phone rang again. *I can't believe this heifer.* "What now, bitch?"

Instead of Ria's aggravating voice, she heard a man's deep dull voice. The voice sounded like it was devoid of all emotion. "I'm going to destroy your world the same way you destroyed mine." The phone line went dead. The man's voice sent chills up Kennedy's back. It took a few minutes to shake them. *Great, now some deranged fan has my number. Guess I'll have to get that changed, too.*

• • •

"Kennedy, wake up," Yatta said, shaking Kennedy.

"What is it?" Kennedy said, pulling the covers over her head.

Yatta pulled the covers off of her. "The white party is tonight and we still have to find you something to wear. We've been calling here for hours. Why aren't you answering the phone?"

"The ringer is off."

"Why?"

"Unwanted phone calls." Kennedy got out of the bed. "I really don't feel like going to this party."

"You better start feeling it; you're performing tonight. It's your introduction to the industry."

"You know, your ass is starting to sound a lot like Strick."

"Shut up. Hurry, we still have to find two outfits for you."

Running around with Yatta looking for something to wear had taken all of Kennedy's energy. After receiving her glamour makeover, she lay down on the couch in her dressing room. She slept with her hands propped under her chin, being cautious not to mess up her hair or makeup. A firm knock on the door startled her out of her sleep. "Who?"

"It's Strick. Are you decent?"

"Yeah, come on in." Kennedy sat up and closed her robe.

Strick entered the room looking quite dapper in a custom-made white linen suit. Kennedy smiled at him; he was so fly and sophisticated. Everything about Strick was smooth. It didn't matter if he was in a two-thousand-dollar Ralph Lauren suit or sneakers and jeans; he gave off the same persona.

Strick pulled up a chair and sat directly across from Kennedy. He looked her square in the face, trying to study her. "You aight, Mama?"

"I'm straight."

"I just wanted to make sure. You know, I want you to shine

tonight. Chaz is going on first. At the end of his performance he will call you onstage to perform your duet. After you perform your two singles, Hassan, S.C., and Joaquin will come on with you."

"Does Chaz know that Hassan is going to be here?"

"Yeah, he knows. Chaz is professional; he not gonna start no bullshit up in here."

"If you say so." Kennedy sighed. "You heard what happened yesterday."

"Chaz ain't dwelling on that shit. Him and Hassan saw each other last night at Slate and didn't nothing happen."

"Who told you that?"

"Didn't nobody have to tell me. I was there. Chaz and I went to a couple of parties last night before we went to the studio."

Kennedy rolled her eyes. "Yeah right. What you trying to do—clean his shit up?"

"Whoa, whoa," Strick said, shaking his head. "Kennedy, what are you talking about?"

"Ria called me last night and told me that he was there with her."

"Ken, baby, you cannot let her get to you. Ria is miserable and she has no plans on letting Chaz be happy with another woman. Don't worry about her, Ken—"

"Oh, trust me. I'm not worried about her at all. She can have her baby daddy back. As far as I'm concerned, Chaz and I are only label mates from here on out."

Strick leaned forward. "Ken, what you're dealing with is a man's pride. I know Chaz kirked out on you yesterday, but look at the way Rob brought it to him."

"Rob? I knew his hatin' ass had something to do with all this." Kennedy shook her head.

"Put that on top of all the grief Ria caused him. Chaz was no angel. He did his share of dirt, but he took care of her. I mean, I don't know what he's told you about that relationship, but ol' girl did a lot of foul shit to him."

"Like what?"

"That bitch was fucking wild niggas, even the ones she knew Chaz had beef with. The worst thing of all was when she burnt him."

"Are you serious? He never told me that."

"And through all that, he still respects her as his daughters' mother and never throws dirt on her."

The door opened and Yatta walked in, carrying Kennedy's freshly pressed outfits. "What up?"

"How you doing, Yatta?" Strick asked, blushing.

"I'm doing great, Strick," Yatta said, displaying a flirtatious smile.

"That's what's up," Strick said, admiring Yatta's beauty as he stood up. He bent over and kissed Kennedy on her cheek. "Tonight is yours, li'l mama. You exude a confidence like no other woman I know. I want you to rock this shit, and afterward we're going to party until the sun comes up."

T.O.N.Y.'s annual White Linen and Diamonds party was huge, to say the least. It was also the venue where Strick showcased his up-and-coming artists before the industry. Kennedy had just stepped off the stage after giving a dynamic performance. She looked stunning in a white off-the-shoulder minidress. As she moved through the crowd people were congratulating and complimenting her, making it hard for her to accomplish her mission of finding her sisters and cousin.

Strick grabbed Kennedy and whisked her into the VIP, where all the execs were located. The room was filled with the real big dogs of the industry. A good portion of the room was filled with Jewish men, European men, and Asian men, some of them over the age of fifty, with young model chicks hanging on to their arms. Strick took her around, introducing her to all of the important people. Kennedy was in awe, and not because of the power around her. She was in awe of the open drug use that was going down. Candy dishes of Xstasy pills were being passed around. Lines of cocaine were being snorted.

It wasn't like Kennedy had never seen people partying with drugs before. She just never thought that she would witness it here. These were some of the wealthiest and most respected people in America. She was even more taken aback by the way that they were offering her drugs as if they were drinks. But she was really disgusted. She remained polite, professional, and decided to keep it moving. On her way out she stopped to talk to Perri, the label's premier R&B singer and its only other female artist. She had been signed right after Kennedy. They were featured on each other's upcoming CDs and the pair had quickly bonded.

Perri stood up and embraced Kennedy. "Hey, mama, you did so good."

"So did you, Perri."

"Come sit with me," Perri said, handing Kennedy a mimosa.

Kennedy put the glass up to her mouth then suddenly placed it back on the table. "No offense to you, but, um, I don't trust no drinks that have been sitting around in here. I'll pour my own."

"No offense taken. I understand with all the dope being passed around in here."

Perri and Kennedy made small talk for a few minutes. Chaz was standing on the other side of the room staring at Kennedy, which was making her uneasy. Rob was also staring, with a sneaky smile plastered all over his face. Kennedy's hatred for Rob was growing every time she looked at him.

Time seemed to suddenly stand still when Hassan and Caz walked through the entrance. Kennedy and Perri were sitting directly to the right of the door. Hassan made a beeline to their table. "Hey, ladies." He kissed each of them on the cheek. "Y'all both did ya thing tonight."

"Thanks," they said in unison. Kennedy's eyes darted over to the corner where Chaz was standing. Instead of staring at her, he now glared.

Sensing the tension, Hassan decided to keep it moving. Kennedy could still feel Chaz watching her. "Perri, I'ma go out and mingle. I'm not feeling this shit in here and Chaz keep giving me greasy-ass looks."

Perri glanced over at Chaz. "He still tripping?"

"I guess, girl. I haven't even talked to him."

"I'm leaving out with you. I have to piss like a Russian race-horse."

As Kennedy and Perri made their way through the crowd, a girl with a familiar face stopped Kennedy. Perri continued on to the restroom. The pressure in her bladder was too intense for her to stop.

The girl smiled at Kennedy. "You did your thing tonight, homegirl."

"Thanks, ma. Do I know you? Your face looks familiar."

"We've met over the phone a few times but never in person. We should have, though, since you took my girls to Disney World."

I don't believe this. No wonder her face looks familiar. Chasity and Tiki look just like her. "Ria?"

"Yes, it's me in the flesh."

Chaz, Strick, Jay, Rob, and Yatta were walking out of the VIP area when Chaz saw Kennedy and Ria. "Oh shit."

"What?" everybody asked him in unison.

"Ria is over there talking to Kennedy."

"Your baby mother?" Yatta asked.

"Yes, I don't even know what she's doing here."

"You and Kennedy may not be speaking right now, but you have to go stop whatever is going on. 'Cause if she say the wrong shit, Kennedy will duff her ass and this is not the time or the place."

Meanwhile Ria, figuring she had Kennedy intimidated, began talking much shit. "Yeah, just like I thought, you uptown hos ain't nothing but some phone gangstas."

Kennedy finally interrupted her. "You're one pathetic, miserable skank. And phone gangsta, ma, I *highly* doubt that. I'm two steps from knocking you the fuck out."

"Try your luck, bitch, and my girls"—Ria pointed to three girls behind her—"will mop the floor with your ass."

"I'm not worried about you or them funky-ass hos. My entire family up in here, so the question is: Do you feel lucky, bitch? Keep poppin' shit and I'm going to drop your ass like you hot."

Just in the nick of time Chaz slipped his arm around Kennedy's waist. He finessed the situation like only he could. "I see you met wifey." Placing a huge kiss on Kennedy's lips.

Ria's friends couldn't believe how he was playing Ria. Usually Ria could make him dis another chick on the strength of being his babies' mother. Ria became heated. "So now you disrespecting me for this bitch?"

Chaz stepped up, pushing Kennedy behind him. "You disrespecting yourself trying to show out for the dizzy-ass broads. You just can't stand the thought of me being happy with someone else, can you?"

Ria threw her drink in Chaz's face. As he struggled to get the stinging alcohol out of his eyes, Kennedy reached around him and mugged Ria in the head, knocking her to the ground. Strick's security team stepped up and expeditiously resolved the situation. While being taken away by security, Ria yelled out to Kennedy, "I'ma see you in the streets, bitch."

Outside, while they waited for the valet to bring the car around, Kennedy was flipped on Chaz. "I don't know what kind of games you play with that bitch, but I'm not for it. How the fuck she just rolling up on me at my own shit? You better put that bitch in her place or your daughters will be motherless! That's word to everything I love!"

Noticing the stares they were getting, Chaz didn't want her to go on anymore. "Kennedy, that's enough. We can finish this in the car."

"In what car? Motherfucker, you can't be *serious*. I'm not going anywhere with you."

Just as the valet pulled the car around, Hassan and his crew walked out of the party. Hassan stopped to check on Kennedy. "You aight, Ma?"

Chaz answered for her. "She straight, my man."

"I asked *her,* fam." Both of their respective crews put their guards up in case something popped off. Not wanting the situation to escalate, Kennedy spoke up. "I'm fine, that shit in there was nothing. You know my family got me," she said, pointing to Yatta and a few of her cousins and friends.

"Aight, ma, if you say so. I'll check you later." Hassan and Chaz continued to stare each other down.

Still trying to smooth the situation over, Kennedy told Chaz, "Come on, baby, get in the car. I'm ready to go."

Chaz reluctantly agreed. They argued all the way to his home in Jersey. Kennedy made the situation worse by holding a phone conversation with Yatta the entire ride. She continued to talk to Yatta once she and Chaz got to the house. Already pissed off at her refusal to hang up the phone, Chaz snatched the phone from her, opened the patio door, and tossed it into the black night.

Kennedy screamed, "You bastard!"

"I guess I have your attention now, don't I?"

"I can't believe you did that. You're going to buy me a new phone! Give me the keys to your car so I can go home. Now! Before I smack the shit out of you."

"You ain't going nowhere and you ain't smacking nobody. So stop it."

Kennedy shook her head, sitting down on the couch. "Chaz, I don't want to be here, just take me home."

"I want you here."

"Yesterday you were ready to beat me about some shit from my past."

"I apologize for overreacting yesterday. I know I could have handled that a lot better. You know I'll never put my hands on you." He sat down next to her.

Kennedy looked over at him. "You are the only man I've truly loved since Pretty Boy died. And as good as that feels, I can't deal with this relationship. I can't deal with the press, the industry, your baby mother, and your boys being in our business. I know in the end I'll be the one who gets hurt."

Chaz removed his baseball cap and ran his fingers over his head. "You can end it now if that's the way you feel. But then I would be the one hurting. If you love me the way you say you do, can't nobody tear down what we build. Not the industry, my baby mother, your people, or my people. Nobody, Kennedy."

Kennedy nodded in agreement. Chaz leaned over and kissed her softly. Gently biting down on her bottom lip, parting her lips with his tongue, he kissed her slowly and intensely. They kissed for the next five minutes. Kennedy had been kissed by the best, but she had never experienced anything like this. The kiss was like something out of the movies.

Chaz pulled back and asked her, "You still mad at me, li'l mama?"

She shook her head. "No. For some strange reason, I can never stay mad at you for long." Chaz pulled her in close and lay across the couch with her in his arms. They fell asleep and slept that way until the next afternoon.

Takin' It to the Streets

New York's most notorious gossip DJ broke the exclusive story about Kennedy and Ria's confrontation at the party live from her morning show. She even touched on the rumors that suggested there was a beef between Chaz and Hassan.

Adding fuel to the fire, Hassan recorded a freestyle rap that was filled with thinly veiled subliminal messages towards Chaz. Chaz retaliated with a no-holds-barred rap of his own. And voilà, a new hip-hop beef was born.

Kennedy was sick of it all. She wanted to run to that back room in Big Ma's house and hide. But this was the profession she'd chosen and she was slowly beginning to learn to handle it. When reporters posed questions about the escalating beef between Chaz and Hassan, or about her and Chaz's relationship, she respectfully refused to comment.

At the end of the week Kennedy needed a stress reliever. This time her remedy of choice was shopping, and she took her niece Jazz and Jazz's best friend, Candace, with her. Jazz was used to her aunt splurging on her, but it was new to Candace.

Kennedy knew that Candace's mother was single and that she worked two jobs to support the child. Candace didn't get a lot of extra clothes and trinkets. Kennedy was more than happy to spoil her because she was a good kid, respectful and not too grown for her age. She even bought a special gift for Candace's mother.

Kennedy spent five thousand dollars on the girls that day. They capped off the evening with dinner at the Hard Rock Cafe.

Day was turning to night when Kennedy parked in front of her building. She told the girls, "Y'all can spend the night with me. We can order some movies or something."

"Okay, Auntie, I'll go see if my mother wants to come over," Jazz said enthusiastically.

After several trips from the car to the stoop, the girls emptied it of their shopping bags, and went into the house. Kennedy was retrieving one last bag from the trunk when she heard someone call her name. She closed the trunk and turned to see who it was. She saw Ria coming toward her screaming, "Talk that shit now, bitch."

Noticing the two girls walking a few steps behind Ria, Kennedy was sure that they were there to jump her. Aware as she was of the rules of street fighting, she knew she had to grab just one of them. She dropped her bags and swung her heavy purse forcefully with her right hand, knocking Ria to the ground. Kennedy jumped on top of Ria. She used her left hand to pin her down by her neck, then pounded her face with hard punches from her right fist. Ria couldn't swing back because she was too busy trying to get Kennedy's hand off her neck. Ria's two friends, Nee and Chula, were delivering hard blows to Kennedy's body, trying to get her off of Ria.

Jazz and Candace came out of Kennedy's house to see where she was only to witness the action unfolding. "AUNTIE!" Jazz screamed out.

"Y'ALL STAY ON THE STOOP, JAZZ! DON'T COME DOWN HERE."

Jazz jumped off the stoop and ran over to her mother's brownstone; she began ringing the bell hysterically. Candace picked up a metal pipe that was lying next to the garbage can. She ran up behind Nee, swinging the pipe like her name was Barry Bonds. Nee fell to the side from the first strike. Candace continued to beat Nee with the pipe the entire length of her body.

Inside, Yatta was stepping out of the shower when she heard the back-to-back ringing of the bell. *Who the hell?* She walked over to the intercom and in a very disgruntled voice asked, "Who is it?"

"Mommy, it's Jazz. Come down quick. Some girls are jumping Auntie."

Yatta ran to her room, searching frantically for something to throw on. She grabbed a T-shirt and a pair of gray sweatpants and stuck her feet down in a pair of old Timberlands. She reached behind the headboard and retrieved the Glock that she kept taped there.

Outside, Chula, one of Ria's sidekicks, spit a straight razor blade out of her mouth and into her hand. She grabbed a handful of Kennedy's hair and pulled her head back. In one swift move she had sliced open the right side of Kennedy's face. Kennedy howled in pain, falling flat on top of Ria. Ria pushed Kennedy off of her. With Chula's help, Ria stood to her feet. She was woozy from all the blows her head had sustained.

Ria began kicking and stomping Kennedy's body. "That's what you get for fucking with me, bitch! I told you Chaz is mine. You see that Lexus. Bitch, he bought that and my new house! Bitch, he don't want your stankin' ass." Ria hawked and spit in Kennedy's hair.

Chula freed Nee from Candace's fierce swings by hitting the girl in the head. She and Ria helped Nee to the car just as Yatta came running out of the house with her gun cocked. Yatta aimed and took a shot at them. The gunshot scared Chula so bad she ran the car up on the curb, almost hitting a pole as she drove away.

Yatta was about to let off another shot when she caught sight of Kennedy lying in the street. Her hair and clothes were soaked in blood. She was going into shock from the pain. Yatta ran to her little sister's side and dropped to her knees. Kennedy's face was stained with blood and her hair was sticking to the open wound. Yatta pushed Kennedy's hair back. "Jazzy, get Kennedy's phone out her bag and dial 911 now. Kennedy, baby, hang on."

Yatta sat in St. Luke's emergency room next to Kennedy's bed. Her pain was being treated with a high dosage of Vicodin. She had also received nearly two hundred stitches in her face. Yatta was ready to call her cousins, who were laying low in North Carolina, and take the beef with Ria to the street. The real bloodshed was about to begin. "Kennedy, I'm calling Kane and E. We going to get that bitch. I'ma stomp a hole in Ria's ass. And that bitch that cut you, I'ma cut from ass to appetite."

"No, Yatta." Kennedy spoke slowly. "You not fighting Ria. Nor am I. This shit is all because of Chaz, so he is going to fight her. I'm not going to keep fighting this bitch over my man. He's going to put her in her place once and for all or we're through!"

At that moment Strick walked into the room followed by a tall, dark, good-looking white man. Strick kissed Kennedy on her cheek. "Chaz will be here in a minute. Let me introduce you to a good friend of mine. This is Dr. Rodstat, one of, if not the best plastic surgeon in the world."

Dr. Rodstat stepped forward and lifted Kennedy's hand. He kissed it softly. "Did we . . . did we meet at the white party?" she asked, thinking he looked familiar.

"We sure did, beautiful." He flashed a smile, showing off a mouth full of sparkling white porcelain veneers.

"Please don't patronize me, Dr. Rodstat. I'm scarred for life."

"Call me Phil. Here, let me get at look at your face." He gently removed the bloody bandage from Kennedy's face and examined it. "Kennedy, I will have your face more beautiful than before this terrible incident. When I'm finished with you, the scar will merely be a memory."

Kennedy blushed, forgetting about the scar already. "How long do I have to wait before the surgery?"

"We can start as early as the beginning of next week. The sooner the better."

"How much is this going to run me?"

Strick, who had been sitting back tripping off of Phil's pimp juice, spoke up. "Don't worry about that, Kennedy. This one's on Chaz."

"Thanks, Phil."

"You're very welcome. I hate to rush out, but I have a very early flight. Take care, get plenty of rest, and I'll see you next week."

Chaz entered the room as Phil was leaving. The two men greeted each other like they were old friends and held a brief conversation. After exchanging a pound and a hug with Chaz, Phil left the room.

Dreading the moment, but greatly concerned, Chaz sat down on the bed next to Kennedy. He leaned over and pulled her into a tight embrace. "Baby, I'm so sorry. I'll do whatever it takes to make it up to you."

"That you will," she stated. Her voice was so cold and empty that Chaz pulled out of the embrace.

"Why did you say it like that? What do you mean?"

"That means you're going to beat that bitch ass and check her once and for all."

"Kennedy, you know I'm going to check her about this. But she is still my baby mother."

Yatta and Kennedy looked at each other. Kennedy looked back at Chaz. "Get the fuck out! NOW!"

"What's wrong with you?"

"What's wrong with me? This is what's wrong with me." Kennedy ripped the bandage off of her face and pointed to the nasty, swollen laceration that was oozing with yellowish pus and congealed blood.

Chaz couldn't form his next sentence. Seeing the damage to her face took the wind out of his body.

"Yeah, nigga, look at it long and hard. It hurts like hell. It hurts worse than it looks, if you can imagine that. Now, what I can't imagine is how you were ready to beat my ass over some shit from my past. But you won't get at this bitch about fucking up my face. Fuck you! You don't love me. I'm not going to keep fighting your baby mother over you. If I have to get at that bitch again, it's going to be a lot of slow singing and flower bringing."

Chaz's blood was boiling now. "Get dressed."

Chaz made two phone calls on the way out of the hospital. The first call was to Jay. As soon as he answered Chaz got straight to the point. "I need you to meet me at the block party."

"I'll be there."

The second call was to his sister. "Shorty, you still got my daughters?"

"Yeah. Why?"

"Don't let Ria take them tonight at all."

"What's going on, Chaz?"

"I gotta get at Ria. Her and some other bitches jumped Kennedy. One of them cut Kennedy's face."

"WHAT? Where is Kennedy?"

"She's right here; we're leaving the emergency room now."

"Let me speak to her."

Chaz handed his cell phone to Kennedy. "What's up, Shorty?"

"Are you okay, ma?"

"I'm okay now 'cause I know my face is going to be fixed. I'm drugged up so it doesn't hurt as bad."

"Ma, you know I will fuck that ho up for messing with you."

"Shorty, there's no need for you to get involved. Your brother has to handle this one."

"I know that's right, girl, make him fuck that bitch up. I don't condone a man hitting a woman, but she is one them hos a man have to beat. I told him a long time ago to punch that bitch in her face. That's the problem now. She knows he won't fuck her up. That's why she keeps on disrespecting him."

Pulling up to the annual block party, Chaz knew Ria was there. Not only because she had never missed the event since they were kids, but because he spotted the Lexus he had bought her months earlier parked a few cars ahead.

Jay walked over to Chaz's car as Chaz, Kennedy, and Yatta were getting out. He didn't have a clue about why Chaz had called him. That is, until he saw the big-ass bandage on Kennedy's face. "What the fuck happen to her face?" he asked Chaz as they exchanged pounds.

"Ria and her dumb-ass friends went uptown and jumped her. Man, one of them hos gave her a buck-fifty. I thought that shit was going to be a little-ass nick. Man, that shit is long and nasty as hell."

People were breaking their necks to speak to Chaz and Jay as they maneuvered through the crowd. The bandage on Kennedy's face attracted a lot of stares and whispers. One girl didn't even lower her voice as she pointed at the bandage and boldly said, "Damn, Chaz, what happened to your girl's face?"

Standing in the middle of seven girls, Ria was giving a play-by-play of her altercation with Kennedy. All of the girls were laughing at her animated account. Oversize Gucci shades covered Ria's eyes, hiding the bruises left by the pounding Kennedy had given her head.

BAM! Ria's shades suddenly flew off her face and shattered all over the concrete. She didn't know what had hit her. But before she hit the ground, Chaz grabbed her by her neck and held her in the air. All the girls who had been laughing at her story stood frozen.

Chaz tightened his grip on her neck and spoke sternly, gritting his teeth. "The games stop now, you deranged bitch. Don't fuck with Kennedy no more! Don't call her house. If you see her don't speak. Don't even frown your face up. If you do, I swear I'll body your little ass." He released her neck. Her body fell onto the black street.

Yatta pulled her leg back as far as she could and swung it forward with great force, kicking Ria square in her left cheek. Then she stood back and pulled all the phlegm and saliva she could lock up from her throat and then unleashed her personal fluids from her mouth onto Ria's face. "I told you not to fuck with my sister, you trifling slut."

Jay pulled Yatta away. "Come on, Yatta, that's enough."

As they approached the car Ria ran up on their heels screaming, "Fuck you, Chaz. You and that bitch ain't gonna make it. When that snooty ho dump your ass, don't come back round here. I hate you, you fucking bastard. How could you do this to me? I loved you when you ain't have shit. I'm your baby's mother! I'm supposed to be number one, motherfucker! I should've sliced that bitch's *throat.*"

Stopping in her tracks, Kennedy turned to Yatta and pulled a gun from Yatta's purse. Ria froze, fearing she was about to be shot. Instead, Kennedy walked over to Ria's beautiful six-month-old Lexus and riddled it with bullet holes, emptying the entire clip. She looked at Ria, smiling. "That should have been you. I hope your insurance is up-to-date. 'Cause Chaz ain't replacing this one."

"You crazy bitch," Ria cried, running over to her car, her baby.

Kennedy giggled as she held the gun to up to her lips and blew the smoke off the muzzle like her name was Annie Oakley. Jay took the gun from her. "Go get in the car, girl. The Jakes is coming!"

But Kennedy had to taunt Ria once more before she left. "When you tell the police I shot your car up, be sure to tell them about the scar I received courtesy of you and your homegirls."

I wonder if I did the right thing, Chaz thought as he lay next to Kennedy in bed. *Knowing Ria's psycho ass, I made it worse. I hate I had to embarrass her, but she had that shit coming. Look at what she did to my baby's face. I can't believe I ever thought about marrying her.*

Full of herself, Kennedy was lying with her body tucked under Chaz's, thinking. *I bet that bitch will respect my gangsta now. How ill is that? I made her own baby daddy handle her. I told these hos, I'm not the baddest bitch or the queen bitch. I'm that bitch! Hmm, I think I'll write a song about it in the morning.*

"Jay, you think that nigga lived?" Chaz asked as he handed his clothes to him to be put in the garbage bag.

"Man, if that nigga survived all that firepower I put in him, God was with him."

"I just want to know what the deal is so I can know what I'm up against."

"Don't you mean what *we're* up against? If he lived he can be finished off. Chill, I'm going to get rid of these clothes and the burner. I got some gear at this chick crib in Laurelton. I'll bring you back something to wear so we can keep it movin'." Jay opened the door, stuck his head out, and looked both ways before stepping outside.

Chaz sat down on the bed and lay back. He looked at the ceiling, constantly running the previous night's events through his head, wondering how they had gone awry. All he had wanted to do was hang out with Jay and Tony, maybe have a few drinks and smoke some weed to ease his stress.

He had been in the studio all day working on a sound track for the label. After the session he and Jay drove Kennedy home. She had been feeling uneasy all day. She was worried about the feeling that was weighing on her heart; she knew it all too well. It was the feeling that always preceded a tragic event. When her body became idle, the feeling took over from head to toe.

"Chaz, why do you have to go out tonight?"

"I'm only going out for a minute. Ma, I'll be back around two."

Kennedy wondered for a moment if he was going out in search of sex. In the seven weeks since her surgery, she hadn't had the urge to have intercourse. All the bandages, followed by the swelling, had been a turnoff even to her. Her face was almost healed, and just as Phil had promised, she was more beautiful than before. Kennedy told herself she was ready to be intimate with her man again and if she wasn't she'd damn sure fake it.

"Baby, we can have sex tonight. I know it's been hard for you."

Chaz could see the insecurities showing through in her eyes. "No, ma, stop. Don't do that. I'm not going out to chase hos. But I'm definitely not going to rush you back into having sex."

"You're not rushing me. I want to."

"Okay, I'm going to have a few drinks and build on some things with Jay. When I get home we can do that—if *you're* ready."

Cruising down Flatbush Avenue, Jay had gone ballistic seeing all the ballers' cars in front of the secret gambling spot. "It's some money in there, kid! You wanna go take some?" he asked Chaz.

"You know I'm game, nigga, but what about Tony?"

"That nigga can wait."

Chaz and Jay had entered the spot, ready to get their gamble on. Chaz's enthusiasm was shattered by the sight of Macon actively engaged in a game of C-Lo. He was betting three Gs at a time. *Can you believe this?* he said to himself. Chaz walked over to him and snatched his betting money out of his hands. "Run them fucking pockets, nigga."

"What the fuck is you doing?" Macon turned around and was facing Chaz. He was shocked. This was the last place he had expected to run into him. Macon knew he was in heavy debt to this nigga. Fuck all that. He couldn't come up in the spot and embarrass him in front of all the major players. "Nigga, I ain't running shit. Business hours is from eight to five."

Chaz threw a mean left upper cut, hitting Macon right under his chin. The sixty-five-year-old man who owned the illegal establishment loved Chaz like a grandson. But the shit couldn't go down in his spot. He had pleaded with Chaz: "Not in here. Please not in here."

Chaz scooped Macon's body up and threw him out the door. He hit the concrete ass first. Macon quickly jumped to his feet and snatched his white tee off. He put his fist up and stood in a fighter's stance. All the gamblers had run outside to watch the action. Some were even placing bets.

Macon took a swing at Chaz, throwing a sloppy right. Chaz ducked quick, narrowly missing contact with Macon's fist, then delivered a crucial blow to Macon's stomach. Then hit him with a mean two-piece to each side of his face. Macon's feet were not planted, so they slipped from under him, sending him to the ground once more.

A little dazed and tired, Macon was ready for the fight to end. He pulled up his pant leg in an attempt to retrieve the small gun that he kept in his boot. Jay saw him going for the gun, but Chaz didn't. Pushing Chaz of the way, Jay pulled out his gun and let off a shot. Hitting Macon inches from his groin, the bullet ripped through his pelvic bone. He let off four more shots. All four bullets landed in his abdomen area.

All the spectators had made a beeline for their cars. The sounds of screeching wheels speeding away could be heard for blocks. Jay and Chaz jumped in their own ride and sped away. They'd driven until they reached the hotel where Chaz now lay. His head began to throb just from the thought of what had taken place the night before.

His head was going to be hurting a lot worse if he didn't hurry up and talk to Kennedy. He opened his cell phone, forgetting that his battery was dead. Closing the phone, he picked up the room phone and dialed her number. She answered on the first ring. "Hello!"

"What's up, li'l mama?"

"You can't be serious, nigga! Where the fuck you been all night that you couldn't call me? Since that bitch pussy that good that you couldn't answer my calls, call her." Kennedy slammed down the phone.

He called right back, deciding he would get straight to the point once she answered. And she answered with her attitude in full swing. "What?"

"Kennedy, some real live shit jumped off last night. I need you to pack me some clothes and come to Queens. Once you get off the Triboro take the Grand Central. Call me when you get on the Grand Central so I can tell how to get here."

Less than an hour later Kennedy felt her skin crawl at the sight of the cruddy hotel. It looked worse than the Bates Motel. It hadn't seen fresh paint in years. Half of the rooms were no longer safe to enter and had been boarded up. Just the sight of it made her want to make a U-turn.

Chaz grabbed and hugged her tight as soon as she crossed the threshold. "Thanks for coming, baby."

Kennedy pulled her head back so she could see his face. "Chaz, I hope some bitch ain't rob you and leave you up in here without your shit. I know the game very well. I used to play it."

"Hell no, ain't no bitch leave me up in here. For the thousandth time, I'm not fucking nobody else. And if I was, I sure as fuck wouldn't bring 'em here. Sit down and let me fill you in."

He spent the next thirty minutes explaining everything to her, minus a few important details, like the fact that dope money was the real reason that he and Macon had been beefing. He had yet to reveal to her that he was still dealing heroin. When he finished telling her the story, her response was, "Sweetie, what do you want to do? We can go wherever you want until this shit blows over."

Her response warmed his heart. The fact that she'd said "we" let him know that she was his rider and that made him love her all the much more.

Hopeful Retribution

A luxurious resort in Mexico was the perfect place for Chaz and Kennedy to lay low. For two weeks they bonded and refreshed their relationship before Chaz received word that it was okay to return to New York. Macon had survived his gunshot wounds, and he didn't snitch to the police. Chaz wasn't sure if his silence was a blessing or a curse, though. Either Macon was scared or he was out for revenge.

Kennedy sat in the chair attempting to get her emotions in check. Her first CD, *Married to the Streets,* was due to be released the next day.

She had a million things on her mind. Like the deranged fan who had gotten her address and was sending her dead white roses almost every other week. The person sent letters filled with threats and vulgar drawings, always signing them *Your Watcher.* Weekly, Yatta would beg her to report the incidences to the authorities or at least hire full-time security, but Kennedy refused. "I'm not letting no fucking coward turn my life upside down. For all we know, it could be Ria's crazy ass."

"Kennedy, explain to me how this person knew that you put white roses on Nina's grave every week?"

"I don't know. Maybe they read the article in *Vibe*—you know, when the reporter visited the grave with me."

"No. The dead roses were coming weeks before that article ran."

"Like I said, I'm not going through *no* changes."

"I still think you should tell Chaz or Strick."

"I'm not telling anyone and neither are *you.*"

As Kennedy's makeup artist, Chichi, finished up her lips, the butterflies flipped harder in Kennedy's stomach. She continued to tell herself, *Breathe deep, li'l mama. You got everything under control. Remember, you're that bitch!*

Next thing Kennedy knew she was stepping out of the limo and walking into Float, where her album-release party was being held. By the time she made it upstairs to the VIP, a hundred pictures had already been taken of her. Chaz grabbed her and hugged her tight. She was glad to see him. Their conflicting schedules had kept them apart for the last few days. He stepped back and looked her over. She was sexier than ever in a beige Roberto Cavali halter cat suit and beige-and-green snakeskin stiletto boots. The cat suit hugged every curve on her body. Chaz was ready to take her home and get rid of his erection. "I gotta start going with Yatta to pick out your clothes. She dressing you a little too sexy."

"If you don't like it, take it off of me."

"Don't worry, I have every intention of doing that."

Yatta and Strick came in at the same time. They'd been doing that a lot lately. The VIP area was overflowing with celebrities from various industries. Ty Boogie was on the ones-and-twos, spinning the hottest songs, keeping the dance floor packed. Everyone was already having an excellent time. But the club went bonkers when Kennedy got on the mike and performed from the VIP section overlooking the dance floor. She gave it her all.

Sitting on the couch between Chaz and Strick after her performance, Kennedy had her first drink of the night. She swayed to the music as Ty Boogie continued to play hit after hit. A steady stream of people came through to congratulate her, make small talk, and network.

A half hour later, there was a loud commotion in the area leading to the VIP. It sounded as if an army was marching up the stairs. Club security along with Strick's personal security team secured the VIP's entrance.

Unfortunately, the people causing the commotion outranked them. Instantly the music came to a halt. Within seconds, the VIP was filled with FBI agents.

Kennedy wondered. A slim, plain-Jane-looking white lady in the navy-blue nylon FBI jacket took control. "Good evening, ladies and gentlemen. I am Agent Sorcosky. I have an arrest warrant for Kennedy Sanchez and Kenyatta Sanchez."

Obviously knowing who Kennedy was, two of the agents grabbed her off the couch and attempted to cuff her. She put up a light struggle, "What the fuck is going on?"

Agent Sorcosky walked over to her and explained. "You are now under federal arrest."

"On what *charges*?"

"Conspiracy and interstate trafficking. Be still and let Agent Rivers cuff you or I will *add* resisting a federal officer. Now, which one of the lucky ladies is your sister? And don't lie, I can get her mug shot sent up."

Without flinching, Kennedy returned Sorcosky's stare. "Fuck you."

"Get this stupid bitch out of my face," Sorcosky ordered the agents.

Yatta stood up and extended her arms so that she could be cuffed.

Facing the stares and whispers of the crowd, Kennedy told herself as she was led through the sea of people, *Hold it together, ma. Never let them see you break. No tears. No tears. You are that bitch.*

She and Yatta were transported downtown in separate cars. Once inside the Metropolitan Correctional Center, the sisters were placed in different interrogation rooms. Agent Sorcosky sat across the table from Kennedy. She gave Kennedy a stare that was meant to intimidate. Sorcosky looked over some notes that she had taken. Then she looked back at Kennedy. "Do you know Peter Jameson?"

"Do you know my lawyer, *Agent Sorcosky*? Can you spell *law-yer*? *L-a-w-y-e-r.* I'm choosing to remain silent until she arrives. You know that little Miranda thing you read to me. Do you comprehend it or just recite it?"

The agent was growing tired of the little charade both sisters were playing. Fuck it. She would have the last laugh once their stupid young asses were put away. "Once the judge hands you thirty to forty years, you'll be running and begging me to let you cooperate." She called out to the guard, "Muñez, get this stupid cunt out of here."

In four days, Kennedy had been allowed only two phone calls. She had not seen Yatta since the night they were booked. The food was grotesque. She refused to eat it and it showed. She felt as if the walls were closing in on her.

Yatta was built for jail. She had been there before. But she worried about her sister.

Kennedy's lawyer, Ms. Bovani, visited her on the evening of the fourth day. She showed Kennedy the motion of discovery, which their arrest had been based on. Kennedy couldn't believe the lies Petey had told about her and Yatta. "Ms. Bovani, we both know I'm no saint. But all this shit is a *lie.* I never introduced him to anybody in Norfolk, Charlotte, or Greensboro. And I sure as hell did not traffic any of his drugs. And these witnesses . . . I've never even heard of these people."

Ms. Bovani could see the hysteria in Kennedy's face. She attempted to calm her. "Kennedy, don't worry. This is the way the sneaky feds work. Paul Mazetti is representing your sister. He and I worked together on your cousin Kisa's case." She looked down at her notes. "He is going to be the lead attorney on this case. He has a very good record in federal court. As we speak, his office is in the process of getting you girls a bail hearing for tomorrow. And Mazetti is writing a motion for dismissal."

"At this moment I just want to get out of here. They're treating me like I blew up the Twin Towers. I've only been allowed two monitored calls . . . And no visitors . . . If I'm not out of here by tomorrow . . . I'm going to spaz."

The next day the sisters were granted a bail hearing. The judge set their bail at $1 million each. Strick and Chaz put the money up, reassuring Kora and Big Ma that they had nothing to worry about.

The girls were released six hours after their hearing, and Strick and Chaz were waiting to pick them up in white stretch limo. When Kennedy and Yatta emerged from the courthouse, their weight loss was more apparent than it had been in the courtroom earlier. Chaz joked as he approached them. "We got to hurry up and get y'all uptown so Big Ma can feed y'all. Y'all looking real slim. People might start talking."

"Boy, shut up and give me a hug," Kennedy said, grabbing him, pulling him close.

"Ma, I'm glad you're home. I was fucked up."

"Me, too, baby . . . Me, too. Let's get out of here. I'm ready for a hot plate of food and my mattress."

Chaz smiled, putting his nose in the air. "I hope you're for a bath, too."

"Fuck you."

"I know you want to."

The smell of Big Ma's cooking welcomed them into Kennedy's brownstone. She had prepared endless dishes for them, which Kennedy was ready to devour. Kennedy ripped the foil from each pan, almost missing the note her mom had left. Yatta walked in while she was reading it. "Who's that from, Ken-Ken?"

"Um . . . um, this is from Mommy. It says she and Big Ma took all the kids to Auntie Karen's house so we can eat and get some rest." Kennedy grabbed a plate and loaded it with fried chicken, barbecued chicken, catfish, collard greens, creamed corn, and macaroni and cheese, all made from scratch.

When she came out of the kitchen Chaz looked at her plate, then back at her. "Kennedy, you know as well as I know you not gonna eat all that."

"I was not playing when I said I didn't eat. All I did was drink water. And I didn't trust that."

Chaz placed a sloppy kiss on her cheek. "I'ma lay down for a minute."

Savagely, Kennedy and Yatta ate all the food in almost ten minutes. Strick laughed at them. "Damn, y'all ate that shit like two wild beasts."

They all fell out in laughter. Kennedy chased her food down with her favorite drink, homemade strawberry lemonade with fresh strawberries and lemon slices. Her lighthearted mood then became serious. "This some fucked-up shit Petey doing to us. And that fucking Agent Sorcosky . . . That bitch got a real hard-on for us. She could have come for me at any time. Why the fuck she have to come to my party and embarrass me?"

"That embarrassment boosted your record sales," Strick told her. "You were on the cover of the *Daily News* and the *Post*. They were talking about it on MTV, BET, and even CNN. You sold almost two hundred and fifty thousand copies in two days! That is unheard of for a new female rap artist. People are even saying we did it just to boost your sales."

"Get the fuck out of here." Kennedy laughed. "That's nuts! I go to jail and my sales go crazy."

Kennedy talked to Yatta and Strick for another hour. After they left, she walked into the kitchen and looked around. *I'm not cleaning all this tonight.* She turned and went to her bedroom. Chaz was lying diagonally across her bed. She hit the power button on her stereo. "Love and Happiness" by Al Green came blaring through the speakers. Chaz jumped up. Kennedy hurriedly turned the stereo down. "I'm so sorry, baby. I didn't know it was up that loud."

"That's aight, ma, I needed to get up anyway. Strick still here?"

"Nah, he left when Yatta did. He said call him later," Kennedy said, peeling out of her clothes. Chaz's dick became rock hard as he watched her move around the room ass naked. Kennedy went into the bathroom and turned on the water, allowing it to steam up the room. She stuck her head out the door into the bedroom. "I thought you were going to take a shower with me. Are you still asleep?"

When he didn't answer she stepped into the shower. She

stood under the hot water, letting it drench her from head to toe. It felt so good. Little things like this she would never take for granted again. She jumped when she suddenly felt a cool trickle run down her back. When she turned around Chaz was holding a bottle of peppermint soap and a bath sponge. She hadn't heard him come in. "I see you decided to join me."

"Why wouldn't I? Turn around so I can wash you."

Kennedy followed his instructions, turning toward the water. Chaz poured shampoo in the palm of his hand. He lathered her hair and began to massage the shampoo into her scalp. "Hold your head under the water." He ran his hand through her hair, helping to rinse off the excess shampoo. He picked the sponge up and covered it in peppermint soap. He washed her back slowly and firmly, making his way down to her ample ass. "Turn around," he whispered. Gently he washed her face, shoulders, underarms, and breasts, working his way across her abs. Squatting down, he washed her smooth thick thighs. Standing back up, he began rubbing her between her legs and kissing her neck. Nudging her under the water, he rinsed the soap off her body while planting kisses all over her chest. He sucked and licked her swollen nipples.

"Oh, Pa-pa," she moaned.

Chaz planted kisses all the way down to her stomach, circling the outline of her navel with his tongue. He traced her pelvic bone with wet tongue kisses, then ran his cool tongue over her hot pulsating pussy. He tickled her clit with the tip of his tongue, causing her whole body to shudder. *Don't come yet . . . Don't come yet,* she told herself. She couldn't hold back as her walls became flooded. He stood up, pressing his body against hers. His dick was at full attention. Grabbing her by both sides of her thighs, he lifted her body up, spreading her wide. He rubbed his dick around her inner folds, teasing her.

"Stop teasing me," she panted.

"You want it?"

"*Lo necesito ahora.*"

"You telling me you need it now?"

"*Sí, Pa-pa.*"

He laughed as he eased inside her, causing her to growl. Gyrating his hips, he rolled around inside of her, stroking at a nice medium-paced rhythm. Kennedy licked his neck, flicking her tongue up and down. His strokes became faster and she became wetter. "*Muy bueno.*"

"Oh, it's very good, Ma-ma?"

"*Sí. Sí.*"

"You ready to come?"

"*Un momento.*"

Chaz fought vigorously to hold the oncoming nut off. He tried to think of other places and things. Kennedy was making his work difficult. The faster he stroked, the louder she moaned. "*Ah, sí. Ah, sí.*"

"Like that, baby?"

"*Sí . . . Pa-pa . . . sí.*" Kennedy screamed, exploding all over him. Her warm cream was kryptonite to his hard dick. He busted an explosive strength-draining nut. Still holding her thighs in midair, he collapsed his head into her chest. Trying to catch their breath, they stayed in that position for almost two minutes, letting the water continue to drench their bodies.

Out of the blue Kennedy let out a deep laugh. Chaz lifted his head and looked at her. "What are you laughing at?"

"I was just thinking . . . I need to go to jail and come home again if it's going to be that *good*!"

After trying repeatedly to reach Yatta on the phone the next morning, Kennedy walked over to her place and let herself in. She walked through the house calling for her. "Yatta, are you okay? Where are you?" The house was completely silent. Kennedy opened Yatta's bedroom door. "What the . . . I knew it—I knew it." She jumped around laughing like a kid at the sight of Strick and Yatta scrambling to put on their clothes. "I knew y'all was creeping around here. I been peeped the way y'all be looking at each other. No wonder you wasn't answering the phone, *Yatta*. My bad for busting in on y'all. I didn't know you had *company*." With that, Kennedy left, not giving them a chance to explain.

She literally skipped back to her house. Once inside, she ran into her bedroom. "Chaz, get up!"

"What?" he asked, still half-asleep.

"You will never guess who I just caught in the bed."

"Who?"

"Yatta and Strick."

Chaz woke all the way up. "Get the fuck out of here."

"I put that on everything I love," Kennedy said with a wide grin on her face. "The funny shit was seeing them trying to throw their clothes on." She doubled over in laughter as she got up from the bed. "Let me get dressed."

"Come here," he told her lustfully.

"No, Chaz, I don't have time. Ms. Bovani said our appointment is ten sharp."

He got out of the bed and wrapped his arms around her. "You sure you don't want me to go with you?"

On the inside she was screaming, *Yes, please go with me. I need you to hold my hand. I don't think I can go through this without you.* On the outside she sang a different song. "No, sweetie, I can handle this one. You've done enough."

"Aight, baby girl, Call me as soon as you finish."

· · ·

During the ride downtown, Kennedy teased Yatta to no end about catching her and Strick. But once they arrived at the U.S. attorney's office, all jokes stopped.

The sisters sat side by side with their lawyers beside them. Kennedy's stomach turned as they waited for the assistant U.S. attorney to join them. Mazetti noticed the perspiration on Yatta's face. And he could feel the vibration on the floor from the shaking of her leg. He gave her leg a firm pat to calm her down. "Kenyatta, stop worrying yourself. I can assure you this bullshit will be so far behind you in a matter of minutes."

Ten minutes later, the assistant U.S. attorney, John O'Malley, strolled in, followed by Agent Sorcosky. He looked to be in his thirties, Irish, with classic American white-boy good looks. He was confident that he had the case in the bag. That was before Mazetti tore into him like a pit bull. He didn't even give the pair time to make acquaintances or have a seat.

"No need to sit and converse." Mazetti handed O'Malley a blue legal document. "Here is my motion to dismiss all charges. Your CI should have informed you that he is using you as a tactic to seek revenge against my clients. We do have recorded phone calls of him threatening retribution toward my clients." Mazetti gave Sorcosky a devilish smile. "And if the case does go to trial, you know I'll destroy your lying-ass witnesses on cross. As far as the dates that Mr. Jameson is saying Kennedy Sanchez transported his narcotics . . ." He reached into his briefcase and pulled out a small stack of papers. "We have notarized attendance records from Norfolk State University that indicate she was in all of her classes on those dates. So you can take you fairytale case and shove it up your tight ass. And, Agent Sorcosky, if you come after my clients again with a half-cocked case, I will sue you personally and the entire U.S. attorney's office for malicious prosecution. Come on, ladies, let's leave."

Ms. Bovani was the first to rise from her chair. She always loved to see the great Mazetti in action. Kennedy and Yatta were too shocked to move. Neither could believe how he had just spoken to an FBI agent and an assistant U.S. attorney. Even more, they couldn't believe the bitch, Sorcosky, or O'Malley weren't saying anything. Slowly Kennedy and Yatta rose from their chairs and followed their lawyers. Mazetti stopped in front of Agent Sorcosky. "After 9/11, shouldn't you be out chasing terrorists instead of harassing the innocent?"

"Fuck you, Mazetti!" she hissed, and shoved past him out of the office.

Mazetti was worth the outrageous fees he charged. Two weeks later, all of the charges were officially dismissed. The family gathered and threw a huge feast to celebrate. The day after the dismissal, Kennedy was back on the grind. Along with Yatta and her personal beauty team, she was off on a ten-week promotional tour. The tour proved to be more challenging, stressful, and exhausting than any of the previous ones.

Reporters and DJs would ask her only a few questions about her album and her career. The rest of the questions pertained to her public arrest, her relationship with Chaz, and the growing beef between him and Hassan. This time around, her professional "no comment" reply was no longer working. So it was a challenge for her to handle herself. She came close to telling a few of the reporters who didn't understand the meaning of her reply to fuck off.

Having to maintain a professional face regardless of the circumstances was driving Kennedy nuts. She started depending on prescription drugs to get her though each day.

Imaginary Friends

Lord, protect me from my friends . . .
I can handle my enemies.

Damn it! I missed six calls," Kennedy told Kneaka. "And all of them were from Chaz." She pressed talk on her cell, calling him back. "Hey, baby, what's up?"

"Yo, where the fuck you at? I been calling you all day!"

"Hold up. First of all, I don't know *who* you think you're talking to, but you can come better than that!" She pressed the end button.

"Did you hang up on him?" Kneaka asked, laughing.

"Hell yeah!" Kennedy proclaimed proudly.

Chaz called right back. "I know you didn't hang up on me."

"I sure did!"

"Why?"

" 'Cause, you need to check yourself before you start feeling like you can talk to me any kind of way."

"Come on with that bullshit, man. I'm at your house right now. You not here, Yatta ain't seen you since y'all got back, and you not answering none of my calls. If that was you looking for me, you would've been breaking."

She smiled at his jealousy. "To answer your question, I'm in the Village eating with Kneaka and her roommates. Since you were *too busy*. And I wasn't answering my phone 'cause it was on vibrate in my purse. I'll be home in about forty-five minutes."

"Nah, don't rush now. I'm going out."

"How you going to go out and I just got off the road? You haven't even seen me! Whatever, Chaz, do *you*." Kennedy hung up the phone. This time he didn't call back.

After dropping Kneaka and her friends off at a club in midtown, Kennedy was focused on getting home and into her bed. Kay Slay's latest drama CD was blasting from the speakers. Kennedy was bobbing her head to the freestyles. Suddenly she felt like her ears were playing tricks on her when Hassan's latest dis song to Chaz came on the air.

"It's senseless to tell Schiz to suck my dick/He already did it when he kissed his bitch."

Kennedy almost hit the car in the next lane as she tried to get off the FDR. She sped over to Sure Gold Studios, parked illegally, and ran upstairs.

Her instincts were correct. Hassan was up there with Caz, his entourage, and some groupies. He stood up smiling when he saw her come through the door. "Ken, what up, ma?"

"No! What the fuck is up with you?"

The room fell completely silent. Judging by her expression, Hassan knew she meant business. "Come on, Ken. Let's talk back in the office."

"Fuck no! So you can have some more shit to say about me on one of your petty-ass songs. We can talk outside." She turned and walked out. Hassan followed.

Kennedy paced around the concrete until she got her words together. "Damn, Has, not for nothing I thought we were better than this bullshit. I know you and Chaz is beefing. And I may be at the center of your beef. But you know it's so fucked up for you to put me on Broadway like that. I mean, before anything, we were friends first. Maybe I'm wrong about that, and you. You've turned into a fake, shysty motherfucker just like the rest of these industry assholes."

Her comments hurt Hassan because he really cared about her. For the first time he saw how his and Chaz's beef was affecting her. "Ken, I know you don't want to hear I'm sorry, but I am. I just went crazy after that shit at the party. Then the way he dissed me on the last song. You have to know I never meant to put you out there like that. I knew it was only a matter of time before you got at me about it."

Shaking her head, Kennedy let out an insane little laugh. "You know, once I got this opportunity, I *thought* that everything was finally going to be okay. Now it seems like everything is more fucked up than it was before. I've lost several good friends, including you. A man hates my sister so much that he sent the feds after us." She laughed again. "At first I was grindin' to keep up my lifestyle. Then I found myself grindin' harder for the sake of my son. Now . . . now I just feel like I'm grindin' to keep my sanity."

Looking her directly in the eye, Hassan told her, "Believe it or not, I know exactly how you feel. I'm sorry that I added to the bullshit. I'll even apologize to you publicly for what I said on that song."

"That's peace. I just hate it all had to end like this." Kennedy got into her 745i and sped away, leaving Hassan on the curb.

Chaz's attention was fully captured by the sexy chocolate grinding her perfectly round ass against his crotch. This shorty was gorgeous and her body was mean. The red leather microminiskirt she was wearing was so short that her ass cheeks were hanging out. She was driving Chaz crazy as he partied it up at Mars 2112 along with Jay and Rob. He was ready to slide her home. *Damn, it's been four months since I fucked a chick besides Ken . . . and shorty right here, she could get it tonight!*

Suddenly an image of Kennedy flipping out popped into his head. He heard her voice saying, "All you trifling niggas is just alike. You claim to be different, but you're all the same." Chaz was determined to prove that he was different. A feeling of disgust came over him. *Why the fuck am I even contemplating sliding with this groupie bitch?*

Chaz looked over at Jay. "Man, I'm going to home to wifey."

"Yeah, you need to go home before you get fucked up," Jay said, eyeing the chick's unbelievable shape.

The crowded dance floor emptied as four guys started fighting, throwing wild blows. The rumble was headed right in their direction. Rob turned and pushed Chaz and Jay toward the back exit, out of the way of the oncoming brawl. Rob ushered them through the door and right into the hands of four masked men. Three of the men grabbed Chaz and pinned him to the concrete wall. It all happened so quickly that he didn't have time to react.

Jay was grabbed from behind by the biggest masked man and placed in a choke hold. He was utterly shocked when he saw Rob go back inside the club and pull the door shut. That would be the last thing he saw. The masked assailant placed a razor-sharp nine-inch blade against his neck. With precision, he sliced Jay's neck open like a piping-hot baked potato. Blood poured profusely from his gaping wound. The killer then released him and stepped back, allowing Jay's lifeless body to hit the pavement. A single tear escaped Jay's right eye.

In horror, Chaz screamed out, "JAY!"

"Shut the fuck up, *nigga*!" Macon said, removing his mask. "Your punk ass ain't shit now that your muscle laying there with his shit sliced open!"

"Suck my dick, *bitch*!" Chaz hawked and spit right in Macon's face, infuriating him. He was supposed to be begging for his life, not rebelling. Macon swung hard and landed a bone-crushing punch to the left side of Chaz's face. His body fell onto the man on his left.

"Straighten that fucker up!" Macon barked. "Now gut him," he instructed the killer who had just taken Jay's life.

The killer moved his five-ten, two-hundred-and-eighty-pound frame closer to Chaz. Through the hole in the mask, his mouth displayed a chilling, evil grin. He drew his blade and rammed it into the side of Chaz's stomach. The squishing sound of the knife splitting Chaz's skin was disgusting. He pulled it out and stabbed it into the middle of Chaz's abdomen below his navel. As if he was gutting an animal, he ran the knife upward. Intense pain ran through Chaz's body, causing him to black out. Macon danced around laughing like a kid, so happy to see his biggest foe being taken out.

Just then, three bouncers, who had removed the fighters from the club moments earlier, were coming in through the back. The first bouncer to turn the corner and see the attack screamed out, "Yo! What the fuck is going on up there?" The other two followed his lead and ran up the alley behind him.

Macon pulled his mask down. "Let's go. Now, nigga, let's go."

The assassin pulled the knife from Chaz's body. The two men who were holding him released him from their grasp. His body fell forward. He hit the pavement face-first, breaking his nose. The first bouncer stopped and turned his body over. "Oh shit, it's Chaz." On his cell phone he called for help. The other bouncers gave chase to the four attackers, but they fled in a waiting car.

Kennedy stopped at the bodega to pick up some snacks to absorb some of the liquor and stress. She parked her car in the garage and walked the five blocks to her building. From the corner she could see Yatta's new Jaguar. *I can't believe she has her baby parked on the street.* As she walked past Yatta's car the darkly tinted passenger window rolled down. "Ken-Ken," her aunt Karen called out to her.

"Damn, Auntie, don't scare me like that. What the hell y'all doing sitting out here?" Kennedy asked, looking over at Yatta in the driver's seat. When she noticed the tears in Yatta's eyes, her heart dropped. "What's wrong? Are the kids okay?"

"The kids are fine," Yatta answered. "Get in."

"No, not until you tell me what wrong!"

Karen looked at Yatta. "Tell her."

Yatta inhaled deeply. "Strick called me from Cali an hour ago. He's on his way back here now." Yatta stopped talking.

Kennedy looked at her, waiting for her to finish. "Why is he coming back, *Yatta?*"

"He got a call . . . Chaz and Jay were stabbed at Mars 2112 two hours ago."

Did she just tell me Chaz was stabbed? I just talked to him. Kennedy's head began to throb. Her stomach bubbled. Saliva filled her mouth. She dropped her purse and bags. Feeling the rush coming from the pit of her stomach, she doubled over. Vomit exploded from her mouth onto the sidewalk.

Karen and Yatta leaped from the car to help her. "Get it all out, baby," Karen told her as she patted her back and massaged the nape of her neck. "Yatta, go in the house and get a cold wet rag and some Sprite or ginger ale."

Once Kennedy stopped vomiting, she sobbed heavily as she questioned Yatta. "Is he okay? Please tell me. He's not dead, is he? I can't lose him now . . . I swear to God I can't."

"Baby, I won't know his condition until we get to the hospital. Please get in so we can go see about him."

•   •   •

Entering the crowded family waiting area, Kennedy saw Chaz's mother, Sal; and his sister, Shorty. She could tell that they had been crying. But now it seemed as if they were more focused on consoling Jay's baby's mother, India. And she appeared to be inconsolable. Chaz's cousins, closest friends, workers from the label, people from the club, and police filled the room.

Shorty looked up and saw Kennedy standing in the waiting-room entrance. She rushed over to her, and they embraced and held on to each other. "Please tell me he's not dead," Kennedy said in a low muffle.

"No, Kennedy, he's not dead. He's holding on. But Jay didn't make it."

"No! Not Jay." Kennedy wailed, causing India to cry harder and louder.

"Come on, Ken. Let's go outside and get some air."

"I don't want to go anywhere. I want to see Chaz *now.*"

"He just came out of surgery. He's in recovery. Once he gets in his room, they said we can see him."

As the hours passed and daylight approached, the waiting room thinned out. Kennedy was staring straight ahead, looking at nothing in particular, when the nurse came in to update the family. "Mr. Harris is out of recovery. He's in room 2610. He's under heavy sedation and will probably sleep until tonight."

"Can we see him?" Shorty asked.

"Sure. It will do him good to hear familiar voices."

Shorty and Sal stood up, but Kennedy didn't. Turning around to look at her, Shorty said, "Come on, Kennedy."

"Nah, y'all go ahead. Spend some time alone with him."

Sal extended her hand to Kennedy. "Come on, baby. If he needs to hear anybody's voice, he needs to hear yours."

Kennedy stared at Sal's hand for about twenty seconds before grabbing it and standing up. Hand in hand, the three women walked down the hallway.

The sight of Chaz lying there battered and banged reminded Kennedy of Pretty Boy's death. She paused and stood by the door while Shorty and Sal went into the room. Sal stood next to the bed, looking down at her son, noticing that his face held the same sad expression it had worn when he was a young boy sitting on a courtroom bench, watching his mother being led away to prison. She'd missed the best years of Shorty and Chaz's lives, but they never judged her. Now here was her child, pulled inches away from dying. And just when she was getting know him.

God, thanks for saving my baby, she said inside her own mind. She picked up his left hand, gently rubbing it with her own. "Hi, Chaz, it's Mommy. I don't know if you can hear me. We've talked so many times since I came home. But I guess we've never had the conversation that counts. I'm so sorry that I wasn't there for you and Shorty when you needed me the most. I hated myself for so long for not being there to do the things that mothers are supposed to do." Sal's tears escaped both eyes despite her effort to hold them back. "I know you had Grandma, but you needed me. Because of my mistakes, the two of you were left to fend for yourselves out here in the world. And you had to teach yourself how to be a man. I'm so proud of the man you've become. I can only hope and pray that I've made you proud." She covered her mouth to mask her sobs as she walked from the room. Shorty followed her out.

When they were gone, Kennedy eased toward the bed. She focused on Chaz's bandaged broken nose. Her teardrops hit his hospital gown, leaving huge wet spots. She took his hand. "I hate that we argued last night. If you would've . . . I mean, I love you so much, baby. If you had died last night, I would've died with you."

Suddenly Chaz squeezed her hand and she jumped. A smile lit up her face. His eyes remained closed, but her heart warmed a little, knowing that he recognized her. Never letting go of his hand, she pulled a chair close to the bed and sat down. Resting her head against the bed rail, she said a silent prayer. *God, I know I don't need any man more than I need you. But I love him so much. Please, God . . . please heal his body. Please bring him back to me whole again. All my faith is in You. And, Lord, I know Jay did dirt, but he had a beautiful heart. God, please let him come home and rest with You. These and all blessings I ask in Your holy and righteous name. Amen.* Kennedy drifted off to sleep. Still holding Chaz's hand.

"Good morning, this is Nancy Michaels with this morning's top story. Chaz Harris, also known as Schiz, a well-known rapper from Brooklyn, was brutally stabbed while leaving a local Manhattan nightclub early this morning." A picture of Chaz flashed behind the reporter's head. "Jason Simms, who was with Harris, was fatally stabbed. Harris is listed in serious but stable condition. Police said they have several suspects who will be brought in for questioning. They are asking for anyone with information to come forward."

Rob hit the power button furiously, turning the television off. He scrolled his cell-phone contacts until he came to the name that he was looking for, then pressed the send button so hard it nearly stuck.

The phone rang four times before there was an answer. "Nigga, don't start callin' me every time a news report come on. Trust, I'm watchin' the same shit you watchin'!" Macon said.

"Don't give me that shit, muthafucka!" Rob yelled. "You promised me this would be eighty-sixed. It's my ass on the line if he lives. Even if he don't put it together, which I know he will, he's gonna think I ran like a little bitch. If your ass hadn't tried to be so fucking personal and put one in his dome, this shit would be over."

"Whoa, hold the fuck up! Who in the hell you think you talking to, nigga? Don't ever try and tell me how to handle mines, dawg. You'll fuck around and have two in your head dun. I gave you your cake, now take it and get low if that's what you feel. Fuck that nigga. He done anyway. He can't go to five-o wit'out blowin' his own spot up. And he can't get at nobody without his muscle!"

Rob couldn't believe his ears. "Macon, you're more foolish than I thought. Chaz got all kind of connections. Damn, don't you listen to the streets? You *keep* disrespecting that man's gangsta. Fuck Chaz, that nigga Strick got some straight wolves on his team. *And* he ain't afraid to let them loose."

"Why do I get the feeling you ready to sell me to those niggas to save your ass?"

"It ain't neva like that! I'm just trying to show you what you up against. I just know I'm not sticking around and waiting for it to get busy."

"I don't need your punk-ass suggestions! Macon don't run from shit. Chaz started this and I'm going to finish it. You ain't got no choice but to run 'cause you a rat! You got tired of being a little go-boy for Chaz, so you decided to sell him out to highest bidder. And that was your man since free lunch. So don't pretend like you give a fuck about me. 'Cause if that's what you'd do to your man, I'd hate to see what you'll do to me. Maybe it *is* best if you get low and lose my number, faggot!" Macon slammed the flip on the cell phone closed and threw it hard on the glass table, cracking the tabletop.

He looked over at his younger brother, Marcus, then over at his cousins Rashan and Damon. Macon lit a blunt filled with dro and laced with dust. Taking a long pull on the blunt, he held the smoke in for about thirty seconds before exhaling. Looking at his brother through slanted eyes, he told him, "Young Marc. Find that nigga before he get missing. When you find him put two in his head."

Awakened by a tap on the shoulder, Kennedy opened her eyes and saw Strick and Yatta standing there. Blinking, she tried to focus in on her surroundings, then feeling Chaz's hand in hers quickly reminded her. Looking at him sleeping brought her an instant sadness. She looked back at Strick with tear-glazed eyes. Her face was pale and she looked disheveled. "What up, Strick?" she asked as she stood up and hugged him, never letting go of Chaz's hand.

"How's my man holding up?" asked Strick.

"I think he's all right. The doctor said that he should make a full recovery. He hasn't woken up yet." She paused. "I just don't understand why . . . why he couldn't stay home and wait for me." Kennedy started to sob and leaned her head on Strick's shoulder.

Yatta was concerned because Kennedy was gripping Chaz's hand so fanatically. She stepped forward and told her sister, "Come on, ma, let's go get some air. You need some food, too. I know you haven't eaten anything since yesterday."

"No, I'm fine, I can't leave him until he wakes up. I can't leave him. I wasn't where I was supposed to be last night and look what happened."

Strick searched his mind for words of comfort to give Kennedy. Before he could utter a single one, Chaz began gasping for air. His eyes were wide open, and his grip on Kennedy's hand tightened. But it didn't matter how bad her hand hurt; all her concern was for Chaz.

Strick ran from the room in search of a doctor. Within seconds, two doctors and three nurses arrived. One of the nurses peeled Chaz's fingers from Kennedy's hand. Strick helped to take

Kennedy from the room. Sal and Shorty, who had been to the hospital cafeteria, ran toward the room to see what all the commotion was about. Yatta explained everything as they walked toward the waiting room.

Fifteen minutes later, the lead doctor walked into the waiting room and scanned it until he saw Sal. "Um, Miss Harris, Chaz is okay. He had a reaction common to a lot of patients coming out of anesthesia. His vitals are looking good and we've stabilized him. He's asking for you, his sister, and his wife."

Chaz's voice sounded like it no longer belonged to him; it was rough and raspy. Everyone stood around his bed. Sal was on his right with Shorty next to her. Yatta and Strick were at the foot of the bed and Kennedy was on his left. Through his drowsy eyes he stared back at them. No one's face stood out more than Kennedy's, marked with her pain and guilt. Her eyes kept apologizing to him over and over as tears slid down her face. She could not look directly at him.

To get her attention, he squeezed her hand. "Don't cry, Kennedy," he said, his voice very hoarse. "It's not your fault."

Kennedy bit her lip and nodded. Chaz closed his eyes to the hurt faces in front of him and drifted into a much happier place—his dreams.

Dreams were his refuge, but that didn't last for long. An hour into his sleep they turned volatile. Chaz dreamed of the night that Jay had shot Macon, but in his dream, he was the one who was shot and killed. He could see himself lying on the ground next to a throat-slit Jay. He relived that same dream for the next three days. He kept hearing the heavy steel door from the club slamming shut, and at that exact moment he would wake up, every time.

On the fourth day, he awoke from the dream with a question

to ask Kennedy. *"Where the fuck was Rob?"* It occurred to him that Rob had intentionally shut the door that night. He needed to talk to someone about the subject immediately.

For the first time in four days, Kennedy wasn't by his side when he opened his eyes, but Chaz knew she wasn't far away. He heard her voice right outside his hospital-room door. She was in a heated exchange with someone. There were three other voices. The only other recognizable one was Strick's.

"Next time you want to talk, call my attorney," Kennedy said over her back as she entered the room and sat down on the bed. "Hey, I didn't know you were awake."

Chaz knew from her reaction and the commotion that something wasn't quite right. "What's up, Ken? What was that about?"

"That was some DTs from homicide. Before I get into what they were saying, let me explain this to you." She inhaled deeply. "The night that you were stabbed, I went to see Hassan at the studio. Before you start thinking some off-the-wall shit, I swear on everything I love nothing happened. I went over there to spaz on him, which I did! 'Bout that bullshit he said on his last dis record toward you. After saying what I had to say, I was out. And of course he used me as his alibi when the jakes went to see him. And just now they right out accused me of being a part of a conspiracy with Hassan and Caz to murder you. All that noise you just heard was Strick and me telling them to fuck off."

"I know Hassan didn't have anything to do with this."

"How come you seem so sure about that?" Kennedy said, reading into his confidence.

"Quiet as kept, ma . . . I already know."

"Know *what*?"

"I know who tried to eighty-six my ass. It was Macon."

"And when were you going to tell me? And since we're on the subject, what are y'all really beefing about? 'Cause between your niggas and Strick, I've been hearing a whole lot of whispering about drug money."

Might as well set this shit straight. "Before I get into all that, have you heard anything from Rob?"

"Hell no, ain't *nobody* heard from that faggot! I heard he ran like the bitch he is."

"Nah, I think he did more than run."

"What? You think he set you up?"

"It's starting to look that way."

"Chaz, what does all this have to do with drug money and Macon?"

"I fronted the nigga some work when his spots down south got raided. That wasn't a problem. I usually fronted him whatever he wanted on top of what he copped. He always paid on time with no problem. I gave him time to get back on his feet before I stepped to him about my paper. Every time I got at him, it was a story. Then that night at the gambling spot, the nigga disrespected me when I told him to run them pockets. And well, you know the rest."

"So this beef is from when you used to move weight?"

"You just don't get it?"

"Get what?"

"I never stopped."

"Wait a minute." Kennedy got up from the bed. "What the fuck? You never *stopped*! I can't believe this shit."

"What you mean, you *can't* believe this shit?"

"Fuck it, I'm not going there with you, not while you laid up in this hospital."

"No, ma, don't ever bite your tongue. Say what you got to say *now.*"

"I mean, I don't understand you. Chaz, you received one of the biggest advances ever heard of in rap and yet you're risking your life and those around you to do the same shit you were doing before. What kinda shit *is* you on?"

"Ma, half that shit went to the fuckin' IRS! The other half I put up. This rap shit only gave me the green light to spend my real money. Do you know how long and spaced out royalty checks be? Fuck that. I'm stackin' for the future right now!"

"So you telling me you can't take that twenty Gs you get per show and stack that versus that twenty-five to thirty you get per brick?"

"Girl, you must be up out your mind. Them is coke prices. That's what you used to dealing with. I move boy. Bricks of that go for fifty to a hundred Gs or more easy."

"I feel you on that, but we've met so many of the same people—people who've shown me how to flip my money legally."

"You so fucking off."

"Fuck you, nigga!"

"No, fuck you! Them same people you braggin' about, them bourgeois niggas and millionaire-billionaire crackers, is some of my best customers. Blew your mind, huh? Here, your fresh-out-the-street ass thought these muthafuckas was so straight and narrow. And how the fuck you even actin' like you turning your nose up at me? You just stopped hustlin'."

"Yes and the key word is *stopped*!"

"And you'd probably still be hustling if I didn't put you on." Chaz paused to get the conversation under control. "Look, Kennedy, it ain't as easy for me to walk away as it was for you. You know how many people eat off the money I make? All I'm asking is . . . for you not to judge me. I didn't judge you when the feds picked your ass up."

"You can't even compare that. And nobody is judging you. The least you could've done was put me on to how shit was going down wit' you." Kennedy's face was red. "I'm not some square broad. You know me: I'm down for whatever. I just can't deal with this deceit. I already have enough to look over my shoulder for." She snatched her purse from the window seat and knocked over a get-well potted plant. The damp black soil spilled onto her beige canvas Chanel sneakers. "Fuck fuck!" she yelled.

"Are you all right?" Chaz asked, truly concerned.

"*Wow,* so now you're concerned with me."

"Yo, stop playing wit' me for real."

"Whatever. I'm out."

"Be out, then, you selfish b—" Chaz caught himself.

"Go ahead—say it! Call me a bitch. That's what you're really feelin', you fuckin' faggot," Kennedy said, jerking the door open.

Shorty walked in as Kennedy was exiting the room. "You all right, Kennedy?"

"I'm good, ma. I'll see you later."

"Damn, Chaz, what's wrong with Kennedy?"

"Man, she just buggin' *again.*"

Consequences

Rob stepped out into the early-morning darkness. Cautiously, he looked up and down the street. It had been a week since the incident at Mars 2112. If he hadn't had so many loose ends to tie up, he would've disappeared three days earlier. Instead, he hid out in Tompkins's Projects with his young girl, Yameek. This wasn't one of his better choices. She had a mouth like the hood rat that she was. Therefore, his hideout wasn't a huge secret. And he had his head so far up his own ass he couldn't see what was going on around him.

Yameek, who Rob so foolishly thought was down for him, had once shared a bed with Macon's little brother, Marcus. Finding out that Rob was laid up with Yameek was priceless information to Marcus. He knew that for a price she would set Rob's snake ass up with no problem. The girl craved money; sadly, she loved it more than she loved life. And her price for a little information about Rob was only three thousand dollars. Yameek might have been ghetto, among other things, but she wasn't anyone's fool. She knew that Rob didn't give a flying fuck about her. So possibly giving up information that could end his life didn't even cause her to flinch.

A sense of relief came down over Rob as he walked over to the Dodge Stratus rental car that his baby's mother had dropped off the night before. *I'll be straight once I make it to Baton Rouge,* he thought as he threw his duffel bag into the trunk. No one knew that he still had family in Louisiana, making it a perfect hideout. He knew that his name had been connected to Macon's. Knowing that it would only be a matter a time before Chaz sent someone after him, he had to get on the road. He hated to make the twenty-hour drive by himself. He'd begged Yameek for two days straight to ride with him, but she promised him only that she would fly down the next week. *Fuck her bum ass,* he thought. *I'ma get me one of them thick-ass, biscuit-eating Creole bitches while I'm down there.*

While the car was warming up, Rob prepared for the long ride, taking out his P89 Ruger and placing it in between the seat and the center console. Pulling out a leather CD booklet, he scanned through the pages before choosing a classic DJ Clue disc. When he heard Chaz's voice come through the speakers, dropping a hard freestyle, the voice sent chills down his spine. He immediately hit the skip button changing the track. "The Best of Both Worlds" came blasting through the speakers. From his coat pockets he pulled out four packs of Newports and various candies and tossed them on the passenger seat. Now he was ready to roll.

As Rob drove up the street, he noticed four guys on motorcycles ahead of him. They were doing all kinds of tricks, driving top speed then popping wheelies. One of the guys leaned his bike real low to the ground, pulled it back up, sped up, and stopped on his front wheel with the back of his bike suspended in the air. Rob smiled, thinking to himself, *These niggas is wildin'. They better calm that shit down before five-o bag 'em.* The bikes stopped at a four-way stop long enough for Rob to pull up behind them. He grabbed a pack of cigarettes and pulled the plastic wrapper off the package. Too busy fiddling with the pack, Rob never noticed the movements of the bikers. One lone biker remained in front of the car while the other three made U-turns, surrounding the car. The first bike pulled up, stopping on the driver's side, the second bike stopped at the rear of the car, and the third stopped on the passenger side.

From the corner of his eye, Rob noticed the bike next to him and he looked up. The biker propped his helmet on top of his head. Rob's heart stopped when he saw Marcus's face wearing an "I gotcha" smirk. Simultaneously the four bikers raised their guns. "I'm not going out like this," Rob mumbled to himself. Sliding his hand between the seat and the console, he reached for his gun. He had trouble removing it, and in a panic he yanked at the gun with his finger around the trigger, causing it to go off, shooting himself in the leg.

A wide grin spread across Marcus's face. *Look at this dumb nigga,* he thought. The feeling of power gave him an adrenaline rush. It was he who decided whether this human lived or died. Marcus squeezed the lever of his gun twice. The window shattered and the back left side of Rob's head exploded. The three other gunmen emptied their clips into the car. Just as quickly as they had appeared, they went their separate ways. Each man ditched his stolen bike in a different location and got in his waiting transportation. Marcus took a cab to Kennedy Airport, where Macon was waiting.

Judging by the murderous smile on his brother's face, Macon could tell that the job had been done. "Is everything copacetic?" he asked as he embraced Marcus.

"Everything is love, nigga. No casualties on our side. Yo, son was so shook he shot his own self in the leg."

"Say word."

"Word! That fool made it easy as hell on us. I put two right in the back of his melon."

Macon still couldn't find any kind of calm. He knew that Chaz had to be terminated and the sooner the better. That was the only way he would be able to regain his sense of security. Macon also knew that it would be impossible to touch Chaz anytime soon.

"Damn, bro, what got you zoned out like that?" Marcus asked.

"Man, I need all this shit to end. I don't know how Chaz survived anyway. And all this shit is fucking up my money, yo. Just gotta lay low and plan this shit right."

"Revenge is best served cold anyway."

Macon agreed. "Yeah, catch that nigga when and where he least expect it."

Running from Love

Chaz's home had been filled with family, friends, and security since his release from the hospital a week earlier. It was way too much for Kennedy. Her stress level had gone through the roof already, but news of Rob's murder sent it up another notch. She had hated him with a passion and felt that he had gotten what his hand called for, but his death shed light on how much more serious the situation was becoming with each succeeding episode. At this point she would've given her left arm to return to the solitude of her own home. But when she even suggested that she wanted to spend one night at her own house, Chaz would call her selfish. That would then snowball into an even bigger argument about her giving up her brownstone in Harlem.

"I'm concerned about your safety," Chaz would argue. "Don't you know them niggas know where you stay? They'll touch anybody to get at me. I told my mother, Shorty, and Ria to find new places and I'll pay for everything. Hell, I'm selling this house. You don't have to leave the city. Just find somewhere downtown."

Just to be spiteful, Kennedy argued back. "I'll move, *temporarily*. But don't tell me where to move. I'm not moving downtown. I want to stay uptown, and I mean Harlem."

"Kennedy, be the fuck reasonable, aight? You know downtown is more secure. You know what? Just fuck it, 'cause your ass is hardheaded."

"I wouldn't have to be making a decision about moving if your ass had kept it gully with me."

"Here we go again," Chaz said with a sigh. "You are so fucking unbelievable. And I'm getting tired of you walking around here saying your little slick shit. You act like I wanted this shit to happen. I shouldn't have told you nothing. This is the thanks I get for keeping it real."

"You should have kept it real from the door and we wouldn't be here now."

"What the hell does that suppose to mean? What you trying to say, Kennedy? You don't want to be with me no more?"

Rolling her eyes, Kennedy answered, "Look, before I say something I don't mean, I'm gonna leave. 'Cause all this is too much for me right now. Since Sal and Shorty are here, I'm going down south to spend some time with the kids. I don't think we should make any crucial decisions right now. We're too emotional."

"There you go," Chaz said with a sarcastic laugh.

"There I go what?"

"There you go with that selfish shit you be on."

"Don't give me that guilt-trip bullshit. I don't need it now. If I don't get away for a little while . . . we're not gonna make it. That's true story."

"Just get the fuck out, Kennedy. I thought you would always hold me down. Damn, even *Ria* wouldn't leave me at a time like this."

"Fuck you. *Fuck you!* And since you feel that way, my man, call her ass over here. She can have this bullshit job back!"

Kennedy stormed out of the den through the semicrowded living room. Without telling anyone good-bye, including Sal and Shorty, she went out the front door and slammed it behind. One of the huge security guards ran behind her. "Kennedy, do you want me to go with you?"

"No! I won't be coming back," she said, hopping into her 745i. After cutting off her cell phone and two-way pager, she headed straight to the New Jersey Turnpike south.

"You aight, baby bro?" Shorty asked, walking into the den to check on Chaz after Kennedy's big exit.

"I'm straight. Kennedy still buggin' on some real live shit. She—" The sound of the ringing doorbell stopped his tirade. "Damn, who the fuck is that *now*? I mean . . . I'm glad everybody coming through showing me love, but it's too much commotion. I see what Kennedy meant. If anybody call tomorrow, tell them the doctor said I need my rest."

Moments later, Chaz was happy to see that his latest visitors were Strick and Yatta. Maybe he could get some insight on Kennedy's irrational behavior from Yatta.

"What up, baby?" Strick asked, extending a pound to Chaz.

"For once it's a different script and movie. Yo, did you find out if that was your people that touched Rob?"

"Nah, it wasn't my team. I think your boy Macon might've got at 'im."

"The nigga got what his hand called for regardless of who gave it to him. If Macon did get at him, he was a smart nigga for that move."

"Enough of that," Yatta said, interrupting their conversation. "How you feeling today, Chaz?"

"I'm feeling a little better. What up wit' you, though?"

"Nothin' much. Where my sister?" Yatta asked, plopping her body down in the plush suede recliner next to the couch.

"I don't know. Somewhere going seven-thirty."

"Oh boy, what's wrong with y'all now?"

"Man, she want to fight about every little thing. Before I got stabbed, we was already talking about moving downtown. Now all of a sudden she's telling me she don't want to leave Harlem. Then all week she been trying to find an excuse to leave here and stay at her house, knowing I need her here."

"You know how she is. She probably just needed a moment to breathe."

"She got her moment. She left out of here a little while ago, going down south."

"What?" Yatta asked with a frown.

"She used the kids as her final excuse. I'm not complaining. I'm never trying to come between her and the kids. And I know she miss them. But at the same time she know I would've paid somebody to drive them up here or fly with them. She just been buggin' since I told her the truth."

"The truth about what?"

"Stop frontin', Yatta. I know Kennedy tell you everything."

"On everything I love, she didn't tell me nothing."

"I told her the real story about Macon and me."

"Which is what?"

"The nigga was into me for a couple of bricks of diesel."

Yatta's face wore a look of perplexity. "Okay, and . . . ?"

"Once she found out that I was still moving work, she spazzed."

"Hell, I thought she knew."

"What would make you think that?"

"*I* figured it out from being around you. Damn, she didn't know? No wonder she flipped," Yatta said, shaking her head.

"But why?"

"First of all, you kept it from her. Secondly, what did she tell you about Pretty Boy's death?"

"She told me that she was in the bed when he got killed and was left with his body for hours."

"Did she tell you what happed after that?"

"No."

Yatta leaned forward, resting her elbows on her thighs. "After his funeral, she stopped talking for about six months. She went to Big Ma's house and stayed shut up in a room the entire time. So when Nina died, we were so sure that she would shut down again. If she didn't have the kids, I think she would have. So much happened to her in the last year and a half, I don't know how much more she can take. Then, when you almost died, it was too much for her. Knowing my sister, she's so scared of hurt and loss that she's probably withdrawing."

"What do I have to do make it right?"

"Don't put her under pressure. You know how she feels about that."

"Let me show y'all something," Chaz said, reaching into the pocket of his baggy sweatpants and pulling out a small black velvet ring box. He opened it, turning it around so that Yatta and Strick could see.

"That is gorgeous," Yatta said, taking the box from his hand and examining the ring. It was a four-carat princess-cut solitaire with a wide band that was covered in two and half carats of diamonds, making it six and a half carats total. The clarity was so amazing that it sparkled in the dimmest of light.

Yatta handed the box back to him. He looked at it once more before closing the box. "I was going to ask Kennedy to marry me the day she came back from tour. We kept missing each other. Then I got mad at her and decided to go out that night. Even after she pleaded with me to stay home and wait on her. Now I wish that I had, and maybe Jay would still be alive."

Ten hours later Kennedy had arrived in North Carolina. She'd driven straight there, stopping only for gas. When she got to her mother's house it was after midnight. She tried sneaking in, but that failed. Her mother was up watching television with Jordan and Mattie. Their eyes lit up when they saw Kennedy. They jumped up simultaneously, screaming.

"Mommy!"

"Auntie!"

They both grabbed her legs and hugged them, hindering her movement. "Hi, babies! I've missed you two so much," Kennedy said, smiling so hard that she was laughing. "And what are y'all still doing up?"

"Watching Disney, Mommy," Jordan said with a giggle. He had grown so much since the last time Kennedy had seen him. Anytime she was away from him, even for a week, she could see the difference. But having been away for two months, she could really see how much he'd grown. He was a rambunctious two-year-old going on three. He was her little handsome man with his beautiful cappuccino-brown skin. Dusty brown curls crowned his head. He was the spitting image of his father. It seemed she'd given birth to him only yesterday. *Boy, where does the time go?* she wondered.

And she just couldn't get over Mattie. Her hair was getting so long and thick, so much like Nina's. For her age, Mattie was tall and slim. Kennedy could already tell that she was going to grow up to look just like Nina.

"Auntie, Auntie, look at my earrings," Mattie said, pushing her right earlobe forward with her finger.

"They're beautiful, li'l mama. Where did you get them from?" Kennedy asked, looking at the obviously expensive diamond earrings. Mattie shrugged.

Kennedy looked over at her mother. Kora shrugged, too. "They were delivered to Klarice's house a few weeks ago. We thought you sent them."

"No, I didn't. Maybe her grandmother sent them, since she *missed* her only grandchild's birthday party."

"Hell, Kennedy, did you really expect her to come, the way you stare her down and interrogate her about her son every time you see her?"

"Whatever, Mommy. Why y'all up *so* late?"

"Now, you know you had your phone off, so Yatta *and* Chaz been calling here back-to-back for the last four hours. And why you leave that boy to come down here? You know I would've brought the kids up there."

"Mommy, it too much going on up there right now for the kids to come up. Plus, I just needed a minute to myself. I just need to clear my head. I'm only staying two days. I have to go back and get in the studio before I go on the road again."

"I understand that you needed a break. But please don't shut everybody out."

Kora's last comment saddened Kennedy for a moment. She knew that her mother was referring to her breakdown after Pretty Boy's death. She looked her mother in the eye. "Don't worry, Mommy. I'll never go back there again."

Over the next two days Kennedy spent every moment attempting to make up for all the time she'd spent away from the kids. Her days were filled with trips to Chuck E. Cheese, Jeepers, and Paramount's Carowinds. Jordan, Niko, and Mattie had the time of their little lives, loving the way that anything they pointed at, Kennedy bought for them.

Kennedy gave Taylor special time in the evening. At age eleven, he was well on his way to becoming a man. Kennedy felt he needed special attention, so each night she treated him to a movie and dinner. During dinner, they discussed girls, puberty, social behavior, and finances. Kennedy enjoyed the special time with Taylor so much that she promised him that when he returned to New York in the fall, they would have a movie night once a month.

When the two days were up, Kennedy hated leaving the kids. But there was work to be done and *too* much drama going down for her to take them back with her in the middle of the summer.

Leaving her 745i with her mother, Kennedy decided to catch a flight back New York. Her short trip had really made a difference. It was so refreshing to get away from the hustle of the city and be able to do only what she wanted to do.

Kennedy promised herself that she would visit the Dominican Republic, where her little sister, Kneaka, would be staying for the summer. She planned to go a week after Chaz got back on his feet.

Kennedy talked to Chaz twice while she was in Charlotte. Both conversations went no deeper than asking and answering basic questions. "How are you?" "What did you do today?" "All right, I'll call you tomorrow."

Before going to the airport, Kennedy stopped at the ultrachic Philips Place shopping enclave and picked up a few expensive trinkets for Chaz just so he would know he'd been on her mind while she was away.

"Hey, Yatta bear!" Kennedy said, wearing a huge smile, when she spotted her sister in baggage claim. "I can't believe you're here on time." She gave Yatta a huge hug.

"I know your always-late ass ain't talking about nobody and time."

"*Whatever.* Let's rock."

"Don't we have to wait on the rest of your bags?"

"Nigga, this is all I took," Kennedy said, holding up her large Vuitton tote.

"Your ass ain't got a lick of sense, jumping on the highway like that. All jokes aside, how are you feeling?"

"I feel a whole lot better. I feel refreshed. I feel like I can deal with Chaz without having to pop a pill daily."

"That's always good to hear. Well, I have a little surprise for you. I think it'll make you feel even better."

"*What* surprise, Yatta?"

Yatta smiled, remembering how Kennedy hated being kept in the dark about surprises. She knew that her sister was going to nag her all the way to Manhattan. And that's exactly what she did—all the way to the front door.

As she opened the door to her home Kennedy's heart fluttered when she saw that her living room was filled with pink roses. Instantly, she knew that her surprise had something to do with Chaz. She turned to Yatta. "Let me guess: Chaz is here, right?"

"Nah, ma, he's not here. But you should go shower, and your outfit is on the bed."

"*Un momento, hermana* . . . What outfit?"

On Kennedy's bed lay a gorgeous pale pink Max Mara sleeveless wrap dress. Lying next to it was a Casadei shoe box. Kennedy picked up the box and opened it, revealing a pair of pale pink-and-cream open-toe stilettos. She eyed her sister suspiciously. "Okay, Yatta, what is this about?"

"I don't know. I was just given the money and told to buy you a pretty pink dress. And also, wear your hair hanging straight with the part down the middle. And wear these in your ears," Yatta said, handing her the red box containing the diamond earrings that Chaz had given Kennedy for Christmas a year earlier.

"What the hell do he want me to do? Get all spiffy to go out to his house and play nurse?"

"You know just as much as I do, Ken. When you finished getting dressed, I'll have more instructions for you."

Kennedy laughed. "Y'all two niggas is funny. So you helping him now? That's what's up. I'm in a good mood today, so I'm game."

After showering, Kennedy slipped on a pink strapless La Perla bra and matching tanga that Chaz had bought her the previous Valentine's Day. She put on some makeup. She used three different shades of pink on her eyes, creating a beautiful shimmering effect.

When she was done, Kennedy walked out into the living room, where Yatta was waiting. Yatta smiled, thinking, *She looks so beautiful.* "You look so *wonderful,* baby sister . . . It's something about you. I just can't seem to put my finger on it. Anyway, here are your final instructions." She handed her sister an envelope.

Pulling the pink embroidered invitation from the envelope, Kennedy looked up at Yatta. "Oh, I know that you had something to do with this." The invitation read: *You're invited to dine with Chaz Harris. Location: where we spent our first date. Time: 6 P.M. Please be on time.*

"Where was our first date?" Kennedy asked aloud.

"Your first date was at Carmine's dingy."

"Technically, that wasn't our first date. Whatever, can you take me to the garage so I can get a car?"

A few minutes later, Kennedy whipped her Aston Martin out of the garage and was zipping in and out of traffic all the way down Broadway.

When she entered the restaurant, a hostess directed her to the table where Chaz was sitting. Butterflies fluttered in her stomach when she saw him. A few tables behind him she spotted two of his security guards. There he sat in a white Lacoste polo-style shirt and blue-jean shorts. His eyes were covered by Dior aviator shades to hide the last traces of bruises. The swelling around his nose had yet to go all the way down, so he wore his baseball cap cocked low.

Chaz looked up in time to see Kennedy coming toward the table. She was so pretty that she looked like a baby doll to him. He stood up, greeting her with a hug, squeezing her as tight as he could without causing his stomach too much discomfort. It felt so good to hold her in his arms. And to Kennedy it felt great to be back in his arms. "Hi, baby. I missed you."

"I missed you, too, li'l mama."

Taking his seat, Chaz asked, "How was your trip?"

"It was great."

"What's up with the kids?"

"The kids are nuts! Jordan is so big and he is off the meat rack. Mattie is so grown and fresh. She is four going on twenty-four. Niko is into his sports. It's just t-ball season and he's already talking about football. And Taylor has discovered girls . . . so you know I'm recruiting all the men in the family, including *you,* to talk to him. And what did I miss here?"

"Not shit," he answered drily. "When you left I went and spent the day in the studio laying down tracks for the new CD. Then I went house shopping. I had to do something to busy myself while you were gone."

Guilt came down over Kennedy; she couldn't even look him in the eye. "My bad for bouncing on you like that. I'm sorry about that, true story. I just needed some time to clear my head so my attitude wouldn't be so hateful toward you."

Reaching across the table, he grabbed her hand. "I hate it when you run from me. Just talk to me. Can you give me that much?"

"I'll try, but what can you give me in return? I need honesty

. . . I need you to confide in me, too. I don't need to find out shit about my man from industry gossip and niggas in the street. And how long are you going to keep slanging them thangs?"

"Ma, I accept you in every way. I need you to accept everything about me—my faults, my flaws and imperfections. And I'm not trying to sell them thangs forever. Just long enough to make sure I'm sitting on enough paper to live comfortably and take care of my people with or without this rap shit. Can you live with that, Kennedy?"

"I guess I don't have a choice if I want to be with you. Do I?"

"Well then, will you marry me?"

"What did you say?"

Chaz pulled the ring box from his pocket. Taking the ring out of the box, he told her, "Let me see your hand." He placed the ring at the tip of her finger. "I said, will you marry me?"

Tears filled Kennedy's eyes. She could barely speak. She nodded. "Yes, baby, yes."

Chaz got up from his seat, and pulling Kennedy from hers, he hugged her tight. "Ma, what are you crying for?"

In between gasps she answered, "I'm . . . so . . . happy. I never thought anyone would propose to me."

"I don't know why you thought that. You're so beautiful inside and out. Everyone around you loves you."

Kennedy blushed through her tears. Her heart was thumping. She couldn't believe this was happening to her. She felt like a little basketball was bouncing inside her. She was nervous like a schoolgirl with a crush. An older, well-manicured white lady sitting at a nearby table with two friends yelled over to Chaz, "What did she say?"

Her question caught them both off guard. Chaz laughed at Kennedy. "Tell her what you said."

Kennedy giggled, with tears still streaming from her eyes. "I said yes."

"She said yes," the lady announced to the entire restaurant. Everyone applauded, turning their attention toward Kennedy and Chaz. "Come here, sweetie," the lady said, motioning for Kennedy. "Let me get a look at the ring?" Kennedy got up, walked over to the lady, and extended her hand. "Beautiful. He must really love you," she said.

"Thanks," Kennedy said, still giggling and blushing.

The lady grabbed her waiter as he walked by. "I want to be the first to congratulate this lovely couple on their engagement. Please bring them out your finest bottle of Clicquot, on me."

"You don't have to do this. Your kind words were enough," Kennedy said.

"No, darling, I insist."

After Kennedy returned to her table, the lady turned to her friends. "Did you see the clarity on that ring? It must've cost thirty thousand or more. I wonder what he does. I can't see his face with those shades and that cap on."

Once the champagne had been brought out, Kennedy insisted that the ladies—who were already tipsy—share a toast with her. Kennedy also properly introduced herself and shook each of their hands. She shook hands with the lady who'd done all the talking last. Holding Kennedy's hand firmly, the lady told her, "I'm Darcy Neal."

"Darcy Neal! Of Manhattan Power Management?"

"So you've heard of me?" she asked, smiling, so full of herself.

"Who hasn't heard of you? I've been trying to get an appointment with your firm for the last six months."

Darcy pulled a business card from her purse, "Give me a call on my personal line and tell my assistant that I said to give you the earliest appointment available. And what business are you in?"

Kennedy caught herself before she blurted out "I'm a rapper." Instead, she said, "I'm a musician."

The rest of the night was spectacular. The newly engaged couple took a horse-and-carriage ride, with security following close by. Kennedy was all smiles. No other man besides Pretty Boy had ever treated her so romantically and Chaz knew it. That's why he'd gone out of his way to make his proposal special. He promised himself that he would be more sensitive to Kennedy in every way.

His heart pounded with excitement during the carriage ride. He watched Kennedy as she looked down at her ring, smiling. The joy that he saw in her eyes made him feel guilty about hiding part of his life from her. "Baby, I really do feel bad for keeping you in the dark and I'm sorry. I know how you get down and I know without a doubt that you ride for me. I just want you to understand that what you don't know will keep you from being my co-de. I *never* wanted to tell you about Jay shooting Macon." He was tensing up so bad that he was he was squeezing her left thigh hard without realizing it.

Kennedy rubbed the top of his hand softly until he eased up on his grip. She looked him the eye. "Sweetie, there is nothing we can't share with each other. No matter what you share with me— even if I don't like it, I'll be there for you. And I'll always-always hold you down." She placed a tender kiss on his lips, sealing her words.

Reality of the Situation

O ver the next few weeks, Kennedy moved through life with
her head in the clouds. She didn't let anything worry or
stress her. Not even the threatening and grotesque letters that she
was receiving from "the fan" could spoil her mood. The letters
and dead roses had started coming more frequently with each
passing week. They were even becoming more consistent, arriv-
ing now on the same days. Kennedy took the letters with a grain a
salt. After a while she began tossing them in the garbage without
opening them.

Despite this, every morning when she awoke she felt brand-
new. It showed in the way her face glowed and her eyes shined.
Even her walk was different. When people questioned her about
her sudden happiness, she'd answer as if she were Jay-Z himself,
"I got my swagger back."

Kennedy and Chaz had even let Yatta convince them to
keep their engagement a secret, even from both their mothers.
Yatta planned a celebration for friends and family at which they
would finally make the announcement. She even started gather-
ing all the information needed to plan a wedding and giving it to
Kennedy.

One day Chaz walked into what was soon to be his old home
in New Jersey. Yatta and Kennedy, in the middle of moving
boxes, were sitting looking through magazines. Shaking his head

at the sight, Chaz joked, "I thought y'all was supposed to be help-ing me pack, not staring at wedding dresses."

Kennedy greeted him with a big hug and a kiss. "Hey, baby, you came just in time. Yatta's been showing me all this wedding stuff and I was thinking we haven't even set a date yet or where we're going to have it."

"Now, li'l mama, you already know I'm leaving all this wed-ding shit up to you."

"I have no problem doing all the planning. But the location and date should be something that we both agree on."

"What date did you have in mind?"

"I was thinking a year from now. You know, a nice fall wed-ding?"

"A year from now? Why so long?" Chaz questioned with a raised eyebrow.

"You mean you want to do it sooner?"

"I was thinking we'd have it in six months or so."

Kennedy gave it some thought. "I tell you what. Let's do it six months from now, in the middle of May."

"So where do you want to have it?"

A sly smile crept across Kennedy's face. "Can we have it in Charlotte?"

Chaz looked at her wondering why she was asking, like that would be a problem. "Kennedy, it's your day. Wherever you want to have it is fine with me."

Excitedly, Kennedy began jumping around the cluttered liv-ing room like a little kid on a sugar high. "We're going to have a big outdoor wedding with lots of flowers and a huge wedding party. The train on my dress is going to be *really long,* just like the one I dreamed about when I was a little girl." She stopped her rambling when she became aware of the stares she was receiving from Yatta and Chaz.

For that moment in time, Kennedy had the most joyful, innocent look about her. Chaz saw a part of her so pure he nearly cried. Even Yatta found herself becoming watery-eyed. Growing up, Kennedy had never let on that she'd dreamed of such things. Now, seeing her so excited made Yatta even happier for her. Yet she was also sad for all the years Kennedy had spent hiding that part of herself from the outside world.

Oh, no, Kennedy thought, *they heard me, they saw me.* She'd never felt more exposed and vulnerable. The room was closing in on her. She needed air immediately. She needed to escape. Grabbing her purse and keys, she ran toward the door, saying only, "I'm going to the store. I'll be back."

After Kennedy's exit, Chaz and Yatta gave each other a look that said, *Leave it alone.* And neither of them ever spoke of the moment again.

The following day Kennedy patiently sat in the lobby of Manhattan Power Management, excited inside to have the opportunity to be represented by such a reputable entertainment agency. Sleeping pills had cured her insomnia, and she was well rested. She was also relaxed, courtesy of the one hundred and fifty milligrams of Effexor she'd popped that morning. Darcy Neal came out and greeted her instead of sending her assistant. To Kennedy's surprise, Darcy was wearing an expensive light blue Yves Saint-Laurent blouse and cream slacks. "Good morning, Kennedy. It's so nice to see you again."

"It's nice to see you again also, Darcy."

"Come on, follow me."

Kennedy's stomach flip-flopped as she followed Darcy down the corridor leading to her office. Pictures of the firm's celebrity clients lined the walls.

Just like Darcy herself, her office said money in a not flashy way. There were only a few pieces of furniture—all very contemporary—which complemented the all-glass corner office that overlooked Manhattan. Kennedy took a seat in a high-backed wood-and-white-leather chair in front of Darcy's desk. Darcy leaned against the front of her desk facing Kennedy. She gave Kennedy a once-over before getting down to business. "Darling, I took the liberty of checking you out. And from what my sources tell me, you're one of the hottest females in hip-hop, with nearly two million records sold. I hadn't even realized that you were the rapper who was arrested at her own album-release party. Then I found out that you were in the middle of some type of rap war between your boyfriend and another very famous rapper."

Kennedy was becoming uneasy. She wanted to know where Darcy was going with the conversation. Darcy got up and walked to the other side of her desk, taking a seat in a white plush chenille-upholstered oversize chair. She spun around, facing Kennedy with a huge smile showing off her beautiful dental work. She told her, "All of those things make you my kind of client. Scandal always sells! Nobody likes boring, goody-goody celebrities. Look at all the scandalous headlines I've made myself."

Darcy's change of pace put Kennedy at ease; she'd almost begun to think that Darcy wasn't going to take her on as a client. "How fast can you get your attorney to look over this contract?" Darcy asked, handing Kennedy a set of stapled papers. "Because I already have something lined up for you with Mischief Jeans. They have a shoot in two days for ads that they're running in *XXL, Vibe,* and *Honey.* The ad pays one hundred and fifty thousand dollars. Mischief is also looking for someone very hot and urban to represent their new line of jeans. That ad campaign pays two million dollars. So if everything goes according to plan, that campaign will be yours."

Kennedy was floored. She could barely process what Darcy was telling her. With a wide smile, she asked Darcy, "Are you serious?"

"Honey, when it comes to money I'm always serious. That's just the beginning. I have a few other things lined up for you, including a possible tour sponsorship. As soon as you sign these papers and get them back to me, I can confirm everything."

"If everything is in order, I will have this signed, sealed, delivered, and back to you in the morning."

Not in her wildest dreams could Kennedy have imagined that such wonderful things were to come to her in the days ahead. Her days were more exhausting yet well worth it for the humungous paycheck. The Mischief photo shoot lasted nearly twenty hours. In one day Kennedy went through five hair and makeup changes and thirty-two wardrobe changes. The following day she met with the CEO of Mischief, Malesa Corbin. Kennedy had not known that like many other fashion execs, Malesa was a black female in her twenties. She was also a huge fan of Kennedy's. She and Kennedy hit it off immediately.

Once the photos and test shots came back, Malesa offered Kennedy the $2 million ad campaign, which included the best of perks and bonuses. Darcy kept Kennedy's days booked with business meetings with companies looking for a young hip spokesperson. Between the meetings, studio time, and the Mischief campaign, Kennedy was absolutely worn out. Anytime she sat down for more than five minutes, she would nod off like a dope fiend.

One day about three and a half weeks into her new hectic schedule, Kennedy was in the studio with Strick and his close friend, superproducer, and CEO of Bricklayers Entertainment, Coco. She was laying down vocals to a track Coco was producing. For some unknown reason, the session had been terribly challenging.

Every fifteen minutes Kennedy needed a break. She complained constantly. "Yo, it's burning the fuck up in here. Can I get some A/C?" she yelled from the recording booth.

"No problem," Strick answered, sending one of his flunkies to turn up the air.

That wasn't enough for Kennedy; five minutes later she was at it again. "I can't breathe in here. I need a break. I want some food and water."

All the complaining was unlike Kennedy, and quite frankly, it was was getting on Strick's nerves. He tried his best to be patient with her. "Ken, can you please give me one more take. If you do that we'll get a two break."

Kennedy huffed as she went back into the booth and slammed the door. Strick looked at Coco. "She is really blowing mines today. I don't know what the fuck is *wrong* with her."

Kennedy placed the large headphones back on her head and Coco started the beat. She bopped her head while waiting for her cue to begin rapping. When her cue came she opened her mouth, but nothing came out. Suddenly her head felt light and she felt the need to sit down, but she couldn't get out of the booth quick enough. Everything went blurry then black as Kennedy collapsed to the floor.

Strick and Coco ran toward the booth. Strick snatched the door open and pulled her limp body out. "Kennedy, wake up. Wake up! *Please wake up!*" he said in a panic. Guilt came over him quickly; he'd pushed her too far. Strick's assistant handed him a wet towel and he wiped it over Kennedy's face a few times in a failed attempt to wake her up.

"Man, watch out, that shit ain't working," Coco said, pushing Strick to the side and dousing Kennedy's face with a bottle of water. The ice-cold water shocked her back to consciousness and her eyes popped open extra wide. Totally forgetting where she was, she jumped up, ready to swing. Strick bear-hugged her to keep her from hitting anyone. Once everything came back into focus and she recognized her surroundings, she told Strick, "You can let me go now. I'm okay."

"You sure?"

"Yeah, what happened?"

"You passed out in the booth."

"I *did*? I wonder what happened."

"I don't know. But I think you need to see a doctor."

Forty-five minutes later, Kennedy was sitting on the examination table of the label's private doctor. Strick sat in a nearby chair. She'd begged him to stay in the room with her. They were both on pins and needles waiting for the blood work and urinalysis to come back. For some unknown reason, Kennedy was fearing that the doctor would return and tell her that it was cancer. Strick was silently praying that her illness wasn't his fault. He was pissed with himself that he hadn't given her a break when she'd asked. The office door opened, and Dr. Steinbeck walked in, followed by a Japanese nurse pushing an ultrasound machine.

Strick's eyes became wide at the sight of the machine. He didn't know what it was, but Kennedy did. "Um, Dr. Steinbeck, what is that for?"

"Ms. Sanchez, your pregnancy test came back positive, and I suspect that you're more than a few months pregnant. This will let us know for sure."

Kennedy laughed. "There must be some mistake. My last period was—" Her smile suddenly faded.

"Just relax and lie back so we can see how far along you are."

Unable to relax, Kennedy lay back on the table thinking, *This cannot be happening right now.* She held her breath as the nurse applied the cold gel to her skin. Strick watched the procedure intently. Having no kids, he'd never seen anything like it before.

Sliding the transducer over Kennedy's abdomen, Dr. Steinbeck focused on the screen. As the view of the fetus became clear he gasped. *"My goodness!"*

"My *goodness* what?" Kennedy asked, stretching her neck so that she could see the monitor.

"By the size of the fetus, you appear to be about five months pregnant, which explains your high HCG levels."

"I can't be five months! I was huge when I was five months with Jordan."

"Your schedule and the stress you've been under most likely had some effect on your weight gain and loss." Dr. Steinbeck continued to stare at the monitor, noting odd movements. He noticed that every time the baby moved, he caught a glimpse of what appeared to be another set of arms and legs.

Studying his facial expression; Kennedy knew that something wasn't right. "What is it now?" she asked with a huff.

"How many surprises can you handle in one day?"

"It depends on the surprise."

Turning from the monitor, Dr. Steinbeck looked her in the eye. "Can you handle twins?"

Hours later, as she walked into Chaz's house, Kennedy still couldn't grasp the fact that she was having twins. Hell, it still hadn't sunk in that she was five months pregnant. Chaz was sitting on the couch surrounded by hundreds of moving boxes, waiting for her. He'd already heard about her fainting spell earlier in the day. By the pale drained look on her face, he could tell that she was still sick. Grabbing her up in his arms and hugging her, he asked, "You okay, li'l mama?"

She buried her face in his shoulder. "I'm pregnant."

"What'd you say, Ken? I couldn't hear you, you mumbling."

Lifting her head, she looked him in the eye. "I said I'm *pregnant*!"

Chaz's face lit up with joy. "You are, baby? That's what's up! Maybe I can finally get my boy."

"You're probably getting more than that," Kennedy said, her words dripping with sarcasm.

"So how many weeks are you?"

Kennedy looked at him, disgusted. "*Weeks?* Nigga, I'm five *months*."

"*Fuck outta* here. You're smaller than you were when we met."

"I ain't lying, nigga. Here, look at the ultrasound pictures. Dr. Steinbeck said my schedule and stress is affecting my weight. And that ain't even the shocker."

"What's the shocker?"

"I'm having twins."

"Ain't no way," Chaz said in disbelief.

"Yes way, *my* man. One girl and one boy."

"This shit is crazy. I'ma finally get my boy. Seriously, Kennedy, you wouldn't play about this."

Rolling her eyes, Kennedy huffed, "Didn't I give you the ultrasound pictures?"

He began hugging her even tighter, rocking her side to side. "Damn, I can't wait to tell my mother and Shorty."

"No," Kennedy protested, pulling out of clutches. "I want to surprise everyone and tell them at the engagement party. The only other person who knows I'm pregnant is Strick and I've sworn him to secrecy."

Chaz couldn't tell if Kennedy was happy or sad about the pregnancy. Her facial expression was neutral. "How you feeling, li'l mama?"

"To tell you the truth. I really don't feel any kind of way. It's not even reality to me yet."

Watching

After a few days of seclusion and emotional changes, Kennedy's pregnancy finally became real to her. She happily began taking everything in stride. She and Chaz moved into a beautiful home in a gated community in northern New Jersey. She was having the time of her life decorating the sprawling twelve-thousand-square-foot home.

Kennedy stood back, admiring the wonderful work she'd put into the informal living room. She'd filled it with neutral colors that were perfect for all four seasons. The room was lined with floor-to-ceiling windows that gave a fascinating view of the swimming pool and grilling area. The bar area looked as if it belonged in a Miami nightclub. Kennedy had even stocked it with various liquors, like a real bar. Above the bar she hung martini glasses, wine goblets, and whiskey glasses. She put on the final touches with a one-thousand-dollar martini shaker on each end of the bar.

Kennedy hated that all the drama with Macon had prevented her from having their engagement party at the house. It was to be held later that evening at a posh, exclusive Italian restaurant in Manhattan. But she felt better knowing that tomorrow she would have the pleasure of hosting a cookout for both her family and Chaz's. The sound of the ringing house phone broke her reverie. When Kennedy spun around she felt light-headed. The fainting and dizzy spells were all new to her. She had never experienced any of those things when she was pregnant with Jordan. She balanced herself on the back of the couch and picked up the cordless phone. "Hello?" she answered, a little short of breath.

"What's wrong with you?" Yatta asked on the other end of the line.

"Nothing. What's up?"

"Everyone is in from the airport."

"Are you bringing Mommy and Big Ma out here?"

"They said that they want to stay at Aunt Karen's."

"Why?"

"Look, I don't know why. I'm picking up li'l sis right now and we're taking all the smaller kids to Toys 'R' Us on Thirty-fourth Street to get some toys to play with tonight so they don't give babysitter hell. Do you want to meet us down there?"

"Yeah, I'll be there."

One thing Kennedy loved about living with Chaz was the car options. When Chaz switched the cribs up, he switched up the cars, too. He bought a black Range Rover just like Kennedy's white one. He traded his CL600 for an S-class 600. He also copped a Denali. Chaz had every car including Kennedy's outfitted with stash boxes for firearms and bulletproof windows.

Today, Kennedy decided to take the Benz. It was top-of-the-line. She had only to run her fingertips under the chrome door handle, and upon recognition of her fingerprints, it unlocked and started the ignition. *This shit is crack,* she thought, and laughed to herself. After backing out of the garage, Kennedy set the house alarm with a push of a button on the remote attached to her key chain.

Kennedy sped through the hilly community, passing some of the most luxurious homes on the entire East Coast. She slowed down only to wait for the security guard to open the gates that separated the neighborhood from the outside world. Living in a gated community didn't make Kennedy feel any safer. From her rearview mirror she watched as the gates closed, thinking, *Them gates and that ol'-ass security guard ain't stopping real niggas from getting in here. It's only slowing them down!*

Seeing the kids ripping and running through the mega Toys "R" Us was a sight for sore eyes. Jordan was terrorizing the store employees. He was pulling down everything in sight that his two-and-a-half-year-old stature could reach. He so busy running and laughing that he hadn't even noticed his mother watching him from a short distance away. He was the cutest little badass she'd ever met, and not just because he was her son. Jordan was the best parts of her and Brian, his father, mixed together. Although Jordan had never met his father, the resemblance between them was undeniable. The older Jordan got, the more he looked like his father, which caused Kennedy to think of Brian quite often. She didn't even hate Brian; nor did she love him. It just hurt her to think that Jordan might never know his father. It would be a void that she would never be able to fill with any amount of money or quality time.

"Mommy!" Jordan suddenly yelled, running toward his mother.

"Hi, baby boy. You're having fun, I see."

"Yes, Mommy. Auntie Yatta has my toys."

"I bet she has a lot of them, too."

"Mm-hmm," he said, nodding. "Mommy, Mommy, he told me to give this to you." Jordan handed her a folded piece of paper.

"What man?" she asked, taking the paper from Jordan's small hands.

Jordan pointed toward an empty aisle, but no one was there.

She put Jordan down and unfolded the paper. Her heart stopped when a single dead white rose petal fell from the paper. Her vision went blurry, making it hard to read the words. She blinked a few times until the words were in focus. They were big, bold, and straight to the point:

SEE HOW CLOSE I CAN GET TO YOU,
Your Watcher

Kennedy had to force herself to breathe deeply and slowly just to keep from passing out. Frantically, her eyes searched the store for her sisters and the other kids. Holding Jordan tightly, she searched a few aisles before spotting Yatta, Jalyn, and Mattie. She ran toward them as fast as she could. Yatta looked up and saw her panic-stricken sister heading her way. "Kennedy, what's wrong?"

"Where's Kneaka? Where are the other kids?"

"Calm down. They didn't come. *What is going on?*"

"He's here!"

"Who's here?"

"The fan! The stalker!"

"You saw him?"

"No, I didn't, but he gave this to Jordan," Kennedy said, shoving the note into Yatta's hands.

Yatta scanned the note. "Oh my God, Kennedy, this is getting out of hand now. You're gonna have to call the police or get security involved. Something has got to give."

Kennedy, overcome by the thoughts of the stalker getting close to Jordan, began crying in the middle of the store. Yatta wrapped her arms around her sister, consoling her. "Don't cry, li'l mama, it's going to be okay." Still embracing her sister, she pulled out her cell and dialed Strick's number.

"Yo?" Strick answered.

"Strick, it's me. Is Chaz up at the studio with you?"

"Yeah, what's up?"

"I'll explain when we get there. I need y'all to send security downstairs to meet us in ten minutes."

"Yatta, what's the problem? Do you need us to come meet you?"

"No, Strick. Let me get Kennedy together so I can get her out of here." Yatta ended the call. Keeping her composure, she paid for the toys. Never showing her nervousness, she kept her family close together and got them the hell out of there.

Chaz, along with two burly guards from his security team, waited in front of the building for Kennedy and Yatta to arrive. When they pulled up and Kennedy got out of the car, he knew that something was wrong. Her face said it all. She couldn't even fake a smile. "Baby, what's going on?" he asked, grabbing her face.

Biting down on her lip, Kennedy began to cry. Yatta stepped up and began talking. "Chaz, can you have one the guards take the kids uptown to Aunt Karen's? 'Cause y'all need to talk."

"That's nothing; come on." Chaz sent the more experienced of the two guards to take the kids uptown, instructing him to stay with them until he called.

Upstairs in Strick's office, Kennedy took a seat on the couch. Yatta sat next to her, holding her hand, giving her full support. Kennedy didn't quite know where to begin the story. And the stares that she was receiving from Strick and Chaz weren't making it any easier. After inhaling deeply, she just let it all out. "Look, someone is stalking me. It started with phone calls, letters, and dead white roses. First it seemed like nothing, but the contacts have escalated. Today the stalker approached Jordan in the toy store and gave him this." She pulled the note from her purse and handed it to Chaz.

Strick couldn't believe that Kennedy hadn't told anyone

about this. Leaning back in his big office chair, he swiveled around and said, "Ken, this shit was serious from the first phone call you received. You should've at least come to me so that we could've provided you with security."

"I just didn't really pay it any attention at first. Before today, I thought this person was harmless—a little crazy, but harmless."

Chaz was pissed. He wasn't buying her justification. "Come on, Kennedy, you got to come better than that, *ma*. You're not naive. What if this is some psycho hit nigga Macon sent after you?"

"This doesn't have anything to do with Macon."

"How do you know that?"

"This started six months before Jay shot him."

"You mean to tell me this shit been going on for over a year and this is the first time *I'm* hearing about it? You got some nerve calling me deceitful, B."

Yatta interrupted. "Now is not the time, Chaz."

"Yes it is. What if this person had just taken Jordan today? You could've prevented all this shit if you would've opened your fucking mouth. I can't understand why you wouldn't say something. Unless it's some nigga you been fucking."

"It's not *that*!" Kennedy screamed at him, tears flowing down her face. "I'm sorry for letting it go this far. Don't you know I would literally die if anything were to happen to Jordan! If I had any clues to who this person is, I would've sent the wolves after them." She placed her head in her lap, sobbing heavily; her shoulders heaved up and down.

Yatta and Strick left the room. Chaz took a seat next to Kennedy on the couch. Rubbing her back, he told her, "I'm sorry I yelled at you like that. All this shit is getting too far out of control. It's nothing, though. We're going to get through this, too." Kennedy's face was still in her lap. "You aight, ma? Say something."

Kennedy looked up at him. Her eyes were dark and lonesome. "I just don't know how much more of this I can take before . . ." She paused, staring off into space.

"Before what?"

Oblivious to Chaz's question, Kennedy continued to stare into space.

Lightly, he squeezed her shoulder. "Kennedy, before what?"

"Oh, nothing, baby . . . nothing for you to worry about. Come on, baby, let's go home and get ready for the party. This bullshit is not going to ruin our night." Wiping the tears from her face with the back of her hand, she stood up and left the room.

Just that quick, she'd gone from sixty back to zero. Chaz stared at the open door, perplexed and wondering, *How the fuck she just switch up like that?*

All of Yatta's planning had yielded a perfect engagement party. She was wonderful at planning events. People told her all the time that she needed to make a business of it. The party was held at Trattoria Dopo Teatro in the theater district. Only family, close friends, and the label staff had been invited. Everyone in attendance received gift bags containing chocolates from Godiva, a miniature bottle of Clicquot, a fifty-dollar gift card to Dean & DeLuca, and a one-hundred-dollar gift card to either Henri Bendel, Barneys, or Bergdorf.

When Kennedy made her entrance, she looked better than ever, worry-free, showing no evidence of the problems plaguing her personal life or the frantic episode with her stalker earlier in the day. She looked fabulous in an olive-green Alexander McQueen halter dress. Keeping her shoe game tight, but slightly comfortable, for her feet were feeling the effects of her pregnancy, she had donned a pair of olive-green-and-white Ferragamo pumps with two-and-half-inch heels—as opposed to her usual four. To complement her beautiful dress, she wore a white-gold necklace with a blinding three-carat-diamond half-heart pendant. Her ears sparkled with two-carat princess-cut diamonds. Kennedy's right wrist was wrapped in a five-carat cuff of yellow diamonds accented with striking green emeralds. The only thing on her lower her left arm was her most prized piece of jewelry: her engagement ring.

Chaz was the most handsome man in the room in a black linen suit and black sling-back gators. For once he'd left his chain at home, wearing only a wide fifteen-carat platinum-and-diamond bracelet and a four-carat pinkie ring. His Caesar haircut was lined up just right and his goatee was trimmed to perfection. Kennedy thought he looked magnificent. She also thought it was a blessing that he didn't show up with his usual doo-rag and Yankee fitted.

Yatta, Big Ma, and Kora all noticed that there was a difference in Kennedy's body. She was still able to suck her stomach in so that she wouldn't show, but there was nothing she could do to hide her huge breasts, which seemed to be getting bigger with each passing day. He already wide hips were spreading like wildfire. Old people would say that she was carrying the baby in her breasts and hips.

The first chance that Yatta got, she pulled Kennedy to the side and interrogated her. "Kennedy, why in the hell is your titties looking so damn big?"

"Huh?" was the only reply that Kennedy could come back with while she got her lie together.

"Don't play with me, Kennedy. You heard what I said. And look at your hips. Come to think of it, you've been on some baggy jogging-suit shit lately."

Kennedy let out a little laugh. "Yatta, you analyzing my body a little too much. I look big because I'm coming on my period. You know how bloated I get. Having this tight-ass dress on only makes it more noticeable."

"Um-hmm," Yatta said, rolling her eyes as she turned to walk away.

Kennedy envied her sister's outfit as she strutted away. She loved the way that Yatta was working the black minidress with the plunging neckline and a pair of supersexy four-inch John Galliano sandals. Kennedy wasn't seriously envious, but she did like Yatta's dress better than her own. It would be a long time before she could again slip into anything that sexy. Kennedy scanned the room, searching for Strick. When she spotted him talking to Big Ma and Klarice, she walked over and politely snatched him from the conversation.

Kennedy pulled him to the side and spoke through her teeth, barely above a whisper. "Did you tell Yatta about me being knocked up?"

"No. Why?"

" 'Cause she just put me through the third degree about my weight gain. And when I told her it was because of my period, she acted like she didn't believe me."

"I didn't tell her shit, *true story.* She probably tripping on you 'cause she swear she been dreaming about fish."

"Oh, yeah, that will do it in my family."

Standing in the front of the crowded room, Yatta took a mike in her hand and called Kennedy up to join her. They shared a short but meaningful embrace. Under certain circumstances, Kennedy could become quite shy, and this was one of them. She grabbed Yatta's hand before she could walk away. "Could you stay? *Please?*"

"You got it, baby girl."

After flashing her dazzling white smile, Kennedy began to speak to the small crowd. It felt as if a thousand butterflies were fluttering in her stomach. "I would like to thank all of you for coming out and celebrating my success as an entertainer. I'm so happy just to be here celebrating anything, because for a long time I didn't think I would ever be able to accomplish anything that I once dreamed of. But this party isn't really to celebrate my career. The real reason for this celebration is to celebrate the growth of the love between Chaz and me. A little over five weeks ago, he proposed to me and I said yes!" Kennedy held her hand up showing off her ring to the crowd.

A wave of chatter and applause swept through the crowd. Chaz approached the stage, carrying tiny black-and-gold gift bags in each hand. He hugged his wife-to-be and gave her a kiss that made the crowd whistle and howl. When Kennedy tried to pass him the mike, he refused to take it.

From the crowd, his sister, Shorty, began to yell, "Speech, speech, speech." Following suit, the crowd joined in, forcing him to take the mike.

With a nervous smile he began to speak. "I think Kennedy and I feel the same sense of gratitude toward all of you. Once again, thanks for joining us. Like I told my mother, I love this girl. I swear I do. And I knew there was nothing else I could do but make her my wife. Physically, I think she is one of the prettiest women I've ever seen. But on the inside, she is even more beautiful. One of the first things that made me fall in love with her was seeing her with Nina's kids. She treated them no different than Jordan, as if she'd birthed them herself. I think it takes a special woman to be so giving. And that's why I love her." Hugging her once more, he told her," I love you, baby."

"I love you, too." Taking over the mike again, Kennedy started rolling her neck. "That's my man, y'all, and what." The crowd laughed at her theatrics. "Aight, aight, let me stop playing so much. I have a few special gifts to hand out. The first two are for my mother and Chaz's mother. Since you will now share children, we thought the two of you should spend some time alone. Inside your bags are gift cards to various stores throughout Manhattan and a gift card from the Bella Spa which entitles you to a full spa treatment."

Chaz passed out the bags as Kennedy continued to talk about the significance of each gift. "The second set of gifts are pretty much the same. And they are for my sisters, Kneaka and Yatta, and my new sister-in-law, Shorty. I want the three of you to spend the day together bonding, since we're all sisters now. I also have a little something for you, Darcy—just a little something to say thanks for taking my career to the next level."

Having already tossed back four martinis, Darcy simply gave Kennedy a thumbs-up from the audience as Chaz handed her her gift bag.

Knowing that the next gift was going to be difficult, Kennedy swallowed hard. "Aunt Klarry, I can say without an ounce of doubt that if Nina were here today, I would be giving her this bag. Thanks for all the late-night calls that comforted me when I should've been comforting you. I love you always."

"I love you, too," Klarice yelled from the audience, blowing Kennedy a kiss.

Kennedy moved on to avoid crying. "Aunt Karen, this only small token of my undying love and appreciation for you. You have always been in my corner, even when I'm dead wrong. And I thank you for that. Last but not least, Big Ma, you are the love of my life, my refuge, and my resting place. I really didn't know what to give you, so I gave you my heart." She walked over to Big Ma, and presented her with a white-gold necklace that held the other half of the diamond heart pendant that Kennedy was wearing.

While returning to the front of the room, Kennedy caught a glimpse of her aunt Kara giving her a pissed-off look. She knew that Kara was hurt that she hadn't gotten a special gift or any type of recognition. If she had been anyone else, Kennedy would have felt bad. But she sure didn't give a damn about Kara's feelings. For as long she could remember, Kara had always looked down on her entire family. Kennedy shot a nasty smirk at Kara before continuing. "Okay, y'all, this is my last gift. And it's for my hus-band-to-be." Taking the small square box from Yatta, she turned to Chaz. "I know that one of your favorite songs is 'If This World Were Mine,' a song made famous by the great Luther Vandross. I just wanted you to always know that if this world were mine, I would give you everything. So I thought that this would be a con-stant reminder for you." She opened the box, displaying a minia-ture yellow-gold globe. The phrase *If This World Were Mine* was encrusted in diamonds around its surface.

"Girl, you gon' make me cry," Chaz said, actually laughing to keep from crying. He hugged her tight, holding her close for a few seconds. "Thank you, ma. I love this."

"It's nothing, baby, you know that." Letting Chaz go, she faced the crowd once more. "I know y'all are ready to get your grub on, so I'ma say this and get out the way. Chaz and I had planned on having our wedding six months from now. But due to unforeseen circumstances, there has been a change in plans."

Yatta gave Kennedy a perplexed look. Kennedy giggled. "Yes, Yatta, this is one that even you don't know about. But you did suspect it. A week ago I went to the doctor and got the shock of my life when he told me that I'm five months pregnant." The news sent the crowd into an excited uproar. Raising her hand, Kennedy got them to calm down. "That ain't all."

"What more can there be?" a voice shouted out.

"I'm having twins." That sent the crowd into a complete frenzy.

From their seats, Sal and Kora jokingly threatened to whip Chaz and Kennedy for keeping secrets. Kennedy just smiled and laughed, loving the crowd's reaction. "I promise y'all, three to four months after I drop this load, there will be a wedding. Seriously, though, thanks again for coming out. I love all of you."

After the party all the family members gathered at Kennedy and Chaz's new home. It was a wonderful night, filled with laughter and joy. The couple's family members shared hilarious childhood stories about them. Big Ma said that she felt like Sal was one of her own daughters.

As Kennedy sat back with her feet propped up in Chaz's lap, watching her family, she thought, *Hands down, this has to be the best night of my life.*

Almost Like Déjà Vu

Over the next weeks Kennedy completed all her open projects, including her sophomore CD, which was slated for release a few months after her due date. She was all too happy after her final photo shoot for the Mischief ad campaign. Finally she could throw caution about weight gain to the wind and eat all the fatty and high-carb foods she wanted. Her appetite seemed to be endless and her weight gain was rapid. In four weeks she'd gained nearly twenty-eight pounds.

Kennedy adored the attention that she was receiving from Chaz on a daily basis. She really appreciated it because she hadn't received that kind of treatment at all when she was carrying Jordan. Chaz loved that she basked in his cooing over her and their babies. He was enjoying his experience with Kennedy's pregnancy. It was the exact opposite of what he'd experienced during both of Ria's pregnancies. Ria had been evil when she was carrying his daughters. By no means was Kennedy a pleasure every single day, especially when her hormones were raging. But living with Ria while she was pregnant had been only one level above hell. When Chaz touched her big belly, Ria cringed and cursed him out. She had done nothing but complain all day. The only time she showed any type of courtesy was when she wanted Chaz to get out of bed in the middle of the night and go out to get her something to eat. Kennedy's positive attitude was a breath of fresh air. On the nights he didn't have to travel or perform. Chaz would try to make it home before Kennedy went to bed. He would rub her belly until they fell asleep together. If she was already asleep when he arrived, he'd slide right up behind her and wrap his arms around her protruding tummy.

Knowing that Kennedy had had to do everything alone while she was pregnant with Jordan, Chaz made it his priority to help her prepare for the babies. He attended every doctor's appointment. He helped design and decorate the nursery. Every Friday afternoon he put aside time to go out with Kennedy and shop for the twins.

On one particular Friday, Kennedy's energy was down and her ankles were swelling up. Her Seven maternity jeans were irritating her stomach. Although it was a cool December day, she was burning up. After only an hour and a half of shopping, she was too tired to go on. "Chaz, baby, I'm ready to go. I'm tired. And I'm starving."

"Aight, let's walk up to Jimmy Jazz first. They got the limited-edition Jordans for babies."

"No," she whined. "Can't you come back and pick them up later?"

"Okay, li'l mama, what you wanna eat?"

"I already know it's somewhere you're not going to want to eat."

"Why, what is it?"

"I'm really craving some sticky wings from BBQ's."

"Now, you know we'll *never* be able to eat in peace in there."

"Just have House or Yak go inside before us and get us a table in the back. And when we go in, just pull your hat real low. Besides, who gonna to recognize my fat ass?"

"Aight, ma. BBQ's. You got that."

"Thanks, baby." Kennedy smiled.

To their surprise BBQ's was not crowded, unusual for the

lunchtime rush. *No crowd means faster service,* Kennedy thought. When her food arrived she demolished it. Eight huge sticky wings, a salad, a plate of fries, and two pieces of corn on the cob. "Damn, Ken," Chaz exclaimed, "you want something to go, too?"

"Ha ha ha, I sure do," she said, sticking her tongue out like a little kid.

Chaz laughed at her silliness. "But yo, seriously, we doing all this shopping, planning, decorating, and we haven't even thought of any names."

"*I've* thought about names."

"Like what?"

"For the girl, I was thinking about Carlie, Tatum, or Brooklyn. For the boy, I like Sy, Angel, Nasir, or Micah."

"You know, I'm feeling Brooklyn for the girl. I don't like any of those boy's names, though. Why can't his name be Chaz Junior?"

"I was thinking about that, too, but you know Chaz is Jordan's middle name."

"Yeah, that is right. We gotta sit down together and come up with some better boy names."

"Maybe if you come home early enough tonight, we can go through some name books."

"We gonna do more than look at name books," Chaz said with a sexually charged smile. "Why don't you just wait til I finish my session and we can ride home together."

"Baby, I'm too tired."

"You can lay down at the studio."

"Nah, I want to go home, eat Almond Kisses, and fall asleep in our bed."

On the short ride to the building that housed the studio and garage, Kennedy fell asleep on Chaz's shoulder in the backseat.

When they arrived inside the garage, he gently squeezed her thigh. "Wake up, baby."

"I dozed off that quick? Damn, I don't have *no* energy today."

"You sure you don't want House to drive you home?"

"No, he can just follow me as usual. Give me a kiss. I'm out."

Chaz pulled her close, giving her deep kiss. "I love you, girl."

"I love you, too, baby. See you later."

Kennedy pulled up to the gate and waited for the security guard to open it. House waited patiently as she entered through the gate. He didn't drive off until the gate was closed and her car was out of sight.

Sitting in the driveway, Kennedy waited for the garage door to open. Suddenly she had an urge to urinate. Once the door was high enough, she zoomed into the garage. Pressing the remote on her key chain, she shut off the house alarm. Leaning over, she picked up her purse and a few of its contents that had fallen to the floor on the passenger side. Sitting up, Kennedy pushed the garage remote, shutting the door, never noticing the two intruders who had slipped in.

A chill ran down Kennedy's spine as she stuck the key in the lock. Shaking it off, she proceeded to open the door. When she'd gotten the door only halfway open, she felt a hard shove from behind. *Oh God,* she thought, bracing herself so that she would fall onto her knees and not her stomach. Her purse and keys fell from her hands and slid across the kitchen floor. Crawling, Kennedy desperately tried to reach her key chain. "Stop trying to be slick, bitch," one of the assailants said, viciously kicking her in the butt, causing her to fall flat on her stomach.

Excruciating pain shot through her abdomen. Suddenly Kennedy was yanked up by her hair and spun around to face a man who was unfamiliar to her. She could only wonder if this was the man who had been stalking her.

"Where the fuck that nigga at?" the man asked aggressively. Never answering his question, Kennedy stared blankly at his face at the same time as she tried to ignore her pain. With the back of his free hand, the man smacked her across her face. Blood gushed from her nose. "Answer me, slut!" he yelled.

"I don't know," she answered through clenched teeth, trying not to cry.

"You're lying!" he screamed, punching her between the eyes. Kennedy nearly blacked out from the blow. Releasing her hair, the man let her body fall to the ground. "Yo, Zee, give me that duct tape." The second man walked over, handing the tape to the assailant, who bound Kennedy's wrists together, telling her, "I don't got nothing but time. We can sit here all day. Shit, I don't care if that nigga don't come home till tomorrow or next week." After taping Kennedy's ankles together, he covered her eyes and mouth.

Pull it together. Think—think. Pull it together now, Kennedy told herself, but she couldn't. Her mind and heart were racing at an unbelievable speed. With the tape covering her mouth, she had to concentrate on catching her breath and breathing through her nose. The entire scene felt way too familiar to her, felt like she was living the night of Pretty Boy's death all over again. Judging by the man's question, she had pretty much figured out that he wasn't her stalker, but that he was there for Chaz. Kennedy found herself concentrating on staying conscious as she started to feel dizzy. Her face, buttocks, and stomach were all aching. *Why didn't I wait to turn off the alarm once I got inside?* she questioned. *My stupidity will probably cost me my life, my babies—oh God, my babies. And Chaz is going to walk right into a trap. God, please let House and Yak come home with him.* She drifted away, slowly passing out.

Yeah, this is how you get shit done, Marcus told himself, sitting back watching Kennedy. *Macon should've let me take care of this shit from jump street. I told him get a nigga's bitch first, then you guaranteed to get the nigga.* He watched Zee rubbing Kennedy's thigh and looking at her lustfully. "Yo, Zee, what the fuck is you doin'?"

"Man, I want some of this," he said, crouching over Kennedy with his short stocky body. "You know what they say about pregnant pussy."

If one needed a good, efficient hit man, Zee was the one to hire. But he had an immaturity about him. Marcus found him childish and highly annoying. He could never fathom how Macon hung around him as a partner. Laying his gun down beside him, Marcus jumped off the counter and walked over to Zee. He yanked Zee's arm, pulling him to his feet. "I don't give a fuck what *they* say about a pregnant bitch! We came here for one thing and that's to merk that nigga and anybody who gets in the way. So you not fucking nothing. That's how niggas get caught slipping."

Having to scold your partner can be a deadly distraction, and neither Marcus nor Zee had noticed that another person had quietly slid into the room. Suddenly the sound of rapid gunfire filled the kitchen. Two bullets ripped through Marcus's back. The first bullet exited through his throat and the second one lodged in the middle of his spinal cord, almost severing it. Catching a glimpse of the man still aiming a gun in his direction, Zee reached for the gun in his waistband as Marcus's body hit the floor. For his effort, he received a bullet in his hand, which went straight through, hitting him in the pelvis. His body fell across Kennedy's legs. Howling in pain, Zee made a second attempt to retrieve his gun.

With his gun aimed at Zee's head, the man stood over him. Then he squeezed the lever, firing three shots into Zee's head. Kennedy sat frozen. She'd been awakened by the initial gunshots. She silently prayed that the body lying across her legs was

not that of Chaz. The silence was deafening. She could only wonder why she wasn't hearing any voices or noises. *This can't be happening again,* she thought.

"Ouch!" Kennedy yelled from the pain of the duct tape being
snatched from her mouth. Gasping for air, she asked, "Who's
there?" There was no answer, just silence, but she could feel the
presence of another person. Kennedy let out a shrill scream as the
tape was snatched from her eyes, ripping out chunks of her eye-
lashes and eyebrows. She couldn't open her eyes, but she could
feel the tape being cut from her wrists and her ankles. She rubbed
her eyes, trying to ease the stinging. Blinking vigorously, she tried
to bring her blurry vision back into focus. Looking down, she
was relieved to see that it wasn't Chaz lying dead on her. A few
moments later, she could see the silhouette of a man standing by
the kitchen sink with his back to her. He had the hood of his blue
Akademics sweatshirt over his head.

"Who are you?" Still standing with his back to her, the man
maintained his silence. Who was this man who had saved her
life? Why wouldn't he face her or answer? Kennedy slowly rolled
the dead body off of her lap. She tried to stand up, but the pain
was overwhelming. She looked down at her pants and realized
they were drenched in amniotic fluid, urine, and blood. "Oh
God!" Kennedy screamed. "Can you help me, please, I'm bleed-
ing. I need to go to the hospital."

The strange man let out an evil laugh, one that Kennedy knew
too well.

It can't be, she thought.

"I'm not the mu-fucking cavalry, bitch. I'm *tha Watcher.* I
didn't come here to save yo' ho ass. I didn't plan on comin' for
you so soon, but I couldn't let them niggas kill you and have all
the fun." Pulling his hood back, he turned to face her. His face
was grossly unshaven, his hair was wild, and he was extremely
frail. But it was him, just as Kennedy had thought when she'd

heard him laugh. It was *Cream.* No doubt about it. He'd never even crossed Kennedy's mind when she was trying to figure out who her stalker might be. Suddenly she felt like a fool for putting him to the back of her mind. She should've hunted him down instead of figuring that she would catch him slipping. Her fear turned to extreme anger.

Cream smiled at her. "Yeah, it's me, you arrogant bitch! Bet you didn't expect to see me, huh?"

"Fuck you, *faggot.*"

"Damn, baby, no 'thank you, Cream, for saving my life'?"

"Die slow, you *bastard*!" Kennedy said, rising to her feet.

"That's so cute and original coming from a bitch that stole my life."

"How did I steal your life? You killed Nina! You killed the mother of your child, faggot-ass nigga!" Looking down at the bodies, then back at him, she said, "I'm glad you finally graduated to killing men."

Cream ran toward her, socking her in the mouth. Kennedy gathered what little strength she had and swung back, landing a hard right to his left eye. The punch did indeed hurt, but he laughed it off. "That's all you got? You big-mouth *bitch*!" Cream violently palmed the side of her head, forcing her body to the floor. He then battered her face and body with blow after blow. He taunted her the entire time, blaming her for the last fight he'd had with Nina. "My girl wouldn't be dead if your nosy ass minded your own damn business!"

Kennedy was slipping in and out of consciousness. She didn't have the strength or energy to combat him seriously. She could barely move to avoid his punches.

In Cream's sadistic mind, fighting Kennedy was turning out to be a major disappointment. "All that shit you popped and you ain't shit but a punk-ass slut. At least Nina could roll with the punches. Damn, I thought you would make this a little fun for me." He unzipped his pants and pulled out his penis then urinated all over Kennedy's face. "Wake up, bitch! Ain't no sleeping."

Wiping the burning urine from her eyes, Kennedy tried to spit the salty liquid from her mouth. From the corner of her swollen eyes, she could see her keys and they were not that far out of her reach. Cream looked down at her, then throwing his head back, he laughed hysterically like a madman. Mustering what little strength she had, Kennedy lifted her leg and kicked him forcefully in the groin. Cream doubled over from the intense pain and fell onto Kennedy's legs. Kennedy struggled desperately to free her legs, and once she got from beneath him, she crawled as fast as she could to her key chain. Pressing the remote, she tripped the silent alarm.

Kennedy slid the keys across the room so that Cream wouldn't catch on to what she'd done. With the pain passing, he rose to his feet. "Whew! That's what I'm talking about. It's on and poppin' *now*! And you not the only one who can kick." Bringing his leg all the way back, he kicked Kennedy in her side. Her amniotic sac exploded on contact and it was very audible. The ringing of the house phone stopped him from delivering the second kick. Cream snatched the phone from the wall and slammed it into the side of Kennedy's head, knocking her out completely.

Pushing his Denali down Route 4 with House riding shotgun, Chaz bopped his head in time to one of his new singles that featured Kennedy. The song was blazing hot. He couldn't wait to get home so that she could hear the final mix. Chaz felt his phone vibrating in his pocket, *This bet' not be another unknown number.* His last four incoming calls had been unknown. He never answered those. Looking down at his phone, he saw that he had a text message.

The message read: *Please call Safe Zone Security concerning an urgent matter immediately. Give code 3117. Thank you.*

Chaz's heart dropped to the bottom of his stomach. "Oh shit!"

"What is it, man?" House asked.

"That was the fucking alarm company."

Wasting no to time, Chaz called Safe Zone. "Good evening, Safe Zone Security, this is Steven."

"Yes, uh . . . code 3117," Chaz said nervously.

"Is this Mr. Harris?"

"Yes."

"Are you at home, Mr. Harris?"

"No."

"Your panic alarm has been set off. The police are en route to your residence. Are we correct by not assuming that this is a false alarm?"

"You are correct. My pregnant fiancée is home alone."

"I'll send an ambulance to your residence also."

After terminating the call, Chaz pressed down on the gas pedal and picked up speed. He couldn't seem to gather his thoughts as he tried calling Kennedy's cell phone again and again with no success. He could only hope and pray that Kennedy had hit the alarm because she was going into labor. *Something must've happened. That's why she never called. It can't be that nigga Macon. I know it can't be.* The more he thought about it, the faster he drove.

Cream took the extra set of car keys from the kitchen wall. Grabbing Kennedy by her hair, he dragged her out to the garage and threw her into the trunk of her 745i. Then he jumped into the driver's seat and pressed the remote on the visor to open the garage door. As he backed out he found himself blocked in the driveway by three police cruisers. Five uniformed Bergen County police officers were walking up the driveway. Two of the officers quickly drew their guns, yelling. "POLICE! TURN THE IGNITION OFF AND STEP OUT OF THE CAR."

Banging his head on the steering wheel, Cream began talking to his self. "You didn't come this far to fuck up now. The bitch has got to die right now." Following the orders he'd been given, he opened the door and stepped out. He thought, *If I could get off a couple of shots into the trunk, I could still kill her . . . or die trying.* He hated Kennedy just that much that he was willing to end his own life in order to stop hers. In one swift motion, he went for his gun and attempted to fire at the trunk.

"HE GOT A GUN!" a young black rookie officer yelled. All of the officers wasted no time firing their guns. The rookie emptied half of his magazine before he stopped shooting. The gun slipped from Cream's hand as his body fell backward onto the concrete. Blood trickled from the corner of his evil grin. "I got her back" were his last words.

The sound of screeching tires coming to a halt took the cops' attention away from Cream's lifeless body. Putting the truck in park, Chaz jumped out, followed by House. The cops pointed their weapons toward them. An older white cop said, "Hold it right there!"

Growing up in the hood, both Chaz and House knew not to act irrational. Not to mention there was already one dead black body on the ground. Chaz calmly spoke to the cop. "Officer, this is my house. The alarm company notified me that there was a disturbance."

The cop gave him a "yeah, right" look. It was a blessing that that the black rookie cop was a fan of Chaz and he stepped up, saying, "Richards, he's telling the truth. He's a famous musician."

The officers lowered their guns. Officer Richards gave Chaz an apologetic look. "Sorry, I didn't know."

"Sure you didn't," Chaz responded sarcastically. The sound of the approaching ambulance sirens brought his mind back to the real situation. He asked the officers, "Where is my fiancée?"

The rookie took over the job of talking to him, "Mr. Harris, I'm Officer Sanders. We haven't been inside yet. We're about to go in now and canvass the house to make sure it's safe. What's your fiancée's name?"

"Her name is Kennedy."

The cops had entered the house and were calling out to Kennedy when they stumbled onto the bodies of Marcus and Zee. They knew the scene could only get worse. The only sign of Kennedy was her purse, its contents scattered across the floor. Looking at Zee, they knew without doubt that he was dead. "Get the medics in here. This one is still breathing," Richards said, looking at Marcus. "And bring Mr. Harris in here so we can find out who's supposed to be here and who's not."

Chaz stepped inside. As he took in the scene a terrible feeling came over him. "Are these men supposed to be here?" Richards asked.

"Fuck no."

"Do you know them?"

Chaz's eyes said yes, but his mouth said, "No."

"What about the man outside?" Sanders asked.

"I really *don't know* him."

The other officers continued calling out to Kennedy and doing a complete search of the house. Chaz watched Officer Richards studying a wide trail of blood and liquid that ran across the kitchen floor to the garage entry. Richards yelled over his shoulder to Sanders, "I think I know where she is."

He followed the trail out to the garage. Figuring it out, Chaz ran past him. Reaching into the BMW, he popped the trunk. His heart stopped when he got to the back of the car and saw Kennedy lying in there. Her eyes were swollen shut. Huge purple-

and-black bruises ran rampant across her face and neck. Chaz pulled her unconscious body from the trunk. He was completely floored by how badly beaten she was. He couldn't even tell if she was alive. He zoned out, oblivious to everyone around him. Holding her close, he rocked back and forth slowly, tears steadily streaming down his face.

Reasons and Seasons

Kennedy continued living in Charlotte with Big Ma, although she had been healed for about a year. She was still not ready to return to New York or the music industry. She and Strick had remained close. They really didn't have a choice about the matter since they were now in-laws, Strick and Yatta having married in Bermuda earlier that year. They were now expecting their first child together and Yatta's fourth daughter.

Chaz had gone on to record his third and most critically acclaimed CD, which sold more than ten million copies worldwide. The CD was filled with songs about his personal struggles, like the pain of growing up without his mother and losing his best friend, Jay. He had also recorded three songs inspired by his relationship with Kennedy. Each song displayed a different emotion toward her; one showed anger, one showed love, and the third showed confusion. The authenticity of the emotions behind the songwriting was what made the CD such a success, proving the old saying that "in order to be a great writer you must first experience pain."

Not a day went by that he didn't think of Kennedy. At every performance, his eyes would scan the audience in the hope that she was there. Sex didn't even feel right anymore, and he had it coming from groupies, executives, female athletes, models, actresses, and singers. But no one could ever fill Kennedy's place in his heart.

Big Ma sat in her rocking chair watching Kennedy looking at Chaz as he was being interviewed on the red carpet at the MTV video awards the night before. Kennedy's eyes could never lie. Big Ma could tell that she still loved Chaz. Kennedy was so engrossed with Chaz that she didn't notice Big Ma get up and walk out of the room.

Closing the bedroom door behind her, Big Ma sat on the edge of her bed. She rummaged through her nightstand drawer until she found the paper she was looking for. She picked up the cordless and dialed the number off the paper. The phone rang a few times before the person answered, "Hey, Big Ma!"

"Hi, baby. Big Ma not calling to trouble you, but I think it's time for you to come down south and get baby girl."

Three days later, on a hot Saturday afternoon, Big Ma was sitting on the porch watching her great-grandkids and a few neighborhood kids playing out in the yard. A black Lincoln Town Car with black-tinted windows pulled up in front of the yard. All the kids paused to see who was inside. The driver got out first, walking to the rear of the car, where he removed two duffel bags from the trunk and placed them on the sidewalk. He then walked to the back passenger door and opened it. A big smile spread across Jordan's face when he saw Chaz stepping out of the car. *"Chaz!"* Jordan, Mattie, and Niko yelled as they ran toward him and hugged his legs.

It made Chaz feel so good that the kids were excited to see him. "What's up, y'all?"

The sound of an approaching ice-cream truck quickly diverted the three kids' attention from Chaz. Niko ran to stop the truck while all the other kids ran toward Big Ma, yelling, "Can we have some money for ice cream, Big Ma?"

"Wait, wait," Chaz told the kids. "Leave Big Ma alone. Here, take this and pay for everybody's ice cream." He handed Mattie three ten-dollar bills. "That should be enough to get all of you whatever you want." All of the kids ran past Chaz, almost knocking him down. Chaz picked up his duffel bags and walked up onto the porch. Tossing his bags to the side, he gave Big Ma a huge hug. "Hey, Big Ma, how've you been?"

"I'm fine, baby, and you?"

"I'm okay."

"It's so good to see you. Stand back and let me look at you. You look good, but you done lost a good bit of weight."

"I don't get those good home-cooked meals anymore."

"How're your girls doing?"

"They doing real good. Getting big. Wanting everything they see in the store."

"What 'bout your mama and your sister?"

"They doing fine, too."

The group of kids floated back into the yard. In unison, they all said, "Thank you, Chaz" as they headed into the backyard. Chaz took a seat next to Big Ma. "So where is your baby girl?"

"She and my grandnieces went for a ride. They should be back at any time now."

Chaz dropped his head and stared down at his feet. "Big Ma, you think she'll come back to me?"

"I know she will."

"How do you know that?"

"Her face lights up when she sees you on the television or in one of those magazines." Big Ma let out a little chuckle. "Then she gets this little sad look about her. That's how I know her heart is still with you."

"I can't thank you enough for staying in touch with me through all of this."

"Y'all babies just needed some time apart. And she needed time to heal. But this time, together you will be stronger. Chaz, you must never forget that there are reasons and seasons and everything on this earth has a reason."

Big Ma's words stuck in Chaz's mind. The events that had led up to the termination of his and Kennedy's relationship were still fresh in his memory. Although he'd gotten through it all, he had never gotten over it.

"My babies didn't make it, did they?" Kennedy had asked, lying in her hospital bed the day after the brutal assault. It was the first time she had fully regained consciousness since being admitted.

Smoothing her hair with his hand, Chaz answered the question that no one else wanted to answer. "No, baby . . . they—they didn't make it."

Kennedy squeezed her eyes tight, trying hard to fight off the feeling of loss. The tears rushed from her eyes as she moaned and hollered loudly. Calling out to her mother, she asked in tearful sobs, *"Mommy, why? Why is it always me?"*

At a complete loss for words, Kora simply got into the bed with her daughter. Kora held on to her girl while Kennedy poured her soul out in tears and mournful screams. Kora didn't let her go until she fell asleep.

Since the twins were stillborn, the hospital had offered to bury them free of charge. Chaz wasn't having that. He had them properly buried in the same tiny white casket. He bought a beautiful headstone for their grave. Engraved on it was a girl and boy on each side, and it read: *Mommy and Daddy's Little Angels, Brooklyn and Micah.*

Chaz also had the funeral home take pictures of the babies in case Kennedy ever wanted to see them. Every time he thought about the twins or looked at their little bodies lying in the casket, he saw red. He saw Macon's blood. It had been on before, but the war was really on now. He'd searched high and low for Macon, but was unsuccessful in locating him. It hadn't been hard for him to find Marcus, who, due to his gunshot wounds, had been recovering at Holy Name, under twenty-four-hour police supervision. And it hadn't been hard at all for Chaz to get Marcus hit. Fifteen thousand to the beat cop who guarded the door to take a five-minute break. And sixty thousand to a beautiful hit woman named Mish to replace his IV bag with highly concentrated pure liquid cocaine.

Chaz had sent the message to Macon loud and clear. *Fuck with mines and I will annihilate yours.*

After a week-and-a-half stay in the hospital, Kennedy was released. Chaz knew there was no way that she could ever return to the house in Jersey. So he rented a five-bedroom condo in midtown just three and a half blocks from T.O.N.Y.'s new offices and studio. He tried to make the place as comfortable as possible for her. He hired someone to come in and cook for her. He even had fresh flowers delivered daily.

A little over a month after the attack, Kennedy seemed to doing fine, at least to judge by her appearance. But it was a front that was becoming increasingly hard for her to keep up when she was actually dying on the inside. She had barely made it through a weekend visit from the kids without breaking all the way down. Watching them laugh and play had only made her wonder what the twins would have been like.

Sunday-morning breakfast with the kids became especially hard for Kennedy often Jordan asked, "Mommy, where-where my sister and brother?"

Then Mattie chimed in. "Yeah, Ken, where *are* my new cousins?"

Chaz, Niko, and Taylor looked nervously at Kennedy.

Smiling, Kennedy explained to them: "Micah and Brooklyn are in heaven now."

"With my mommy?" Mattie asked.

"Yes, baby, they're with your mommy. Excuse me, ya'll," Kennedy then said, getting up from the table. She walked briskly down the hall straight to the bathroom. Shutting the door, she balled over from the hurt in the pit of her stomach. She covered her mouth to keep from crying aloud. After a good long cry, she left the bathroom only to go into her bedroom and fall into a deep sleep. She woke up just in time to get the kids ready for Yatta to pick them up for their flight back to Charlotte.

When Yatta arrived and saw her sister, the first thing she noticed was the drastic amount of weight that Kennedy had lost. When Kennedy greeted her with a warm smile and a hug, Yatta held on to her, wanting to cry. She could see through Kennedy's smile and she saw nothing but pain. Yatta didn't want to leave her sister, but she had to chaperone the kids on the flight. With her styling and party-planning businesses both thriving, Yatta had not had much time to spend with Kennedy. She promised herself that when she returned the next day, she would spend the entire day with her.

That night Kennedy was sleeping peacefully when she was awakened by the sound of crying babies. She sat straight up in the bed and looked around. Chaz was next to her snoring, deep in his sleep. Suddenly the noise stopped. Shaking it off, Kennedy lay back down. As soon as her head hit the pillow the crying started all over again. For two hours Kennedy tossed and turned, unable to fall asleep, still hearing the sound of the crying babies.

Finally she got up, grabbed her purse, and went into the bathroom. Sitting on the edge of the tub, Kennedy rambled through her purse until she found her old bottle of prescription sleeping pills. Although the instructions said *Take one pill before going to bed,* Kennedy poured three pills into the palm of her hand and popped them into her mouth. And when her head hit the pillow that time, she fell into a coma-like sleep instantly.

The following morning she was still feeling drugged up from the sleeping pills. She was so incoherent that she could barely return Chaz's kiss before he headed to the studio around noon. Kennedy crawled out of bed around one-thirty that afternoon. Not five minutes after she woke up, she was sitting on the toilet urinating when she began to hear the crying again.

Kennedy turned the radio and television on full blast, attempting to drown out the cries of the babies. When that didn't work, she sat in the middle of the living-room floor for two hours with her knees close to her chest. Rocking back and forth, she covered her ears with her hands. Huge tears slid down her face as she chanted over and over, "Stop crying. Please . . . please stop crying." Suddenly, as if something had clicked in her head, she jumped up and ran from room to room searching for the twins.

When she was unsuccessful in finding them, she burst from the apartment still wearing her green silk nightgown and matching robe, her hair very disheveled. People stopped and stared as a barefoot Kennedy ran three and a half blocks to the studio.

The security guard of the building where the studio was housed recognized her when she ran through the door. Allowing her to pass, he picked up the phone and called upstairs to the studio to warn them about her appearance.

Chaz was already in front of the elevator when the doors

opened and Kennedy stepped off. She fell into his arms screaming, "I can't find the babies! They won't stop crying. Can you
please come home and make them stop?"

Wrapping a blanket around her, Chaz held her tightly. He
didn't know what to say. He couldn't lie and tell her that everything was going to be okay. He himself didn't know if *anything*
was going to be okay ever again. With his arm around her, ignoring the stares from people in the hall, he led her back to Strick's
private office. He took a seat behind the desk with Kennedy in his
arms. The room was completely silent as Chaz rocked her slowly,
like an infant, until she fell asleep.

Beaten down by jet lag, Yatta had been enjoying a wonderful afternoon nap. The constant ringing of her house phone and cell
phone brought an end to her peaceful slumber. Never opening
her eyes, she reached out to her nightstand and grabbed her cell
phone. "Hello?"

"Yatta, this Chaz."

"What's up?"

"Yo, that thing we talked about the other day. I think it's happening."

Yatta's heart sank. She sat up in the bed. "Oh God. What happened?"

After Chaz explained to Yatta what Kennedy had done, the
only words she said were: "Yeah, we have to take her to get some
help before it's too late."

The thought of putting Kennedy in any kind of mental institu-
tion killed Chaz. He closed his eyes to fight off the oncoming
tears. "Damn, Yatta, but I don't even know if can take her to one
of those places. I want and I do need for her to get better. I mean
I want *my* Kennedy back. She's here physically, but she not my li'l
mama. When I look into her eyes they're just blank."

"I understand what you're going through. She's my sister and I love her more than anybody else. But we can't be in denial. For two years she's been self-medicating with pills and alcohol. She needs to get help now."

"You right. Can you bring her some clothes, a brush, and one of those things to put her hair in a ponytail?"

"That's nothing. I'll see you in a half."

A deafening silence filled Strick's truck as he drove to the facility in Eastchester. Yatta sat in the passenger seat staring out the window. Chaz sat in the back holding on to Kennedy, who was still sleeping. None of the passengers were up for conversation. All their minds were focused on one thing: getting Kennedy the help that she needed.

Kennedy finally awakened once Strick had stopped the car at the facility. She sat up stretching and looking around. "Where are we?"

None of the three knew how to tell her. Feeling that Kennedy was her responsibility, Yatta turned around and grabbed her little sister's hand. Looking Kennedy in the eye, she told her, "Baby, everyone who loves you feels that you're very tired and you need a little help resting. There are people here who can help you with that."

Like a helpless child, Kennedy whined, "But why can't I go to Big Ma's house?"

"No, Kennedy. This time you need professional help." The sad look on Kennedy's face crushed Yatta's heart. She began having second thoughts. *Maybe I should take her to Big Ma's house.* "I would much rather take you to Big Ma's house any day than to leave you here. But that wouldn't be getting you the help that you need."

"How long do I have to stay?"

"Until you feel better."

"Will I get to see y'all?"

"Yes, sweetie. They have visitation days and I'll be here for every one of them."

Kennedy lowered her head, sniffling like a child. "Will you bring Big Ma and Mommy to see me?"

"I'll do whatever you ask me to."

From the outside, the Better Days Therapeutic Center looked like a resort spa. The center had been the temporary home to some of the top celebrities and wealthiest mental patients and recovering addicts in the Northeast. A young, beautiful, dark-skinned female greeted them at the door. "Welcome to Better Days. I'm Dr. Kisha Webster. Here, we're all on a first-name basis, so feel free to call me Kisha."

"Hi, Kisha. I'm Kenyatta Sanchez. We spoke on the phone earlier. And this is my sister Kennedy Sanchez."

"Yes, I remember our conversation. How are you, Kennedy? I hear that you're exhausted."

"I'm okay . . . I guess."

"We're going to help you get the rest you need. I'll give you a few minutes to say your good-byes."

"That's okay, I've already said them," Kennedy responded, coldly cutting her eyes at Yatta, Chaz, and Strick. She walked into the building, never looking back.

Her sudden coldness was a hard blow, especially to Yatta and Chaz. Chaz wasn't feeling it. "Yatta, let's just take her to Big Ma's."

"Chaz, we can't turn back now. One day she'll thank us for this."

Kennedy spent her first two days at the facility sleeping, only waking up to eat and shower. On her third day, she had her first meeting with one of the resident psychiatrists. Kennedy walked into the office and plopped down on a brown suede chaise. She sat up straight on purpose, thinking, *It'll be a cold day in hell before I lay down on this shit and pour out my life story to this bitch.* The ultrapetite therapist had golden blond hair and piercing ocean-blue eyes. From the outset, the perkiness of her voice irked Kennedy. "Hi, I'm Dr. Irena Kapolski. You already know that you can call me Irena. And you are Kennedy?"

"I am," Kennedy answered with a slight attitude.

"In reading your file, I saw that you've had a breakdown before."

"If that's what you wanna call it," Kennedy said snidely.

"It appears that a lot of the issues in your life begin with the men in your life."

"You're the shrink. You tell me."

"According to your file, your first breakdown came right after the death of your boyfriend Malik when you were just a teenager." Kennedy tensed up as Irena continued to talk. "Being a single mother with no help from the child's father can be a great source of stress—"

Kennedy cut her off immediately. "Raising my son without his father has never been and will never be a source of stress, so that's where you're wrong."

Irena continued on as if Kennedy had never stopped her. "And the latest traumatic event in your life was your miscarriage. It happened because you were attacked by the man who killed your cousin."

Tears burned the back of Kennedy's eyes as thoughts of the twins and Nina danced through her head. "So, Doc, it is your opinion that the men in my life are the problem?"

"I do believe that maybe your choice in men does play a major role. But let's focus on why you pick these men. Tell me . . . what kind of men did your mother date when you were growing up?"

"Despite what you think, Marcia *fucking* Brady, all black and Hispanic women are not single mothers raising a bunch of crumb snatchers."

"I never said that."

"You didn't have to *say* it. I can see it in your eyes . . . the way they judge me. My mother didn't have to date any men while I was growing up. She'd been married to my father since before her children were born, you perky *bitch*. You know what, I don't need this shit. I'm out of here."

"Kennedy, please sit back down."

"Fuck you," Kennedy said, yanking the door open. She ran down the hallway, straight to the pay phones.

Humming "Precious Lord," Big Ma placed the lid on top of the collard greens she was cooking. Opening the oven door, she checked on her squash casserole, but quickly closed the door when her house phone began ringing. She made her way to the phone hanging on the wall as quick as aching knees would allow. "Hello?"

"This is AT&T with a collect call from Kennedy. Will you accept the charges? If yes, please press one now."

Anxious to find out why Kennedy was calling her collect, Big Ma hurriedly pressed one.

"Thanks for using AT&T. Caller, go ahead." Barely giving the automated voice a chance to finish, Big Ma began talking. "Kennedy, baby, where you at?"

"Don't you know, Big Ma?"

"Nah, I wouldn't have asked if I knew!"

"I'm at a mental facility upstate."

"No, grandgirl, I didn't know anything about you being there. How did you get there?"

"Yatta arranged it, but that ain't important right now. I want to leave here now. I want to come stay with you, Big Ma."

"You know you can come here, chile."

"I don't have any cash or credit cards on me here. Can you charge my flight on your card?"

"Sure, baby."

"Thank you, Big Ma. And whatever you do, don't tell Yatta I'm leaving. And don't tell my mother because she'll tell Yatta. As a matter of fact, don't tell anyone."

Three days after Kennedy's call to Big Ma, Yatta and Chaz arrived for Kennedy's first visitation day. Chaz brought with him two dozen multicolored roses, Kennedy's favorite. Carrying a Vuitton duffel bag full of new clothes for Kennedy, Yatta anxiously approached the reception desk. "Good afternoon. We're here to see Kennedy Sanchez."

"One second, let me pull up her room number and I'll call her." After keying in Kennedy's information, the receptionist looked at the screen, then nervously at Yatta. "Let me get Dr. Webster for you."

"Is there a problem?" Chaz asked.

"No, Dr. Webster has requested that all phone calls and visitors for Kennedy be directed to her first."

As Dr. Webster approached, the serious look on her face spoke volumes. "Good afternoon. Please follow me into my office." The warm smile and kindness that she had greeted them with days earlier was now gone. Yatta and Chaz sat down in the two chairs directly in front of her desk. Getting right to the point, Yatta asked, "Is everything okay with my sister?"

"Your sister left the program."

"What do you mean she left?" Chaz demanded.

"She checked out yesterday."

Yatta shook her head in disbelief. "This is fucking un-believable! Why didn't you call me? And why did you let her leave?"

"Ms. Sanchez, you know that she signed herself in voluntarily. So therefore she could check herself out. She also requested that we not inform you. If I'd called you, it would've violated doctor-client privilege."

"I don't care about that privilege shit. My sister is unstable. She could be somewhere DEAD!"

"I can assure you that your sister is very safe." Reaching into her desk drawer, Dr. Webster pulled out two envelopes. "Kennedy left these for the two of you."

Sitting in the parking lot of Better Days, Chaz and Yatta both stared at the envelopes in their hands. Opening his first, Chaz pulled the paper out. Pain literally shot through his heart when he unfolded the paper and Kennedy's engagement ring fell out. He held it tightly in his left hand while he read the letter.

Chaz,

I need space to clear my mind. For some reason, I can't get past the recent events. Maybe it's because I still haven't gotten over some of the painful events in my past. Please don't pursue me. I need time to heal my mind and my soul. I cannot do that and build with you at the same time. In the meantime, if you find an-other woman, that's okay. I have too many issues to expect you not to find someone else better. Whatever happens with me, please know that I will always love you and will never forget you.

Sincerely, Kennedy

Seeing the single tear fall from Chaz's eye had Yatta afraid to open her letter. Putting her fear to the side, she opened it and began reading.

Yatta,
I know you probably think I'm mad at you for bringing me here. Well, I'm not. I know that your intentions were good. Better Days just was not the place for me to heal. I'm going back to that same old room I had to go to eight years ago. If you really care about my healing process, do not lead Chaz to me. Please reassure him that I never blamed him.

See you soon, Kennedy

Neither spoke a word on the drive back to the city until they pulled in front of Yatta's brownstone. Yatta looked over at Chaz in the driver's seat. He was staring straight ahead, lost in a trance. Reaching over, she touched his shoulder gently, getting his attention. "Chaz, she loves you very much. She just needs time."

"I know," Chaz said, turning his head and looking out the window so that Yatta wouldn't see the tears forming in his eyes.

Feeling his pain, Yatta told him, "Come in and hang out with me and Strick for a while. We can watch a few movies and I'll cook you something good. You look like you ain't ate since Kennedy's breakdown."

"Nah, that's okay, Shorty's gonna bring the girls by the house later on."

Yatta could tell that he was lying, but she decided not to press the issue. She planted a sisterly kiss on his cheek. "Be safe, okay? See you later."

"Aight, Yatta, I'll hit you tomorrow."

Chaz watched Yatta until she got into the house. After she closed the door, he looked over at the town house where Ken-

232 | Danielle Santiago

nedy used to reside. It was now rented out to a young white couple. He sat there for a minute staring at the house, thinking, *I remember the first night I ever came over. All those late nights after the studio . . . Kennedy would hide me from the kids. She always had a hot plate waiting for a nigga. It was all love back then. I miss those days . . . I miss her.* Banging his fist on the steering wheel, he yelled out, "WHAT THE FUCK, MAN? On everything I love, I'ma kill that nigga." Speeding away from the curb, he drove recklessly all the way to his midtown apartment.

Even in his apartment Chaz was still unable to find solace. Everything inside of those walls reminded him of Kennedy. Pictures of her, him, and their kids lined the foyer. Her clothes, shoes, and handbags were spread throughout the house. Walking into the den, he snatched an unopened liter bottle of Hennessy from the bar. After cracking the top, he chugged half the bottle down in one swig. He removed the bottle from his lips and let out a loud deep cough. The burning sensation moved from his throat down to his chest before warming his entire body.

Chaz fell back on the couch as the liquor slowly crept over him. He picked up the CD-player remote that was lying next to him and pressed play. The sounds of Anthony Hamilton's "I'm a Mess" poured through the speakers like thick molasses. "I'm a Mess" just happened to be one of Kennedy's favorite songs. It was also very ironic how the song mirrored his exact feelings at the moment. *"I'm a mess right now. Can't believe I lost you, my soul mate, my best friend. We invested in a set of twins."* Listening to the words, he stared at a beautiful poster-size picture of him and Kennedy on the red carpet at the *Vibe* awards. It was displayed proudly between his first platinum plaque and Kennedy's.

Out of nowhere, Chaz hurled the Hennessy bottle right at the picture. Glass shattered everywhere and the brown liquor splashed against the wall. The wooden frame slid down the wall, breaking into huge pieces when it crashed against the hardwood floor. Enraged, Chaz ran over to the wall and began snatching all the plaques and pictures, throwing them all across the room. He knocked over everything in sight. Angrily, he put his fist through the wall with one punch. He pushed over the huge entertainment unit, completely smashing it, the plasma television, and the home-theater system.

Chaz dropped to his knees in the middle of the destruction; looking toward the sky, he moaned loudly from a broken heart, "Why now? *God, why now?*"

His answer would come soon enough. He had to learn that God moves in mysterious ways. And all His ways are not meant to be understood by the human mind.

Now, more than a year later, three loud motorcycle engines roaring up the street brought Chaz back from his trip down memory lane.

"Here they come," Big Ma said, "riding them bikes like damn fools."

"Who is *they*?" Chaz asked.

"Kennedy and my crazy grandnieces. They been down here since they got into some problems back in New York."

"Since when Kennedy been riding motorcycles?"

"She's been riding them things. Reckon she didn't mention it because she didn't ride for a long time after Nina died. Nina's purple bike is still back there in the garage. Kennedy don't let *nobody* touch it."

The three girls pulled into the driveway all wearing helmets, which made it hard for Chaz to tell which one was Kennedy. The two other girls had the same Sanchez tattoo on their right arm as Yatta, Kennedy, and Nina. Chaz spotted Kennedy by the black panther tattooed on her left leg.

From the driveway, Kennedy couldn't see Chaz where he was

234 | *Danielle Santiago*

sitting on the porch, but he had a perfect view of her. Kennedy pulled off her helmet and shook out her hair. Chaz could see that she had dyed it burgundy. He thought that she looked more beautiful than before. Her new hair color complemented the red tones in her skin. When the two other girls removed their helmets, they looked, at first glance, like twins. "Are they twins, Big Ma?"

"Nah, they first cousins—just been together like sisters since the cradle."

"Man, E, I dusted y'all bum asses," Kennedy taunted her cousins as they walked toward the porch.

"You should have! The way you got that bitch kitted out," E replied. They continued laughing and joking as they stepped onto the porch. Seeing Chaz stopped Kennedy right in her tracks, causing her cousins to bump into her and making her fall down on the steps. Chaz jumped up and ran over to help her. "Are you all right?"

"Yeah, I'm fine. What are you doin' here?" Kennedy said, getting to her feet.

"Damn, what happened to hello? How are you?"

"Hi, *Chaz,* how are you? Now, what are you doing in Charlotte, North Carolina?"

"A little birdy told me that it was time I came down."

Kennedy glared at Big Ma. Smiling, Big Ma turned her head and looked the other way.

"Now, Kennedy, I know Kora taught your high-yella ass some manners."

Kennedy gave her cousin the evil eye. "Sorry, didn't know your red ass was so big on manners. Chaz, these are my cousins Kisa and Eisani. Y'all, this is Chaz."

"Nice to finally meet the two of you," Chaz said, extending his hand toward them. "I was starting to think that you were figments of her imagination."

"We're real," Kisa replied.

"Yes, flesh and blood," Eisani added.

Jumping back in, Kisa told him, "And your baby mother better be glad that we *wasn't* around when she decided to play Edward Scissorhands."

Eisani jumped right back in, too. " 'Cause it would've been a lot of slow singing and flower bringing."

Big Ma stood up. "Come on in the house, you two troublemakers. Stop starting shit."

"We just messing with him, Auntie," Kisa said, winking at Chaz.

"I know you two very well and you're not joking," Big Ma replied.

"Did Sincere pick up the kids?" Kisa asked Big Ma as the girls followed her into the house.

Eisani went through the door last, leaving Kennedy and Chaz alone on the porch. There was an awkward moment of silence. "I want to see more of Charlotte," Chaz said.

"Well, my mother has my truck right now."

"I was thinking we could take the bikes."

"Can you ride or would like for me to pull you?" Kennedy teased with a smirk.

"Pull me? You can't be serious, homegirl. And can *I* ride? I could beat you on a moped."

Kennedy laughed. "Now, don't write a check your ass can't cash."

It turned out that Chaz was a very skillful rider and Kennedy barely beat him. She knew that he had wanted to visit the Bank of America Stadium, home of the Carolina Panthers. Slowing down in front of the two giant panthers on Mint Street, Kennedy parked in front of the stadium. Chaz pulled up, parking behind her, gloating even though he'd lost the race. "Baby girl, you gotta get your skills up if you want to beat me."

"I did beat you, punk!"

"Only 'cause you got a little something extra in that engine, plus I don't know my way around."

"Whatever. Don't be a sore loser. Take it like a man."

Chaz focused his attention on the stadium. "This is real nice on the outside. I can't wait to see the inside. Maybe we can go to a game when the season starts."

"Yeah, maybe." They stood silent for a few seconds, making it another awkward moment.

Chaz reached into his pocket. "Here, you forgot this," he said, extending his closed hand toward her.

"What is it?"

He opened his hand, revealing its contents to Kennedy. A nervous smile lit up her face. "My ring. I can't believe you still have it."

"I kept it hoping that you would wear it again one day."

Kennedy's heart melted as she became overwhelmed with guilt. "Chaz, I'm sorry that I hurt you. But I had to do what was best for me so that I could get better. I need you to understand that I wouldn't have been any good to you as long as I was messed up in the head. Most of all, I need you to forgive me."

"I forgave you a long time ago. I just wish you would've let me decide if you would've been any good to me."

"Chaz, you yourself knew that I was a heavy burden. I would've only stagnated you. And at that time you needed to focus on your career and all that shit that was going on in the streets."

"Kennedy, do me a favor. Stop always trying to think for everybody. You don't know what I could've handled." He placed the ring in the palm of her hand. "I'm not trying to pressure you, but I would like for you to wear this again."

Shaking her head, Kennedy placed the ring back in his hand. Chaz felt his heart breaking all over again. "It's like that? You couldn't even think about it?"

"No, it's not like that at all. I just wanted *you* to put it on for me."

Smiling hard, Chaz quickly slipped the ring onto her finger. He pulled Kennedy into him, embracing her tightly. "I love you so much, girl, you just don't know."

"I love you too, baby."

"Let's go so I can get you out of those little-ass shorts."

"I suggest that you go around the corner to the Westin 'cause ain't no sleeping together up in Big Ma's house unless you're married."

"You know that's nothing."

Kennedy stood on her tiptoes and gave Chaz a soft peck on the lips. Looking her in the eye, he told her, "Don't ever leave me like that again."

"I won't. Just don't ever give me a reason."

They both climbed back onto the bikes. Chaz called out to Kennedy as she was putting her helmet on, "Baby girl, a little birdy told me that you weren't ready to return to the city yet."

"I'm going to hurt Big Ma."

"It's okay if you're not. I think I'm going to like Charlotte. Might even buy a house out here."

"I've been looking at town houses and condos. I do plan on moving back to New York one day."

"Let's get a big house so we can fill it up with five or six more kids."

"You had some more kids?" Kennedy asked, laughing.

"I'm talking about the ones that you're going to give me."

"Nigga, you good if you get one baby out of me. You see my body? I wear size six now. I'm in the best shape of my life. That's courtesy of Dr. Atkins and Peak Fitness."

"You're so vain."

"And you love it."

As Kennedy pulled away from the curb she thought, *Mommy always said if a lost love is meant to be, it will find its way back.* Looking up, she spotted a beautiful rainbow spread across the sky. She thought about Nina. *I wish you could've met this one, Nina. He's a keeper. And I know he loves me for me, even with all my flaws. Guess I can move on now. It's back to grinding . . . grinding for keeps.*

Acknowledgments

Thank you, Heavenly Father, for saving me through your most wonderful grace and mercy. I'm so grateful for all the many blessings you've given me, especially the blood of your son, and your divine favor.

Kaden, you are still my greatest creation and my best inspiration. Mommy loves you always.

Carlos, I'm here and I will always be here. You are my best friend, and I'm so happy I'm yours. I love you.

Mommy and Daddy, quite often I thank God for blessing me with you. Yeah, we fuss and disagree, but at the end of the day we're smiling and joking again. I'm most thankful for the loyalty, pride, morals, and love that you've instilled in me.

Aundi, I could not have asked for a more perfect little sister. There is nothing in the world I would not do for you. You were my first and biggest supporter. Thanks for always holding your big sister down.

Darion, baby boy, keep following your dreams. No matter where they lead you, your big sis will be there.

Mont, over the years, due to our hectic lives, we've grown somewhat distant and a lot of that is because of me. I promise that soon we're going to get together and take a long family vacation. I want you to know you're an excellent big brother, a wonderful man, and I think the world of you.

TT, I'm grown now! Stop being so overprotective and let ya li'l sis live! Trust me—I know you got my back.

Teon and Shani, you are the most wonderful godparents to my Kaden. You love him just as if he were yours, and I thank you for that.

Special thanks to my loving grandparents. Many hugs and kisses to my all my aunts, uncles, and cousins for all of your love and support.

I would like to acknowledge a few special ladies who are helping me develop spiritually: Nikki Long (my beautiful stylist), Doris Mumtaz, Prophetess Brittany Woods, and Ms. Betty.

Thank you, D. Adams, for being my emergency hairstylist and one of my best friends for more than ten years. To all my true friends, you know who you are, and just because I didn't name you individually doesn't mean I don't cherish our friendship.

Thanks to a few of my favorite authors who happen to be my friends: Tu-Shonda Whitaker, K. Elliot, TN Baker, Kiesha Ervin, Tonya Blount, and Kwan Foye.

Thank you, James Muhammad and Two of a Kind Publishing, for every single thing you did to help me take my career to the next level.

A special thanks to Miss Nakia Murray and As the Page Turns Literary.

Malaika Adero, thank you so much for taking a chance on a li'l ghetto chick like me (lol). I promise I won't let you down. Krishan, I know I can be a pain in the ass when you're trying to catch up with me, but I don't mean to be. Thanks for all your hard work. Thanks to the entire staff at Atria and Simon & Schuster who worked hard to make *Grindin'* happen.

Vickie Stinger, I've told you before, you are more than my agent. I can't thank you enough for going above and beyond your duty of looking out for me as an agent and a friend.

I would like to extend a heartfelt thanks to Charlotte, the

"Queen City," for welcoming me home, supporting *Little Ghetto Girl,* and all the love. Shouts out to the Chop Shop, Dynasty Books, *Power 98* morning show, Imaginations, and Salon Retro.

They say home is where the heart is, and mine is still in Harlem. Thank you, uptown, for all the love. I've been around the world and back, and I still haven't been anywhere like Harlem, USA. Somehow I even believe the air is different in Harlem.

And last but not least, to my fans: I love you all. It makes me feel so good when I meet you and you tell me you enjoy my works. Your support makes me work harder on my next story, because I want to make sure I give you something you enjoy every time you purchase a Danielle Santiago novel. Thank you so much for all the love and support.

God bless all of you.